Plan B: Revised

(Book 1 of the Siege of New Hampshire series)

Mic Roland

Plan B Revised

ISBN: 9781520158013

To my wife, for all her patience and support,
And to my many pre-readers who helped knock off the rough
edges and kept the characters from doing anything
too incredibly stupid.

Table of Contents

Chapter 1: Trying to get out of town

If movies and books were reliable guides, the collapse of modern civilization was supposed to come suddenly. A comet impact, a nuclear attack, or a giant lizard rising from the sea — it would be something that sent people running into the streets screaming. Square-jawed heroes with cool tactical gear would swashbuckle their way through all adversity, hot brass flying, against all odds.

Starting out quietly — as an inconvenience — was not the usual movie plot. Giant lizards sell better. They are not only more exciting, but have the added benefit of making it obvious which way to run.

Who runs screaming from an inconvenience? Most people just grumble and wait, assuming that things will return to normal. But what if "normal" does not return?

Martin pushed through the revolving door into the brightly lit lobby. Between the doors and the teller windows stood a woman holding brochures. Seeing Martin enter, her professional smile warmed slightly.

"Good morning," she said in an official sing-song tone. "Welcome to Bank of Boston."

"Hey. Hi, Susan." Martin smiled back. "Not at your window this morning?"

"No. It's my turn to work the lobby." She held up her handful of brochures.

"I see the curls are back," he said.

"What? Oh." Susan looked down and reflexively pulled at her curly hair. "Yeah, I don't like to straighten it too many times."

"That's okay," he said. "The curls look good."

Martin could see over Susan's shoulder, one of the bank managers frowning at them from within his glass cubicle.

"I guess if you're working the lobby, you won't be taking my deposit this time."

"Guess not. I've got another hour 'on deck' to go."

Over Susan's shoulder, Martin saw the frowning manager stand up quickly, and stride towards them. Martin plucked a brochure from the cluster in Susan's hand.

"Was there some question here?" The manager said. Susan, startled at the sudden voice behind her, stepped aside. The manager looked back and forth from Martin to Susan: a schoolmaster on a mission to ferret out bad behavior. His smile carried a hint of menace.

"Actually, yes," Martin answered calmly. He glanced down at the open brochure. A headline caught his eye -- something about linking accounts. "Your employee, here, was just explaining to me about linking accounts. My firm has a corporate account with your bank…" Martin held up his deposit bag. "I thought I might, um…" His eye quickly scanned the brochure again. "… qualify for…one of your premium personal checking accounts. Is that right?"

The manager's face quickly switched from angry schoolmaster to smooth maitre d'. "Oh? New accounts? Yes sir. I would be happy to assist you with that." He held out his hand for Martin to shake.

"I'm Mr. Skinner, branch manager. Why don't we step into my office?" Without looking away from Martin, the manager said over his shoulder, "I'll take it from here, Ms Price. You may resume your duties."

As the two men walked towards the glass cubicle, Martin glanced over Mr. Skinner's shoulder. Susan mouthed the words "thank you" and gave a sympathetic little smile.

Halfway to the manager's cubicle, the lights flickered a moment, then went off completely. A mixture of worried gasps and annoyed groans rose from the other cubicles. A pair of emergency lights popped on in the lobby corners, even though the room was well lit by morning light through tall windows.

Mr. Skinner stopped and looked up at dark ceiling fixtures for a few seconds. He cocked his head, expectantly. "Where's that generator?" he muttered to himself.

"Um. Please excuse me, but I have some issues to attend to." Martin gestured his approval. Mr. Skinner walked briskly towards the back room door. He impatiently poked at a keypad a few times with no results, then, fumbled with a ring full of keys.

Seeing the other tellers apologizing to their customers and the worried look of Mr. Skinner scurrying from teller to teller, Martin could tell he would not be making the deposit for awhile. He ambled back towards the front door with half a plan to return on his lunch hour. Susan glanced around, holding her brochures like a bouquet, looking unsure if she should stay at her lobby-greeter post or not.

"Looks like I won't be talking with your Mr. Skinner, *or* making any deposits for awhile. Guess I'll come back later when the power's back on."

"Sure. I hope it's not out for too long." They parted with smiles and shrugs.

Outside of the bank, State Street looked as it always did. Pedestrians walked toward their offices with briefcases, coffee cups or donut bags. The cars, delivery vans and cabs still flowed along, albeit slowly.

The traffic lights at State and Congress were dark, but the drivers were cooperating with each other, even negotiating left turns and cross flow. Boston drivers have a reputation for being rude, but that is usually towards outsiders who do not follow the unwritten rules. These drivers all seemed to know the rules and were making the best of it.

Further up State Street, beyond the traffic lights, stood mesh construction fences. Martin wondered if the work crew had severed a power cable. Workers in hardhats were slowly climbing up from their pit. They looked more annoyed than alarmed. If they had cut a power cable, they clearly did not realize it. As Martin walked back to his office, everything looked like a normal autumn morning in the city.

Nothing stood out as unusual in the lobby of Martin's building either. Large windows always kept the small lobby bright. The elevator button did not light up when he pushed it. The floor indicator lights were dark too. Martin groaned. *Is this dumb thing broken again? They just had it fixed.* He noticed the two ceiling lights were out. *Ah. Our building lost power too.*

The old, narrow elevator was out of service almost more than it was in-service, so the trudge up the five flights of stairs was nothing new. The darkness in the stair well, however, was new. A soft glow from emergency lights at the third floor landing cast long angular shadows. None of the other emergency lights had come on.

The fifth floor offices of EdLogix were twilight dim, even though it was 9:30 in the morning. Light from the small windows did not carry very far inside the old brick offices.

"Hey Brian," Martin stood before his boss's desk. "No deposit for now. The bank lost power. I see ours is out too…" Brian had not looked up or replied, but stared at his iPhone. Martin dropped the bank bag onto the desk. "Hellooo Brian."

"Oh, sorry, what?" Brian pulled the ear buds out of his ears.

"Couldn't do the deposit." Martin pointed at the bag. "Bank lost power. Us too, I see. Wonder how long it will be out."

Brian held up his phone. "I was listening to the news, hoping to find out what's going on. WBZ was off the air for awhile, but they're back on now. So far, no one knows much."

"I'm wondering if it was that construction they're doing up on State Street," suggested Martin. "You know, workers cut something they shouldn't have?"

"I don't think so," said Brian with a little shake of his head. "It's bigger than just State Street. News is spotty so far, but it sounds like all of Boston is out." He tapped at his phone and studied the screen.

"BostonDotCom was listing neighborhoods affected, which was most of them. But they haven't updated for over 10 minutes. CNN's got nothin'. FoxNews said there's power outages in New York and DC. Tweets have been rolling in like crazy."

Martin took out his phone and pulled up his feeds. "Hmm. I'm getting them too."

City of Manchester NH@*Manchester_NH*: Serious traffic delays due to power outage. Avoid downtown. #manchtraffic

WMUR TV*@wmur9:* State budget meeting postponed. Power out in Concord. #nhbudgetmeeting

Professor Calhoun*@HistoryCzar15:* Cultures 101 test postponed. Exeter Academy closed due to power outage. #peahistory

"Looks like parts of New Hampshire are out too. We must be having another good ol' fashioned New England power grid failure." Martin sighed.

Brian was still looking at his phone. "I'm getting some retweets from my brother. Lincoln Park is out, Englewood. Shedd Aquarium, Near North Side. So this extends out to Chicago too? Oh, now something from St. Louis. Check out the hashtag #outage."

Martin tapped that in and scanned the feeds as they quickly scrolled down his screen. Most were the inane reactions of the clueless, with little useful news.

Jared Dunkel *@ShowMeCity54*: *St. Louis trying to save on elect. bill? Laaame!* #outage

Chad Inumbral *@ChadsBaltimore*: What's going on with the lights? #outage #wantmypowerback

Rebecca Sophia *@BeccaInBedford:* Hey, No power!! Seriously!? I'm missing my shows!!! Someone will pay! #outage #noTV

One tweet caught Martin's eye as he scrolled.

Southwest Airlines *@SouthwestAir:* Due to #outage, SWA offices and website temporarily offline. We hope to be back online soon. #southwest

"Southwest is offline?" Martin said. "Their headquarters is in Dallas. Weren't you saying Texas is a whole other power grid from us?"

"Yes it is," said Brian. "So, this is something bigger than just another one of our usual Northeast blackout things."

"You were talking about EMPs a couple weeks ago. Think that's what it was?" Martin asked.

Brian shook his head. "I thought that at first too, but I don't think so now. I mean, a burst big enough to take down that much of the power grid should have totally fried delicate stuff like our cellphones. But they're working fine."

"A solar flare then? I see some tweeters out there think it was a solar storm."

Brian shook his head and shrugged. "That would only fry stuff that was plugged in, but my phone was plugged in. There's no scorching, or signs of a surge. This is more like when an ice storm takes down power lines, but without the ice."

Martin pocketed his phone. "Anything this widespread doesn't sound like it'll be back online in an hour or two. What do you want to do about the Madison proposal. It's due Friday."

Brian tilted back in his creaky chair and ran his fingers through his hair. "I know. I know. We're actually in pretty good shape on Madison. Without power, no server, router or internet, it's not like we can do much around here today. I already told Amy and Shree they could go home. You should go too. We'll see how things look tomorrow."

"Sounds good. I've got my sections of the proposal on my laptop. I can finish them up tonight. We can merge it all together tomorrow morning. I'll just go get my stuff and catch an earlier bus."

At his desk, Martin picked up his desk phone to call home. No dial tone. He felt stupid at forgetting so quickly. *Force of habit,* he comforted himself. He tried his cell phone, but all he could get was the "All circuits are busy" message. He tapped out a quick text message home.

"Mon.9:30.Pwr out in Bos. Office closed. Going 2 get bus."

The screen said "Message Sent," but he wondered if Margaret would get it. At least the voice call's "all circuits busy" recording was a clear-cut failure. Text messages were more like notes in bottles. Who knew when — or if — they ever washed ashore?

He began shoving his laptop into his messenger bag, but stopped.

Wait. What if there are no busses? He remembered a previous long and fruitless wait for busses that never came.

He plopped back into his chair and blew out a long breath through pursed lips.

If there are no busses, I might have to resort to Plan B. Better take the other bag, just in case.

He pulled a scruffy gray backpack from under his side table. A quick inventory confirmed what he already knew: his Plan B bag was not ready. There were extra clothes, a rain poncho, some basic first aid tidbits and miscellaneous small camping items, etc. The water bottle was there, but the energy bars had long ago fallen victim to snack attacks and never been replaced. If he caught a bus, the energy bars would not be missed. But if he could not get a bus? Fifty miles was a long way to walk on an empty stomach.

He shook his head to dismiss the thought. He told himself he would not have to walk. That was simply a remote possibility: a Plan B. He wanted to believe that the day's worst-case scenario would be a tediously long bus ride. He assured himself he would be home by dark.

Martin slid his laptop between the clothes in the backpack and traded in his leather business shoes for a pair of worn sneakers. In the office fridge, he scrounged up a bagel, leftover from their client meeting the Friday before. It was a bit dry, but there were no mold spots yet, so he stuffed it in the backpack.

It could be a long bus ride. He was avoiding thinking about the alternative.

"Guess I'm on my way, Brian," said Martin. "See you tomorrow, hopefully."

"Eh, maybe, maybe not." Brian pointed to his phone. "Getting unconfirmed reports that London might be down too."

"Whoa." The news impressed Martin, but he did not let it sink in very deep. He had a bus to catch. "Well, one day at a time. Let's touch base tomorrow and see how things are then. Get that Madison thing all buttoned up. I'll call you in the morning. Take it easy, Brian."

"Yeah, I will. Be careful out there."

When Martin stepped back out into the bright of day, the city looked different. The sidewalks were full of people. Most of them stood motionless, looking at their phones. They reminded Martin of an old sci-fi movie where the army of invading robots all stopped in their tracks for lack of instructions because the hero had destroyed the mother ship.

Those not staring at phones milled around in small groups, talking, like they did when a fire alarm emptied a building. In this case, it appeared to be every building. Some chatted together, but most were tapping on, or staring at their phones. A few looked like they were talking to someone.

Did they get a connection? Martin tried his phone again. The same circuits-busy message played.

As he made his way through Liberty Square, he heard a familiar loud voice over the murmurings of the crowds.

"Spare Change Nee-ews. Only a dolla. Help da homeless help demselves." On the steps in his usual archway, stood a wrinkled old man with a Popeye face and white walrus mustache.

"Hey Tony." Martin called out and waved. "Where ya been?"

"Hey pard'ner. Yeah. Had to take a few days off. My hip was killin' me." Tony held out his plastic cup and armful of newspapers. "But I'm back in the saddle, so to speak. Paper mister?"

Martin slid a five dollar bill into the cup and took a paper. Tony nodded his thanks, then waved his cup at the crowds. "Heck of a crazy show goin' on today, eh? Lookee all these people."

"Yeah," Martin said, suppressing an impish smile. "What did you do, Tony? Pull some fire alarms to get more customers on your sidewalk?"

"Wha? No. I never even…" Tony's eyes flared wide, but then squinted from a broad grin hidden beneath the mustache. "Aw, ya got me dat time. Heh, no, but that's a good idear. Have to remember me that for later. Nah, these folks ain't in a buyin' sorta mood. All nervous nellies. Guess power's out in all these buildings 'round here. Heard there's people trapped in elevators in that tall glass one over there. This one over here had a generator going for awhile up on the roof, but something went kablooie." He pointed to a roof across the square where a ribbon of black smoke trailed up over the cornice.

Tony pointed to the left. "People from that brick one there were talking about folks in wheelchairs trapped up on the ninth floor. No elevators, ya see. A bunch of them young lawyer types from over in that other building just went in to carry 'em down the stairs. I might have to stop doin' my weekly lawyer jokes. Them guys are alright."

"So, Tony." Martin said. "Sounds like this crazy show isn't just around here, but all over. You gonna be okay? I mean, with the outage and all?"

"Outage shmoutage. I jus walks. Don't take no power for that."

"But what about at…" Martin almost said 'home' "…where you stay?"

Tony laughed. "That ol' Impala ain't never had 'lectricity. But it's got the best bench seats *ever*. Outage won't be changing much for me."

"Hmm. I suppose not. Still, a guy's gotta eat. if you were going to get groceries or something…" Martin slipped Tony another five-spot. "You should probably do it quick. You know how people get when there's a storm or something. Strip the shelves of bread and milk. Best to get there early. Beat the rush."

"Hmm. Might be yer right about that. People ain't buying papers anyhow."

"Well, I gotta get to South Station," Martin said. "Gotta catch me a bus."

"Okay, pard'ner. You take care of myself, ya hear?" he winked.

"I will if you will, Tony." Martin winked back.

The scenes of congestion and confusion were the same along Congress, High and Federal streets. People stood around on the sidewalks as if they were attending a large, but boring, block party, or like a crowd that had shown up hours early for a parade. Instead of peering up the street to catch the first glimpse of sports champions on duck boats, they looked up at their buildings or their phones. Some wore their coats and jackets. Others shivered and rubbed their arms, regretting having left their offices without their coats.

From the fragments of conversation Martin picked up as he passed, people were unsure on what to do. Go home? Go back to work? Wait for 'services to be restored'? How long would that be? Call someone to complain? Who do you call? How do you call?

Some of them shared news tidbits and guesses for why the power was out. Amid the banal were some colorful theories. Terrorists had blown up Niagara Power. One woman heard that a train full of chemical weapons blew up in New Jersey. Her friend heard it was a train full of nuclear waste that blew up and it was in Connecticut. Each passed along their theory-news as if it were a revealed secret truth.

Martin smiled and shook his head at the creativity that fills a news vacuum. He wondered why the power was out too, but was more focused on getting home.

The drivers on Atlantic Avenue were not playing as nicely as those at State Street and Congress were. Cars inched along in close order. They allowed no gaps for side street traffic to enter the glacial flow. The shut-out drivers honked their displeasure. As far as Martin could see up and down Atlantic Ave, the four lanes of stalled traffic *did* resemble an automotive glacier, slowly inching towards the sea. Pedestrians filtered between the cars, two or three abreast, like sand running through fingers.

A sizable crowd had gathered around the Red Line T station entrance. People were filing in. Others were wandering out. It looked like business-as-usual, though Martin wondered why. The T ran electric trains. Why were those people going down the stairs? Did they think their train would be an exception?

The bustle around South Station reminded Martin of the day before Thanksgiving — thousands of people hurrying to get someplace. Except, this time, no one had holiday smiles.

Then a sudden tinge of deja vu gave him a chill. The worried faces and urgent jostling was more like what he saw back on 9/11. Back then, his carpool had left without him. Back in 2001, catching a bus to New Hampshire was his seldom-used backup plan to his carpool.

The bus station was mobbed back on 9/11. No one was smiling then either. Martin remembered waiting around the crowded station for over five hours, but there were no busses going north. A few busses departed for points west or south. After that, no new busses came for anyone. Hundreds began setting up indoor camp on the concourse. They were stuck in the city. So was he.

This day was different from 9/11 in one big way. This time, there was no power at the bus station. People marched up frozen escalators. Without all the ceiling lights, the main rotunda lobby resembled a man-made sinkhole. Soft daylight filtered down from the ring of glass block around the dome. The station hummed with a thousand conversations.

Martin merged into the mass of people trudging up the central escalator. A woman pounded on a dark ATM kiosk. She tried profanities when fists did not work. It was unacceptable that the ATM did not accept her card. Apparently, it was also unacceptable for the kiosk to be dark as well.

Martin worked his way through the swirling eddies of people on the dark concourse, towards his usual gate door. There were no HubExpress busses waiting outside.

Was this normal? He was familiar with the afternoon and evening schedule, but had no idea when the morning busses ran. He made

his way back to the HubExpress ticket counter to pick up a
schedule or ask when the next bus might be.

The ticket bays and food vendor bays resembled dark caves in the
sink hole walls. Most were totally dark. The occasional wavering
flashlight beam from within one or two of the bays resembled
guided-cave-tours in progress. In the HubExpress ticket bay, the
rows of jostling people were silhouetted by the soft glow of a
flashlight shining on the colored back wall. Would-be riders were
pressed up against the counter, three and four deep, all asking
questions at once.

Most of what Martin could hear was the whining or angry demands
of people wanting tickets. Martin already had his commuter
tickets. What he needed was schedule information.

At one point, the agent's phone bleeped. Martin was surprised that
push-to-talk service still worked. From the snippets he could
overhear, the news was not good. The 10 o'clock bus was stuck in
the tunnel from the airport. When the lights went out, a chain
reaction fender-bender stopped everything. No one was hurt, but
the bus was blocked in. The agent announced all this to the crowd,
trying to reassure them that the 12 o'clock bus would take an
alternate route, though it might be a little late.

The agent's announcement answered Martin's question, but not in
the way he had hoped. If the stalled traffic he had already seen was
any indication, that 12 o'clock bus would be stuck somewhere, but
not getting into or out of Boston. The ticket agent probably knew
that. Whether he was following company policy to report only
happy news, or from a sense of self-preservation, the agent was not
going to tell all those impatient people that no busses were coming
for them.

Martin pushed out of the crowd that had formed behind him. He remembered seeing a Concord Coach bus a few gates down. His HubExpress tickets were no good for Concord Coach, but their busses drove up into New Hampshire too. He overheard two women talking about their bus being the 10 o'clock Concord bus and gate 16. He felt a rush of optimism. It was 9:55. He did not know where the Concord busses stopped – Salem, Manchester then Concord? It did not matter. All were closer to home than Boston. His challenge was getting on without a ticket. He thought he could offer the driver cash.

He maneuvered through the cross flow of people as if fording a neck-deep river. He hoped there was enough time to reach the bus. A stop in Manchester seemed likely, and a good compromise. That was not where he parked his truck, but close enough. It would mean a four or five hour walk to get to it. That seemed a small price to pay. Even if he had to ride all the way up to Concord, he could have Margaret come pick him up. Maybe the phones were not all jammed up further north. She would not like having to drive all the way to Concord, but she would do it.

The windowless concourse was darker than the rotunda. The only light came from puny emergency floodlights at both ends, and from the headlights of a few busses shining through the glass walls. For a brief moment, the scene reminded Martin of old black and white war movies: prisoners of war massed in the yard for a surprise night inspection with spotlights in guard towers.

Too many old movies, Martin muttered to himself.

The concourse was packed like a stadium lobby just before the gates opened. The air was getting stale with the scent of breath and many perspiring bodies. Martin overheard more fragments of conversations as he squeezed and zigzagged through the jumble of shoulders, backs and butts. Some were angry at the inconvenience. Some were worried about family.

Others shared news and questions. Was it all the work of terrorists? Someone heard there was a leaking LNG ship in the harbor, so officials cut all the power in the city to prevent sparks. That at least sounded logical, even if wrong.

Why would they cut the power in Chicago because of a leaking tanker in Boston?

One middle-aged woman was certain it was all the work of Tea Party extremists intent to destroy America. Martin was not sure how that worked, but did not have time to listen for more.

The people near Gate 16 were silhouetted by headlights beaming through the plate glass wall. It was the Concord bus, lights on and loading. People had compressed themselves into a solid mass struggling to get through the single door. Gate 14 had no bus and no crowd at its door. Martin slipped out that door and joined the side of the crowd on platform 16. Everyone was talking loudly, jostling and trying to climb through the bus door at the same time. Clearly, the driver was inside taking tickets from the driver's seat.

Martin inserted himself into the mass of people that flowed towards the bus door. He had a $20 bill folded in his fist. Once onboard, he planned to hand it to the driver and step down the aisle. Maybe the driver would accept it, maybe not, but Martin figured that once he was aboard the bus, the inflowing stream of passengers would make it nearly impossible to send him back off. Being aboard was nine-tenths of a ticket, or something like that.

The opportunity never came. The bus began backing up while Martin was still several people back. A man and a woman continued trying to jam themselves into the still-open doorway as the bus backed out. Neither got on. They scowled at each other. The remaining crowd at the gate stared in disbelief, bathed in red light from the taillights, until the bus rounded the bend and out of sight. Many in the crowd loudly vowed to wait right where they stood -- to be first in line for the next bus.

That assumes there will be a next bus, Martin thought.

Martin felt an odd tingling on the back of his neck. Something about the sight of those people scrambling to get onto the bus as it backed away, and those left behind, reminded him of old news footage. During the evacuation of Saigon: crowds on rooftops left behind, reached up for a rising helicopter.

Was this how it felt to watch the last helicopter leave Saigon?

Martin dismissed the thought as an overactive sense of drama and too much History Channel.

Things are not that bad. It was just a bus, he told himself.

He worked his way back through the station crowds slowly, not quite certain where he was going next. He could stay and join the hundreds in the station waiting for another bus. He had no confidence there would *be* another bus. Waiting did not work for him last time, when it was only a nervous city that still had power. This time, there was a functional problem.

Another option was go back to the office and sleep under his desk again. He shook his head. That was still waiting, but with fewer people around. He was not giving up yet. There was still his Plan B, to walk home. His mind had been avoiding eye contact with that option.

If the outage was as serious as it seemed, the city would probably open up shelters for all the stranded business travelers, tourists, and distant-commuters like himself. Martin wondered who he would ask about shelters. A cot would be more comfortable than carpet, but how long would he be there? Days? Weeks?

The only mental images he had of shelters were from news photos of the Superdome after Katrina. He cringed at the prospect of becoming trapped in the quicksand of government benevolence.

Then, an idea flashed into his mind. *North Station! Maybe I could catch a train!*

Martin was surprised he had not thought of the trains before. They did not go anywhere he needed to be, so he seldom thought of them.

He knew the conductors sold tickets onboard. Martin would happily pay the higher onboard rate — even if they tacked on some opportunistic "crisis fee." Paying out a few extra bucks was the least of his worries. The train might only take him as far north as Haverhill or Lowell. But, he reasoned, that would leave him maybe a half day's walk up to his truck. He might still be home before midnight. That was far less intimidating than a fifty mile walk. This new alternative salvaged his hope. His pace quickened, once he had a destination.

Re-crossing through the snarled traffic on Atlantic Avenue was more difficult than before. Traffic had tightened up such that the cross-flow of pedestrians could only sift through in single file. Most pedestrians were still streaming towards the station. The air in the street was hot from all the idling engines, and acrid with exhaust fumes.

The extra effort required to cross Atlantic gave Martin time to wonder if he was overreacting. Was he letting himself get spooked? What if the power came back on in a few hours? He could find himself on a northbound train, halfway to no place he really wanted to be. Had his memories of 9/11 taken on inflated drama over the years? Was sleeping in the office really all that bad?

Back on the night of 9/11, sleeping beside his desk had been passable enough. Some sort of blanket would have made it easier to stay asleep. The offices got surprisingly cool after hours.

The mayor had "closed" the city, more or less, so on the day after, nearly everyone stayed home. Businesses were closed. Venturing too far from his ad hoc office campsite did not seem wise. He had nothing but the clothes on his back and three dollars in his pocket, so he roamed only a half dozen blocks in any direction.

The few convenience stores in the financial district and waterfront were all closed. The city was a virtual ghost town. An occasional siren wailed up a side street. Some "important buildings" (banks and government offices) were guarded by jittery security personnel or policemen. They stood with hands on holsters and eyed Martin (a lone pedestrian) with nervous suspicion. By the end of the second day, Martin had eaten what little there was in the office's kitchenette. For all the time he spent walking the empty streets looking for food, he reasoned, he could just as well have been walking home — had he been equipped for it.

That experience had been the start of Martin keeping a backpack under his desk. If he ever got stranded again, he would at least have the option to walk home. Over the years, he added things to his bag to make his Plan B walk more manageable. That went in cycles. Occasionally, he thought it was a silly waste of time and stopped adding anything more to the bag. After Hurricane Katrina, he resumed, adding a few more things: a disposable lighter here, some paracord there.

Martin vowed to himself back then, that he would rather walk the fifty miles home — even if it took three or four days — than stay stranded downtown again. *Better to be moving slowly than sitting still*, became his motto, even if he never said it out loud to anyone.

Egging him on to continue adding to his bag, was a nagging feeling that never quite came into focus — that being stranded in Boston the next time could be worse than a couple of chilly nights on the carpet and meals of old cream cheese on oyster crackers.

Maybe what made him uneasy about staying in town were the horror stories from Katrina and Sandy, or travel restrictions like Boston had after the Marathon bombing. Also in the corners of his mind was the frequency with which other cities had erupted into bloody riots for the thinnest of reasons — an unpopular jury verdict, a racial incident, or a sports team *not* winning their championship. It took surprisingly little for cities – those cathedrals to Kumbayah enlightenment – to turn savage.

Chapter 2: Good deed quagmire

Retracing his path up Federal Street, the people were not milling around on the sidewalks any longer. Instead, the scene resembled a heavy evening rush. People wore coats and carried bags: all walking briskly. Some had worried expressions. Most looked annoyed at the interruption of their routine.

The triangle of streets where Pearl, Milk and Congress joined at Post Office Square, was more of a challenge to cross. The stalled traffic was a chaotic jumble. A T bus, blocked in mid-turn, formed an effective dam for the flow of traffic on Pearl and Milk. Cars continued to try to come up out of the underground parking garage, but there was no open street to absorb them.

One impatient driver from the parking garage decided to drive his big BMW along the wide sidewalk in an attempt to bypass the motionless traffic. Pedestrians jumped out of his way. The driver of a neon blue Corolla with skirts and a spoiler must have seen the BMW and thought the sidewalk was a good idea. The Corolla bumped up onto the sidewalk, trying to get ahead of the BMW, but only got one wheel up before bottoming out on the curb. Martin guessed that the Corolla was not the driver's usual car or he would not have tried such a move. Lowered tuners and granite curbs do not mix.

The BMW driver veered around the beached Corolla, but this forced him to the left of a cast iron lamp post that stood in the middle of the sidewalk. He must have thought he could get around it. He was wrong. With a fingernails-on-blackboard scraping and a crunch, he had only managed to get his shiny black car wedged between the lamp post and atop the granite planter. It was his turn to be beached. His left front wheel spun uselessly in the flower bed, flinging up mulch and shreds of mums. The pedestrians who had to jump out of his way a few moments earlier, kicked or pounded on his car as they climbed through the planter to get around him. A few of them threw dirt on his car and yelled hostile sentiments about equality and justice.

Once Martin made his way through the traffic maze at PO Square, the northbound side of Congress was smoother going. Fewer cross streets meant less weaving through stalled traffic. The cooperative spirit was no longer present at the intersection of State and Congress. It was yet another jumbled parking lot. Martin preferred to cross in front of cars whose drivers were standing beside their cars, yelling and gesturing. Drivers behind the wheel were prone to suddenly lurch forward if they saw an opening.

On the north side of the intersection, the threads of pedestrians re-formed back into a thick column marching down Congress. In contrast to the steady flow of pedestrians, a couple dozen people stood in front of the doors to the State Street T stop. Among them, Martin saw a familiar face. Susan looked up and down State Street with a mild frown.

"Hey, Hi again," Martin gave a small wave to catch her eye. "What's up?"

"Oh, Hi." Her face brightened a little.

"You know," Martin said. "It's kinda strange seeing you outside of the bank. Are you off work now?"

"Yeah. Mr. Skinner closed the branch a little bit ago and told us all to go home for the day. I usually take the Orange Line," She pointed behind her at the T stop doors. "But not now. I got as far down to the turnstiles, but it was pitch black beyond that. The T's not running. Some people coming up from the platforms said there are still some trains stuck back in the tunnels. They could hear voices, but couldn't see anything."

"Makes sense that the T isn't running," Martin said. "Being electric and all."

"I guess so, but now I'm looking for other ways home. I was going to try and take a cab," she continued. "But look at this traffic! Even if I could find an empty cab, which I haven't, it couldn't get anywhere."

"So, what are you going to do?"

"Walk, I guess. Where I live in Somerville takes about an hour to walk. I walked to work several times in the summer. What about you? On your way home too?" She pointed to his bag.

"Yes. I'm on my way up to North Station to see if I can catch a train. Sounds like we're both walking north. Okay if I walk with you, at least as far as North Station?"

"Sure." A small smile erased the last of her worried expression.

They merged into the northbound flow of pedestrians headed down Congress.

"Man," said Martin. "There is a *ton* of people out here. I've never seen the sidewalks so full. Is this what rush hour is like every day? Maybe I just leave before it gets like this."

"This is the worst I've seen it."

"With all these heads bobbing up and down," Martin said. "I feel like I'm floating downstream in some white-water river of heads."

Susan tapped Martin's arm to direct his attention to the left. "Bet that's why there's so many people here. Look. They've got the sidewalk closed in front of City Hall. Everyone's got to be on this side of the street."

Behind the lines of white sawhorses and yellow tape stood nervous city cops in regular uniforms. A few men wore helmets, face shields and full black tactical gear, their hands on grips of black ARs hanging from monopoints. It reminded Martin of the nervous cops on 9/11, but this time, much more heavily armed.

The scene around City Hall looked peculiar and set Martin's mind to musing. The massive concrete building always did look like a post-modern fortress with its tall concrete walls and slit windows. Now it had a cleared perimeter protected by a ring of armed guards. City bureaucrats inside could rest easy, knowing they were safe. Safe from what?

It seemed odd that in the face of a possible crisis, local government's first response was rush into their bunkers to protect themselves. Did they fear that Boston would quickly devolve into riots and looting like LA, Fergusson or Baltimore?

Years ago, city employees used to be called "civil servants". With this outage, the peoples' civil servants were more intent on hiding behind concrete than being servants. Were local officials afraid that terrorists had staged the blackout as cover for kidnapping a city councilman, the Registrar of Deeds, or the Parking Clerk?

"Weird about the blackout, huh?" Susan interrupted Martin's musing.

"What? Yeah. It sounds like a big one this time."

"Oh? Have you heard some news about it? We were too busy closing out our drawers and stuff, so we didn't hear much."

"My boss, Brian, heard on his radio that it's not just Boston or even just the northeast. This time, it's Chicago, LA and other cities too, maybe even London."

"Really? Weird. What's London got to do with us?"

"That's the odd part. When we had our last big blackout, it turned out to be some petty mechanical failure and a bit of dumb human error, you know, that made the northeast's grid collapse like a house of cards. We're kind of used to that happening, right? Ice storms, leftover hurricanes, it doesn't take much. The cards fall pretty easily. We're used to that."

"I guess, but where's the odd part?"

"The odd part is Chicago going dark too. Other parts of the grid, like Chicago's, or Atlanta's were unaffected when we went dark the other times. They weren't as connected to us. This time, though, it's not just OUR card house. It sounds like it was all of them. The usual dopey failure in one area shouldn't make all of the card houses fall at the same time."

The human river slowed down to a quagmire near the Haymarket T Stop. A sizable crowd of frustrated would-be subway riders blocked the sidewalk and spilled out into the street. Angry drivers honked at them, although no one was going anywhere.

Traffic on Sudbury Street, as it crossed Congress, was impassible. The cars were literally bumper to bumper. The slow river of pedestrians had met an automotive dam. Yet more cars were lined up on the parking garage's exit ramps, waiting for a gap in traffic which never appeared. It seemed like all of them were trying to out-honk each other.

Susan threw up her arms. "This is crazy! There isn't even room to walk between the cars now! Why are they doing this? It's not like being twelve inches closer is getting them home any faster."

Martin glanced at the many scowling drivers. "Maybe they're jealous of us pedestrians. If they can't get anywhere, maybe they figure nobody should. Kind of the dark side of equality."

"Well that's just silly. I mean, c'mon…"

Martin interrupted. "Look over there. See that W.B. Mason truck? Come on. I've got an idea." They pushed through the crowd and headed to the back of the truck.

"Just like I thought," he said. "Lift gate. Little ladders, handles and a deck. We have a bridge!" He helped her climb up and across the deck. The driver immediately behind the truck honked long and loud. He edged the long snout of his silver Infiniti beneath the truck. It was a futile gesture. Martin and Susan were walking across the lift gate deck above his car.

The driver silently shouted inside his chrome and glass box. He gestured vulgarities to add visuals to his disapproval. When several other pedestrians followed Martin up onto the lift gate, the angry Infiniti driver got out and pulled a man off the ladder. Mr. Infiniti was intent to stop such flagrant cheating. A disorganized brawl developed.

"Man, I'm glad people are handling this outage like mature adults," Martin said. They sidestepped between a few more cars and quickly left the brawl behind.

Passage under the Government Center parking garage was slow going. Thick crowds swarmed towards the various stairwell doors. Martin considered the irony of them all struggling to get to their cars, only to be unable to get them out of the garage. Driving home was probably their only plan, so they were acting on it.

"Last time we had a big blackout," said Susan. "The power was out for two days at my apartment. Do you think the power will be back on soon? Tomorrow, maybe? I sure hope so."

"I don't know. This sounds like a bigger problem than last time. Something special about tomorrow?"

Susan's brow furrowed. "I was supposed to take my test tomorrow."

"Test?"

"Yes. I've been a teller for six months now. It's okay, but the pay is low. Then Katy had her baby, which created an opening for Associate. I've been studying for a couple months, but cramming hard ever since Katy left."

"Whoa. Studying for a couple months? Is this Associates test like the bar exam?"

"No. The test itself is pretty minor. It just covers the bank's various products and services. No big deal."

"Then where does a couple months of studying come in?

Susan shrugged. "It's kinda complicated."

Martin glanced up the crowded street. "Looks like we've got time."

"I suppose. Well, it's like this. In order to take the test, Mr. Skinner, my manager, has to schedule you for it."

"Oh, Mr. Skinner." Martin rolled his eyes. "I have to confess, he didn't make a very good first impression."

"He can be a bit gruff at times, but he's not that bad deep down. He keeps a picture of his cat on his desk. How mean-spirited can a man truly be if he has a picture of his cat on his desk?"

"Anyhow, Mr. Skinner won't schedule tests unless he thinks an employee is serious about banking principles, economics, etc. He used to be an economics professor or something, back in the day. He's always grilling us on the economic news. Us tellers call it our daily pop quiz. It's usually some random questions about

Keynesian Economics, or Fed policy, or Marginal Utility and Value theory. Stuff like that."

"Even if you didn't need to know it for the test? That doesn't seem fair."

"Maybe not, but I figured Mr. Skinner just wanted to see who had a head for financial issues. You know, promote worthy employees, not slackers. I wanted to prove that I was that worthy employee. So I read books and listened to the financial news, stuff like that."

"Ouch. Didn't that turn your brain to mush?"

Susan laughed. "At first, but it got better. Once you get past all the silly jargon, it starts to make more sense. I tried to be ready for his pop-quiz questions."

"So, were you ready?"

She partially concealed a beam of pride. "I guess Mr. Skinner thought so. He scheduled me to take the Associates Test tomorrow. I am so excited, and nervous at the same time. I really want to move up. I could use the pay raise."

Martin frowned. "But wait. If you become an Associate, you won't be at the window to take my deposits on Mondays. I'll have to go to...Angry Eyes."

"Angry Eyes? You mean Laurie? You call Laurie 'Angry Eyes'?"

"Well, not to her face, only to myself...oh, to Brian too, but that's all. You have to admit, she has seriously angry looking eyebrows."

"No she d...well, maybe a little, but still, that's not very nice." The corners of her mouth betrayed a suppressed smile. "She *can* be a little cranky sometimes."

"Does she have a picture of her cat at her teller window?"

Susan chuckled. "No. Laurie doesn't like animals."

"Well, there ya go." Martin continued. "So I don't know if I'm liking this news that you'll be in a cubicle and I'll have to face Angry Eyes every Monday."

They walked without words for a block. After a long pause, Susan offered. "But, if you ever had any questions about your account..."

"Well, here we are at North Station," said Martin. "Crowds are pretty thick here too, I see. Guess this is where we part ways."

Susan looked down. "Yeah, I guess so."

Martin felt a bit sad that they would part ways, then felt guilty for it. He had no business enjoying her company.

Looking over her shoulder distracted him from his guilt. The platforms at North Station were crowded like a refugee ship's deck. He stood on tip toes to see over the cars in the parking lot. "Hold on a minute." He climbed up on a jersey barrier for a better look. "Where are the trains?"

"What trains?"

"Any trains. There aren't any. There's all kinds of people waiting on the platforms, but no trains. All the years I've driven past North Station, I don't think I've ever seen all of the tracks empty. There's always been at least one or two trains."

He hopped down and sat on the barrier. First, his alternative bus plans fell through. Now it looked like his alternative train plans were falling through too.

"Now that you mention it, neither have I," said Susan.

"This kinda ruins my plan to catch a train. Gotta have trains for that."

"Maybe they're just running late. You could wait for one."

Martin rubbed the back of his neck. "I don't think so. I'm not keen on waiting."

"Why not?" she asked.

"I don't like the idea of waiting. I could be sitting there all day — and for nothing — if no trains come."

"Okay, if you won't want to wait for a train, what else were you going to do? There's no T, no busses. Cabs are useless..."

Martin sat on the jersey barrier in silence while his mind searched for any other alternatives beside the one symbolized by the pack on his back.

Try to buy a bicycle? Where? Bum a ride? he thought. *That might work. Do people pick up hitchhikers anymore?* He had not hitchhiked since college.

He unzipped a little pocket on his pack and pulled out a small folded map. He had highlighted I-93 in yellow marker, from the Bunker Hill Bridge, to his usual exit in New Hampshire. He imagined hitchhiking up 93 to get to his truck. It was a hybrid of his original plan to walk home, but with much less walking, if he could convince someone to give him a ride. On either side of the bold yellow line were thin lines in red pencil, marking out alternate side roads in case 93 was blocked.

He stood up and adjusted his backpack straps on his shoulders. "Looks like I'm back to my old Plan B. Walk home like you are."

"Oh. Okay. How far do you have to walk?"

"Um, well, it *is* a bit of a hike."

Walking to New Hampshire still sounded outlandish, even to him, and it was *his* plan. He was certain it would sound absurd to her. He was not eager to sound absurd in front of her.

"Guess we'd better get moving." He tried to sound enthusiastic, mostly to encourage himself. "You said that in the summer you walked home from the bank, which way did you go?"

Susan looked around to get her bearings. "Hmmm. I'd go up that way and take the bridge past the Museum of Science. Then over that long bridge past the college and on up to Rutherford Circle. It's not the shortest route, but it's a lot nicer than going over the rail yards."

"Ah. That's north…ish." Martin studied his map. "Works for me. Mind if I walk along with you awhile longer?"

"That'd be okay, I guess." She suppressed a smile.

Martin liked the idea of continuing in her company, but then felt guilty at the pleasure. He mollified his guilt. *It's just a few more blocks. No big deal.*

Traffic in the intersections near the river were jammed too. Pedestrians zig zagged through the cars like nervous lab mice. Martin noticed many of the drivers had the usual traffic-jam body language: rapid arm flailing, leaning forward to shout at their windshields, pounding on their steering wheels. Martin had sat through many three-hour commutes and not seen drivers get testy so quickly.

Maybe when there's an obvious reason for slow traffic, like snow or rain, people accept the delays better. There's no good reason now, so tempers are short.

Once Martin and Susan got onto the left side of the long bridge, there was no need to deal with traffic for several blocks.

Susan pointed up at people leaning out over balcony railings of the tall apartment buildings. "Boy, I'm sure glad I'm only on a second floor. Can you imagine what it must be like for those poor people without elevators? Ten, twelve flights of stairs each way? That would really stink."

"Oh yeah. I wonder how long tall buildings like these keep water pressure." Martin wondered out loud. "I suppose when it does, at least they've got a water source nearby. Not that you'd want to drink Charles River water. Perhaps if they had one of those really good filters. Still, they'd have to carry water up all those stairs."

"What? Why would they do that?"

"Oh, never mind. I was just thinking out loud."

She shrugged it off.

"So, I took your deposits every Monday, and I always wanted to ask you what kind of business EdLogix is."

"It's kind of hard to describe. We make corporate and educational apps, like for schools, companies, or special events."

"You're a programmer?"

Martin chuckled. "Well, I used to code, but the past few years I've become more of a researcher. We've got a couple wünderkinder now who crank out the code at warp speed. Things change so fast in development. I'm not so cutting-edge anymore."

"Research?"

"Yeah. I work up the content, the words and pictures. History, famous people, geography, data, stuff like that."

"Like for games?"

"Nothing quite so fun. Usually boring corporate stuff. Like one we finished this summer: ConTracker™. It was for a shipping company. Most of it was a pretty front end accessing the company's database for shipping containers, rates, schedules, and routes. All really boring stuff. Brian sold them on jazzing it up a bit by adding a 'fun' layer of explorer's routes. You know, Columbus, Magellan, Cabot, guys like that. Brian's idea was that maybe people would think it was cool that their shipping container would follow the same route as Cabot, etc. The client liked the idea, so, I researched explorers."

"Sounds fascinating."

Martin smiled skeptically. "I like to think so, but most people I talk to about my work develop a deep glaze. Darn near comatose. It's the sort of stuff only nerdy Education Directors or PhD types think is fascinating."

Susan smiled. "Huh. I think you just called me nerdy, or a PhD type. I'll go with the latter."

They pushed through the students milling around on the sidewalks around the community college. Most of them stared at their phones — more robots waiting in vain for instructions from the mother ship. Some of them were talking into their phones. Maybe they were getting through. Martin tapped his home number and listened to the same circuits-busy recording. He tried to pull up a news site, but only got the spinning wheel and server-not-found messages. "I've got some signal, but no lines open yet. Does yours work?"

Susan tried her phone. "No. I get a recording to try again later."

"Text messages might get through, so if you wanted to let someone know you're headed home, it might be good to do it soon."

"Good idea." She began tapping. "If my dad hears that Boston has a blackout, he'll get all worried. I'm thirty-five years old, but in his mind, I'm forever six. That used to bother me, but now I think it's kinda cute. There. It says 'Message Sent'."

"Your folks live in the area?" Martin asked. He wondered why she did not text whoever was waiting for her at her home in Somerville, but quickly shut down that line of curiosity. It was none of his business.

"No. We used to live out north of Turner's Falls, in western Mass, when I was a kid. But after I went to college they moved out to Ohio." She put her phone away.

"That's it? One text? I don't want to sound like I'm stereotyping or anything, but I thought girls had zillions of friends they texted back and forth with all the time."

"Not this 'girl'. Besides, I'm not into texting all that much. I prefer face to face. That's why I like my bank job."

"I'm hearing sirens mixed in with all the honking," said Martin. "Police cars maybe?"

"Yes. I do. They don't sound like police cars, though."

"Fire trucks is my guess," said Martin. "Look across the river."

They had walked clear of the tall Schraft's building, giving a clear view of the Mystic power station across the river. Black smoke rose from the base of one of the white metal buildings. "That's not coming from the smoke stacks. Must have an equipment fire in there."

"You think that's why the power went out? A fire at the power station?" Susan's voice carried a hint of hope. "That seems like something fixable, right? They could have the power back on by morning."

"I don't want be the wet blanket, but I don't see how a fire at Mystic station would take down Chicago and L.A. too. Might be related, but it's got to be bigger than just a fire at Mystic."

"Hmumph. Well I can still hope you're wrong." Susan stopped at the edge of the curb. "Well, this is Rutherford Circle. This is where I go left, up that way. Which way for you now?"

"Actually, I hadn't thought about it much: been too busy talking." Martin surveyed the low skyline, devoid of useful landmarks. "North, generally. There's 93. I'm gonna try hitchhiking on 93. Yeah, yeah, I know it's not legal, but these are desperate times. Hitching beats walking, and I'm more likely to find a longer ride on 93 than down here on the surface roads -- which aren't moving much anyhow. What about you? How much further 'that way' do you have to go?"

"Oh, not far at all. I live over on Wheeler Street." She pointed under the elevated deck of 93. "It's maybe a half dozen blocks."

Half a dozen blocks sounded like a lot of exposure to angry, impatient people. He felt a boy scout's obligation to escort her home. He was about to offer to escort her home, but stopped. Years of feminist browbeating had made chivalry old fashioned and politically incorrect. Despite all that chivalry within Martin refused to go away.

"Tell you what. I could walk you to your door, just to make sure you get across all the crazy traffic and stuff. If you want."

Susan's smile was gone. "That really won't be necessary." Martin could see subtle defensive body language cues.

Oh great job, Bozo. Now she thinks you're some sleazy stalker weirdo, he berated himself.

"I'm not trying to get all forward or anything. It's just that, well, people are being kinda cranky today. Like that guy behind the W.B. Mason truck? I'd feel better knowing you got home okay before I headed on. That's all. Nothing else. Honest."

She still looked reluctant. With chivalry expunged from the culture, men were left with only one sinister motivation for being nice to a woman. Noble intentions had to buck a hundred years of feminist diatribe.

He surrendered with a sigh. "But, you're probably right. Well, take care. Hopefully see you around the bank sometime soon."

Martin expected to see Susan turn, perhaps with a polite wave, and hurry away, having escaped the clutches of a sleazy stalker. Instead, she stared into his eyes for a long moment. He wondered if it was better for suspects in a police line-up to maintain or avoid eye contact.

The furrows disappeared from her forehead. She glanced around at the noisy traffic congestion. A burst of honking and shouting underscored his point. "I guess people *have* been a little weird today, but I don't want you to be going out of your way."

"No bother at all." Martin felt a rush of relief, like when he needed just one more act-of-kindness for his citizenship merit badge and old Mrs. Nymore finally agreed to let him rake her leaves.

Susan shrugged acceptance and they set out west on Washington.

"I'll veer off whenever you want. You just say when. Totally up to you," added Martin, trying to sound indifferent and as un-creepy as he could.

"Okay."

Within the regular chorus of honking, the wail of sirens grew louder. Some sounded like police sirens, some more like ambulances, or some other emergency vehicles.

"Not a good day to be trying to rush to a hospital," said Martin.

"That's for sure."

"Say, this is a neat looking old neighborhood you have here. Bow-front Queen Anns. Some Greek Revivals. A classic Mansard. Oh, and a cool Gothic across the way there. All very quaint," said Martin.

"You researched old house styles?" Susan asked.

"No, it's just one of my nerdy hobbies. I grew up in a cookie-cutter subdivision where all the houses looked alike. So, the old styles always fascinated me. The narrow streets around here are kind of old-world too. Of course, that means it doesn't take more than a couple cars to completely choke them off. Where does everyone think they're going?"

"Don't know," said Susan. "Judging from the bundles and boxes strapped on their roofs, I'd guess they're trying to go stay at a friend's or relative's house for awhile. But, from what you said, they won't have power either." Susan and Martin threaded through a jumble of cars at one intersection, then another.

"Do you live in one of these neat old houses?" Martin asked. "That would be so cool."

"I do, and it *is* kinda cool. It's a really cute Victorian. Blue with white gingerbread trim. I was really lucky to get it. When I was…well, looking for an apartment, I didn't have a lot of time, so I couldn't be too choosy. Most of the places I looked at were pretty rough, or in a sketchy area, or way out of my price range. Then I saw the listing online for this one and jumped at it. My apartment is on the second floor. Just three small rooms, and not much of a view or anything. But the kitchen has pine wainscoting and chair rails! I was totally sold just from the pictures."

Martin thought she must not be too worried that he was a shady creeper, or she would not have described her house to him. "Sounds charming."

"It is. Still, it has its down sides. Next door is an ugly old triple decker they rent out to college kids. The boys on the second floor can be pretty obnoxious at times. They like their loud parties late into the night. "

"But that's enough about them. What about your house?" she asked. "You never said where *you* were going…just 'north'."

"Oh, well, I...have kind of a plain white house. Not old or quaint…"

"No no no. That's not what I meant. *Where* is your house? How far do you have to walk?"

Martin's face felt hot. He felt embarrassed at his plan to walk home. He felt foolish at being only partially prepared for it. He had never hiked that far before, and had only vaguely figured he would just deal with whatever came up when he got to it. As a 'plan' it sounded half-baked at best, but closer to stupid.

His ego whispered that this was a prime time to lie. He could say just about anything — he lived in Winchester or Stoneham or any place up the road. What did it matter? He could lie to alcoholic panhandlers. He could lie to a pushy bank manager. He hardly knew Susan, yet somehow he felt uncomfortable lying to her.

"Um…New Hampshire?" He winced.

"Wait. What?" Susan stopped and grabbed Martin by the arm. "You're going to try to walk to New Hampshire?"

"Well, not if I can hitchhike most of the way."

"But still. New Hampshire?"

"You say it like it's the North Pole or something. It's only fifty miles."

"Only fifty miles." She mocked his tone.

"Sure. It's totally do-able." Martin tried to sound like it was old-hat, though he had never done it before.

"Even if I had to walk all the way, which I hope not to, fifty miles at three miles per hour would be only sixteen hours. I'll grant you that I won't be able to keep that pace for sixteen straight hours. So, it might take a couple days. I camp out one night under the stars. How bad is that? Regardless, I am *not* sleeping in my office again."

"So, sleep in a hotel instead. Walk to New Hampshire? That sounds crazy and dangerous."

"Hotel? No, I want to get *out* of town, not find someplace else to stay in it."

Susan continued her scolding tone. "I'll admit, sleeping in an office doesn't sound all that appealing, but walking fifty miles sounds…" She was stuck for stronger words. "That just sounds crazy."

"It's not that sleeping in my office would be all that bad by itself. It's just that this time I've had this little feeling in the back of my head that staying in the city is a bad idea. Given the scope of this outage, I feel like, if I don't get out now, I may not be able to get out later."

"And why not?" With her hands on her hips she was clearly expecting a darned good reason.

Martin felt cornered and looked away. He had never articulated his concerns out loud to anyone, so he had no well-practiced lines or phrases. "It's nothing I can put into words easily, but more a collection of little things. Like, after Katrina, officials talked about what a headache it was with all those suddenly homeless people to deal with. That whole Superdome thing looked far worse than a night under the stars. Or hurricane Rita, with thousands of people stranded on the highways for days. Then after the Marathon bombing, all the travel restrictions with the city in lock-down and authorities telling everyone to 'Shelter In Place.' That's all fine if you're already home, but at the office? There's other stuff too, but it all boils down to a feeling that if I don't get out of the city quickly, I might not be able to get out at all."

Martin looked at her with a feeble forced smile. His explanation did not sound as compelling out loud as it did in his mind. "I suppose it still sounds nuts."

"You're right. It still kinda does." Her tone was softer. She pointed to the gridlock in the streets. "But, given how the traffic keeps jamming up, no one else is getting out of the city anyhow."

"That's why I plan to keep moving. Get as far as I can before dark. But, the first order of business is to get you home. Then I can get started hitchhiking."

They walked along without speaking for several blocks. Martin broke the silence, pointing at a plume of black smoke rising over the rooftops. "Really a bad day to have a fire. I doubt the firetrucks could ever get up these blocked narrow streets."

Susan looked at the smoke for moment, then her face went pale. "That's coming from near my house." She bolted and ran.

Martin ran behind her. He could hear sirens in the distance, but he could also see another plume of black smoke rising further south. Were the trucks headed towards this fire, or that one? The sirens sounded roughly between them.

As they rounded the corner onto Wheeler Street, Susan stopped. "Oh thank God. It's not my house. It's the triple-decker."

They ran along the opposite side of the street. A crowd of neighbors had gathered there, gawking blankly as if the fire was street theater. Martin and Susan stood and watched too for a few minutes. Fire filled the second floor deck, curling up to consume the third floor deck. Thick smoke poured out of the second floor windows.

Martin turned to Susan, "I really don't think the fire department is going to get here very soon. Look how those sparks are carrying. The way those flames are spreading, your house might go up too."

Susan gasped. "It can't! This is all I have."

"Maybe we better run in and save some of your stuff — just in case." Martin pointed to embers floating down onto the roof of the Victorian.

Susan let out a little scream, then rifled through her purse for her key. They ran up the wooden porch steps, through the heavy door and up the switch-back stairway. She struggled to get the key into the lock. She pushed open the door, ran in, but halted in the middle of the living room.

"What do I save? Where do I start?"

"Start with things you can't replace: important papers, things like that. I'll go grab some clothes out of your closet, just in case." Martin rushed into the bedroom while Susan plucked family photos from the mantle and shoved them into a canvas shopping bag.

Martin threw open the closet doors. He grabbed an armful of clothes from the bar and tossed them on the bed. The gap in the closet revealed some luggage. He opened the roller bag on the bed and tried to fill it with roughly equal quantities of shirts, pants, sweaters, etc. The roller bag filled up quickly. He pulled out a duffle bag from the closet.

He yanked open the dresser drawer, intent to scoop out socks and things. His hands froze in mid-scoop. Bras and panties. It had not dawned on him that volunteering to get her clothes would mean bras and panties. He hardly knew Susan. Chivalry had no business touching her underwear. Why had he not thought there would be bras and panties?

He was startled out of his paralysis when Susan rushed into the room. "I've got my photos and papers."

Martin, feeling both relieved and guilty, quickly pulled back his hands. He pointed to the bed. "I put as much as I could in your roller bag. Here. I'll hold this duffle and you scoop out...um...what you want from the dresser." He was content to hold the bag, but still had to look away while she filled it.

Susan grabbed a thick sweater from the pile on the bed. They hauled their burdens into the living room. "My dishes?"

"Replaceable?"

"Yes."

"Then never mind." Martin pointed to the bathroom. "Prescription meds?"

"None."

"Okay good. Man, it's getting warm in here. Winter coat? Boots?"

"Closet." Susan flung open the door. She draped a long coat over her arm and grabbed a pair of boots.

The side window shattered from the heat. "Come on. We've got to get out of here!" Martin pushed Susan towards the door. The stairway was starting to fill with lazy wisps of smoke.

Once back across the street, in the cool air, there was nothing much to do but watch the fire among the rest of the neighbors. The radiant heat was becoming uncomfortable, even from across the street.

A little balding man came up to Susan sheepishly. With a heavy Portuguese accent, he said apologetically, "It was those boys. No has power. They try cook on porch, deep fry, on grill. Grill fall on old sofa. Big fire. Boys try to put out." He looked to his right. A young man stood among the spectators, staring in shock, his hands wrapped in towels. Another young man stood beside him with a red face and no hair on the front of his head.

The bald man shook his head. "No can put out."

"This can't be happening! It just can't," Susan said to no one in particular. "My house can't burn down. Where will I....Why isn't somebody doing something? Where's the fire department, for God's sake?" She paced quickly up and down the sidewalk. "How can they NOT see this fire?"

"I hear some sirens," offered Martin. "I'll go see if they're coming." He trotted to the end of the block. At the intersection, he peered up and down the street. It was full of gridlocked cars and many pedestrians, but no fire trucks. The sirens did not sound any closer than before.

He walked back to Susan, not eager to bear bad news. She was rushing from one bystander to the next, half-shouting at them and flailing her arms. The bystanders gave little response, as if they did not understand her or were deaf. Martin thought some of them had an it's-not-my-job look on their faces. They were there to watch, not to *do* anything.

He was still a dozen yards away when Susan turned and their eyes met. There was a flash of wild expectant hope on her face. Martin's stomach knotted. Such a pleading look for rescue, and all he had was bad news. He shook his head.

Susan slowly collapsed, as if she were an inflatable lawn Santa whose blower had been unplugged. Martin rushed over to help her up off her knees. She stared blankly. The roof of the old Victorian burned vigorously. Then flames crept down the siding. Through the crackle and roar of the fire, sirens continued to wail in the distance. No fire trucks came. The street-side windows burst. Billows of gray smoke poured out, followed by licks of orange.

Susan's shoulders began to quiver with silent sobs.

Chapter 3: No room at the Inn

The three porches of the brown house collapsed onto each other when their posts had burned through. The semi-circle of spectators jumped back or ran a little further up the street, only to turn and resume gawking, like zebras the lion had not caught. Sirens continued to howl in the distance.

Martin felt uncomfortable interrupting Susan's vigil for the Victorian's last hours, but watching it burn did not seem like a healthy thing to do.

"Um. Susan? Susan. There's nothing we can do here."

She continued to stare.

"I think we should get you to someplace else where you can stay. Can you stay with one of your neighbors?"

"What?"

"Can you stay with one of your neighbors for a few days? I'll help carry your things there. Do you know one of your neighbors well?"

"No. I've only been here a few months." She continued to stare as the fire slowly consumed its prey. "The only one I know is Mr. Mendes." She glanced towards the little bald man. "Sometimes I'd say hi as I walked home, if he was out watering his tomatoes."

"Good good. So maybe you could stay with the Mendes for a couple days until..."

"No, His little house is full. Grandmother, Mother-in-law, his sister and her kids, a nephew and his kids."

"Oh. I see. Any other neighbors?"

Susan turned away from the fire with her eyes shut tight. "No. I hardly ever see any of them. They're all strangers."

"Okay, well, what about friends somewhere else in the city? I'd be happy to help carry your..."

"No. No friends in the city." Her voice turned impatient. "I moved here from Marlboro six months ago. I had a couple friends out there, but not here."

His Good Samaritan detour was turning into quicksand. "Oh. Um. Geez. Marlboro. I don't think that's gonna be possible, at least not by tonight. What about co-workers? Does, um...Laurie live in town?"

"I don't know where she lives. We don't talk personal that much, okay?" She snapped.

Martin felt neck-deep in the quicksand. He pulled at his collar. As much as he did not like pressing the matter, he felt he had no choice. He could not just resume his travels north and abandon her out on the streets. Helping meant prying questions at a bad time. He swallowed hard and went on.

"How about family?" He recalled her saying her parents lived in Ohio, but perhaps there was a sister or an aunt nearby.

"No! There's no one!" She started to shout, but dialed back her tone. "I'm all alone out here, okay? There's nobody. After my stupid boyfriend...*EX*-boyfriend... *He* said it was over between us, but *I* was the one who had to leave. His condo. His car. He got to keep our friends. I got *nothing*!" Her eyes flashed with rage, but got moist a moment later. Her voice sank to a whisper. "He said we were forever."

Martin felt like an animal stuck in a snare. Usually, when things went wrong — a broken fan belt, a ruptured water pipe, his mind quickly figured up some Plan B. This time, however, his knack for Plan B thinking had abandoned him. He had no idea how to actually help her.

Susan wiped her eye with the back of her hand, sniffed hard and straightened up. "I had to start all over. So I did. I found a job at the bank downtown. I found this cute little place to start over…"

She looked back at the burning Victorian and paused. "That was my...new life." She closed her eyes tightly and shook off a sob. Martin felt awkward. What does one say? He started to put an arm around her, but stopped. That felt even more awkward.

"Um...I'm sorry. I didn't know about…I mean, I'm sorry about your house. But, we have to, you know, find you someplace to stay. There's nothing we can do here. Let me help you with your stuff."

He picked up the coat and sweaters and rolled them into the canvas bag. He felt relieved at having a task he could do — some way to help. With some cord from his bag, he lashed the canvas bag and duffle to the roller bag's long handle. He stood up to survey his progress. The roller bag bundle was bulky, but a fairly manageable load. His minor feeling of success faded away when he realized it was also all she had now.

His Plan B intuition returned. *A hotel!* She had recommended that he stay in a hotel instead of walking.

"You could stay in a hotel until you found a new apartment. How's that sound?"

Susan did not respond.

"We should get you a hotel room to stay in," Martin repeated.

"Hmm."

Martin took that as agreement. He realized that someone should know what he was doing. He told Mr. Mendes that he was going to find a hotel for Susan. He left his name, address and cell phone number with Mr. Mendes. Cell phones were useless at the time, but he wanted to leave some sort of record, in case someone came looking for her. Though, from what she said, who would that be?

He pulled at Susan's elbow to start her walking away from the fire. "I saw a Holiday Inn down the street when we were coming under 93. What do you say we go get you a room there? Hmm? You'll have a bed for the night, get some rest."

"Sure," she said flatly.

They walked slowly, and silently, for a couple blocks. Martin had to portage Susan's bag bundle on his head to get through the stalled traffic. A frustrated policeman was trying to clear an intersection, but with little success. Each opening he created was quickly filled by some other driver who thought the open space was for them. The cats refused to herd.

Martin felt uncomfortable. A Boy Scout does not lead a woman, whom he barely knew, to some unknown place. It felt like all kinds of wrong. Someone else needed to know. "Maybe you should text your dad and let him know you'll be in a hotel tonight," Martin suggested.

Susan did not respond at first, but eventually pulled out her phone. She looked at the screen, then showed it to Martin.

"Oh, no signal. Well, you could try again later. You should let him know. He worries, you said."

"Hmm." She dumped her phone back in her purse.

As they made their way through the lines of cars that filled Washington Street, Martin could see a fire engine several blocks up the street. Flashing lights, siren, it was the very image of urgency, but it was not moving. The way the big red truck towered over its surroundings of gray, white and beige car roofs, it looked to Martin like an automotive reenactment of Shackleton's ship *Endurance*, trapped in the polar ice.

If that fire company is trying to get to Wheeler Street, they won't find much left by the time they get there, he thought. Pessimism is not good for sharing, so he kept that thought to himself.

"Hey look, there's that Holiday Inn I saw." Martin tried to sound upbeat. Susan did not look up, but trudged along beside him, eyes down.

Several clumps of people stood under the carport in front of the hotel lobby as if it were at a neighborhood barbecue. The lobby itself was full of people standing in pairs and trios, cocktail party fashion. People sat on every chair. They sat upon the tables and even the planters. People sat along all the walls with bags or boxes beside them. The lobby looked more like an airport gate of a long-delayed flight. The air was heavy, humid and smelled of perspiration.

Martin pulled Susan to one side of the lobby doors. "It's really crowded in here. How about you wait here, with your bag, and I'll go see about a room for you." Susan didn't look up or answer, but took the handle of her roller bag.

Martin stepped over the legs of people sitting along the walls, and through clusters of people standing around. The desk clerk seemed very busy writing things on loose paper. "Excuse me? Um. Excuse me? Hi. I'd like a room?"

The clerk scoffed, but composed himself. "Ahem. No sir. No rooms."

"None? Don't you usually..."

"None at all. I was three-quarters booked with a convention before the power went out. Between conventioneers, stranded travelers and locals who think they should stay in a hotel 'cuz their house doesn't have power... We don't have any power either. Why is this better? I don't know. Anyhow, people have been pouring in here all morning, offering cash for a room. I've been booked solid since 10:30."

"Alright then. How about another hotel in the area?" Martin asked.

"Don't count on it, pal," offered a man in a rumpled tan suit. "I've been working my way out from the center of town all morning. Marrott's full. They sent me to the Sonesta. They were full. 'Try the Marlow on the river,' they said. Full. Marlow said I should try the Hampton. I schlep all the way over there, but wouldn't ya know, they're full too. Hampton guy told me to try the Holiday Inn, but it's the same story. Full. My next try's the La Quinta."

"Without phones," the clerk added. "I've got no way of knowing who has rooms or not. My 'Spidey Sense' hasn't picked up any vibrations of empty rooms either. You're kinda on your own."

"Look," Martin's tone was more impatient than angry. "That young lady over there needs a room. Her apartment house just burned down and she's got no friends in town, no family, nowhere to stay. Don't you have something? Anything?"

The clerk scowled, raised a jabbing finger at Martin, but glanced at Susan. Her orphan look melted him. His arm dropped to his side.

"Aw crud. I wish I could help, but I've got nothing. The conference rooms are full of people camping out. I've been letting people hang out here in the lobby and along the halls, but as you can see, that's pretty full too. Truth is, if the fire marshall came in here, he'd go ballistic and order everyone out. I'm already on thin ice as it is. What I can tell you is that some people with rooms have been doubling up, kinda like subletting. I'm not supposed to allow that, but what can I say?"

A portly man, face glistening, sidled up to Martin. "Pardon me, but I couldn't help overhearing. You say the little lady over there is in desperate need of a place to stay?"

"Yeah?," said Martin cautiously. *Is this guy part of the hotel staff?*

"We would hate to see anyone left out on the streets during a crisis like this, especially when we had the means to help them."

"We?" Martin asked.

The glistening man pointed with the neck of his beer bottle. "Yes, that's Jimbo, my associate, over there by the windows. We're in town for the medical devices convention, so we've already got a room. We're...doctors, ya see."

Dr. Jimbo?

"Our room has two big beds, ya see. It was Jimbo and his...wife in one and me in the other."

Martin could only see Jimbo having a hearty laugh with two other portly men. No Mrs. Jimbo.

"So I figured he and I could double up in one and the little lady could double up with Jimbo's wife." The glistening man beamed proudly at his clever generosity.

Mrs. Jimbo doesn't have a name? Martin's "Spidey Sense" shouted: *No Way.*

"Thanks for the offer, but I think we'll look for something else."

The glistening man's smile dropped. "So, what are you, her brother or something?"

"No, I'm just a guy trying to help...." Martin turned to look towards Susan.

The man took advantage of Martin's distracted attention to elbow him aside. "We'll just let the lady decide for herself."

This is definitely bad, Martin thought.

Martin stumbled over someones legs. The sweaty man got to Susan before Martin did.

"Excuse me, Miss, but I hear you need a place to stay."

Susan's eyes came up and brightened. "Oh?"

"No. No she doesn't." Martin inserted himself between the man and Susan, grabbed the handle of her bag with one hand, her elbow with the other. "Come on, Susan, we have to go now."

The man grabbed Martin by the shoulder. "Hey Pal. Mind your own business."

Martin reflexively batted the man's hand off his shoulder. The man looked indignant for a moment, then reeled back to throw a punch.

Maybe it was the way the man took a little half step back, or maybe it was something else, but the thought flashed across Martin's mind: *off balance.* With his hand still in front of him, he made a quick jab to push the man in the chest. The glistening man started to topple backwards. He took faltering steps back, arms flailing, and stumbled against another man. While the two were entangled, Martin pushed open the door and ushered Susan out.

Once outside, he pulled the disoriented Susan and her bag across the parking lot, through the line of trees and up the street. He looked back to be sure the man was not following them. He was not.

The air outside felt cool and refreshing. Susan looked around. "Hey. Where are we going? Did you push that man?"

Martin hesitated. "Let's just say he was being a jerk and needed a push."

"Why? What did he do?

"Never mind." Martin mumbled.

Susan stopped and gasped. "Oh my god. My apartment is gone. I can't go home. I have no home. The fire…"

"Yeah, I'm sorry we couldn't save more of your stuff."

"No no no. We were crazy to go in there at all. We could have been killed!"

"Well, I wouldn't go that far. I thought we had a little time. We had to save *something*. At least you have your important papers, photos, and some clothes. Sorry about your furniture and dishes and all."

Susan waved off his apology. "The furniture came with the apartment. The clothes, well, I can get more. But where am I going to stay? I don't have any place to stay. I don't know anybody in town."

"Right. That's why we came here, to the Holiday Inn, remember? I said I'd help carry your bags to a hotel?"

Susan's brow furrowed. "When did you say that? Never mind. But if that's why we came here, why did we leave?"

Martin did not have any easy answers, but was relieved to hear her using more than monosyllables. He thought it best to skip the part about the sweaty man.

"They were all full up. We'll have to look somewhere else."

"Full. Oh. I see. Look somewhere else. Hmm. I have to find a place to stay. I can't just stay out on the streets tonight. Oh, I remember. There's a Hampton-something down on McGrath. I walked past it a few times. Here. It's down this way."

"Hold on. A guy back in Holiday Inn said hotels downtown were full, so they sent him to the Hampton. It was full too. Hampton sent him to Holiday Inn. Apparently, all the stranded people in Boston are working their way out from the center of town: all looking for a place to stay tonight."

"What? Shoot. All the other hotels I know about are downtown." Her shoulders slumped. "If all the hotels are full, that probably means a shelter, but I really don't want that."

"Can't blame you there. Another reason why I'm walking. But don't give up yet. There are more hotels." Martin slung his backpack around to dig out his map. He was glad she was finally focusing on the problem at hand. The situation felt like a Good Samaritan deed again, and not a creepy abduction.

"That guy said he was going on to the La Quinta. I know where that one is. It's north of here, beside 93. I've never stayed there. Just pass by it every day. Not a fancy place from the look of it, but fairly new." Martin studied his map.

"La Quinta, huh? Sure, I could go there." Susan sounded like she was trying to sell herself on the idea. "That would be okay. I just need someplace — a room. Get some sleep and figure out what I do next. Huh. Looks like I'm starting over — again."

Martin studied his map. "Hmm. If we go up this road, Mount Vernon, Broadway. That connects with Mystic Ave. Then up to this triangle here. That should be where La Quinta is."

Susan stepped in front of him and faced him, somewhat sheepishly. "Umm. I don't remember much after…the fire got… but I do remember yelling at you…back there." She pointed towards the smoke above the rooftops, but did not look in that direction. "That wasn't right..."

"Don't worry about it. You were just upset, that's all. Totally understandable."

"Thanks. I really do appreciate you helping me find a hotel. But you need to be getting home too. I don't want to keep you from…"

Martin raised a hand to cancel her concern. "Not a problem. I can't just leave you on the streets, all stranded, now can I? What kind of Boy Scout would that make me? I'll help get you to a room. *Then* I'll head home. Besides, La Quinta is right on my way. See?" He pointed to the yellow highlighter line beside his finger on the map. "A win-win."

"Oh." Susan's worried look softened with hints of a smile. "Cool."

Martin felt encouraged. "You're right. After a good night's rest, you can see what the situation is with your old place, find out when the bank is open, etc. So, it's not like you're starting over completely from scratch."

"Yeah. You're right. Not quite from scratch. I do have my job, and my test coming up. These are just wrinkles along the way — some really really big wrinkles."

As they portaged back across the several lanes of Washington, Martin glanced up the street. *Endeavor* was still trapped in the ice. The walk up Mount Vernon was more of the same weaving around gridlocked cars. Martin noticed Susan deliberately looking in the opposite direction of the rising smoke beyond. He wanted to make distracting conversation. The task of finding passages through the cars, however, proved distraction enough.

"Wait a minute," Susan said at one point. "You're pulling all my stuff *and* carrying your own. I'm not carrying anything."

"So?"

"So, that's not right. It's my stuff. I should be carrying it." She grabbed the roller bag handle away from him. The weight of it surprised her a little, but she put on an oh-this-is-nothing face and walked on.

"Okay, but if you get tired, you just say something," Martin said as he caught up to her.

With his hands free again, Martin checked his phone. None of the news sites would load. No email servers. No messages. The last tweet was over an hour old. His other feeds were even older. They reported nothing new: power out all over, there were many wild theories for why. The #SasquatchUprising thread proved that even in the midst of a national crisis, some people still did not have enough to do. The theory that al-Qaeda used a thousand little radio-controlled planes to simultaneously crash into power lines, was at least technological, even if absurd. His phone still had two bars of signal, so he tried to send a couple more short text messages.

"Mon.2:45pm. Pwr out here. How u doing? -dad"

"Mon.2:47pm. Pwr out here. U & Judy ok? -dad"

"*Mon. 2:50pm. Somrvil. Doing ok but slo. Going 2 hitch on 93.*"

"Texting home?" Susan asked.

"Yes. I have no idea if she'll get it or not. Most cell towers have backup power, but some less than others. One of them nearby must still be working. I'm getting two bars. Even then, who knows if the network behind them still has power?"

"Who is 'she'? Your wife?"

"Yes. Margaret."

"Oh." They walked for a full block without talking.

He could picture Margaret getting the house ready for a night without power, hauling up a couple armloads of firewood, getting the oil lamps topped up and positioned. She would probably have one of her frozen tubs of soup thawing for supper. He had not received a text from her. Did she try to text him, but the system was down? Was she worried about him? He mentioned his Plan B to walk home only once. Her scoff was a few points shy of encouraging.

Martin felt uncomfortable with the silence. "She's probably worried about me, and afraid I'll do something dumb like walk home." He chuckled at his own irony.

"She'd be right. It *is* a dumb idea." Susan muttered to herself and shook her head. "Walking fifty miles."

"I prefer to think of it as Bold or Brave or maybe Daring." He struck a heroic pose, as if he had a cape to flap in the wind.

Susan rolled her eyes. "No. She's right. It's dumb."

The hero pose collapsed. "Hey, I'd rather not walk either, but waiting could be worse. She wouldn't like it if I got stuck down here for days...or longer."

Susan just frowned disapprovingly. "What is it with you and waiting?"

More quiet walking made the blocks pass slowly.

"So, do you and Margaret have any kids?"

"Two. Dustin just graduated college and got married. He's up north. Lindsey is out in Wisconsin going to college, in her second year." Martin felt like the rules of conversation dictated that he then ask her about her home and family situation, but he had already run afoul of those topics. The weather? The Red Sox? No good alternative topics came to mind, so he accepted the awkward silence.

He wondered how his son and daughter were getting along. From the sounds of things, they were probably without power too. As kids, they seemed to enjoy the periodic winter outages: board games played by oil lamp, s'mores in the open wood stove. Martin could imagine them both seeing this massive outage as another no-electricity adventure, though he felt that this outage was going to become more trouble than adventure.

"My bag seems kind of heavy," Susan said after a while. "Even with wheels."

"This stretch is somewhat uphill. Want me to take it awhile?" Martin offered.

"No, no, I can manage. But, can we take a little rest? My feet are killing me."

Martin wanted to keep going. The day was already three-quarters spent and he was still in the city, more or less. His plans for a three mile per hour pace were not panning out. But, he had no defense against big sad eyes.

"Okay, but we shouldn't rest too long. We're not there yet. You can have a good long rest when we get you to La Quinta."

Susan draped herself over the concrete steps of a shabby yellow house close to the street. Martin did not want to admit it, but getting off his feet did feel good.

"Maybe you should change out of your work shoes," he suggested. "I put a pair of sneakers in your duffle."

"That's okay," said Susan. "We're only going a little further, right? I just need a break."

He began to visualize the rest of his day. After his Boy Scout duty was done, he would hitchhike on 93. Ideally, he would find someone bound for New Hampshire who could drop him off at the exit near the bus station and his truck. If all went well, he might still be home by dark and enjoying some of Margaret's soup. The sooner they got going again, the sooner he could be home. Margaret had been through enough outages to know what to do in the short term. Martin wanted to get started on longer-term arrangements around the house in case the outage lasted more than a week.

"How about we trade bags?" suggested Martin. "It's like cross training. Uses different muscles." Susan looked skeptical, but agreed.

The traffic at the Broadway intersection was more troublesome to cross.

"Whoa!" said Martin. "I think I liked gridlock better. This traffic is moving just enough to get scary. A gap appears, and someone rushes up to fill it."

"Over here. Quick" Susan shouted. They bolted through a gap caused by a distracted driver. The driver looked up and honked long and loud. Another car nosed into the gap he left. The driver was shouting something out his window, but Martin and Susan ignored him as they walked briskly between the lanes.

"I feel like I'm in a giant 3D game of Frogger," Martin said. "Over here. Behind the blue car." They ran through.

Once under the 93 overpass, they paused for a shared sigh of relief. Mystic Ave, however, was yet another Frogger river.

"Tell you what. Let's stay on this left side. It's a bit bleak and we'll have to go single file, but we can avoid those intersections up ahead."

Susan nodded wearily.

Martin looked back at Susan as he walked in the lead. "La Quinta is a bit further from downtown, so maybe it won't be full. But it should be near bus service -- when they can get the streets clear enough for busses to run again."

"That would be good," Susan half-shouted up to Martin. Horns and driver shouts echoed off the concrete wall of 93's elevated deck. "I'll have be able to get in to work when they reopen the bank. Take my test."

At one dark traffic light, two cars sat locked with crumpled fenders. One car steamed. Their drivers stood on opposite sides, flailing their arms at each other. The rest of the traffic tried to creep around them, creating gaps in the flow.

"Look," Martin hollered back. "See the sign up there?"

"Yes."

"We should cross now. You ready?" She nodded. They managed to cross all three lanes without breaking stride. The drivers were either being kinder, or Martin and Susan were getting better at Frogger.

"Oh hey. That's good to see." Susan pointed between two low brick buildings. "That glass building back there? That's the Orange Line's Assembly Square stop. That's pretty close to the hotel, actually. This will work out great. I can get a good night's sleep and when the power comes back on, and the T is running. I can get back in to the bank almost as fast as I did before."

They made a beeline for the hotel, over curbs and grassy strips and up through the rear parking lot.

"I am *so* ready for a huge long nap," Susan said. "I don't remember being this tired in a long time."

"This place won't have power either," Martin cautioned. "But at least you'll have a bed. Should still have water pressure for a while, I'd think, so you can clean up -- with cold water anyhow."

Susan laughed softly. "Cold is fine. I just want to get off my feet. I need some quiet time to clear my head."

"You know," she continued. "Maybe you should get a room here too. Walking to New Hampshire still sounds crazy to me. What could be so bad about waiting until tomorrow? Things are bound to get better in a couple days."

"Thanks, but I still don't like waiting." Martin said. He did not think things would get better in a day, or maybe even a week, for that matter. He had no clear notion of why the roads had become impassible, but it seemed imprudent not to travel while it was still possible.

Susan frowned at him. "I don't see the big deal about waiting."

"That's okay," said Martin. "Just call me crazy. The important thing is that we're here at La Quinta, and *you* will have a place to stay."

Martin smiled at the prospect that his Good Samaritan detour was nearly done. He visualized her happy smile upon hearing there was a room for her. He imagined that he would shake her hand, wish her well, and perhaps say something upbeat like, *hope to see you at the bank again soon*. He would try to end their joint adventure on a positive note about the future — her future. Then, he could get going and maybe catch a ride up to his truck.

They rounded the corner to the front of the building, but stopped cold. Something was wrong. A sizable crowd stood around the lobby door. Many of them were shouting. Martin could not make out what they were shouting, but the tone was unmistakably angry. Others stood braced, as if expecting a strong gust of wind.

"What's going on? Susan asked.

Just then, a man in a tan suit came sailing backwards out the double doors. He landed on his back and rolled.

"Hey, that's the guy from Holiday Inn I was telling you about." Two other men came running out, trying to grab the tan-suit man. A man and a woman in the crowd pulled at the two men, not so much to save the man in tan as a chance to get in some licks of their own. The melee broke up into smaller schoolyard scuffles of three or four people, slapping, kicking and pulling at each other's clothes. One of them made a break for the lobby doors. The other fights ceased and their combatants also rushed for the doors.

"What the heck?" Martin asked rhetorically. His visions of smiles and handshakes clearly had no place here.

The doors flew open and two different people were pushed out. An opportunist from the parking lot crowd pulled them out of the way and ran into the open doors. The less ambitious in the crowd shouted and shook fists from a safer distance.

Susan stared in disbelief. "What on earth are they fighting about?"

"Got me. I really didn't think things would get bad that fast."

"What do you mean 'get bad that fast'?"

"Brian thought the city would go all chaotic soon after a crisis. Sometimes, when we were working late, he'd talk about how he figured people in the city would go crazy if the system ever broke. How, just a few days without power, water and food, hordes of starving city people would totally freak out — fights, riots and…" Martin decided he should stop there.

"A few days?" Susan said. "The power hasn't even been out for one whole day yet. These people haven't hardly had time to get hungry, let alone starving."

"True. This can't be what Brian talked about. Maybe it's more like too many Type-A personalities in the same place at the same time, not finding any rooms here either, they just snapped."

"Snapped? More like flipped out! There's no way I'm going in there," Susan pointed at the door. "Those people are dangerous."

Martin knew she was right. He could not leave her at La Quinta. His Good Samaritan deed was not finished after all. Her trouble finding housing was turning out to be similar to his problem finding a bus or a train. He should have resisted the urge to make a little gotcha dig out if it, but he did not.

"Hmm." Martin pulled at his chin. "I suppose you could wait, though." He put extra emphasis on the word *wait*. "The fighting is bound to stop eventually. If you waited until things calmed down you could go see if there's a room."

"Wait? That's crazy. They may only stop fighting when there's nothing left to fight over. I don't want to wait. Where is the next hotel?"

Martin smiled a smug little smile.

"What?" Susan asked, irritated.

"You're sounding like me now."

"What? Am not. And walking fifty miles still sounds dumb. I'm talking about maybe a mile more. Totally not the same thing." Susan peered around the cityscape. "Where *is* the next hotel?"

Martin regretted his little irony dig. She was under a lot of stress already and certainly did not need someone making wisecracks. He decided to be all-business the rest of the time and hoped she would forget his lame attempt at humor.

"Ahem. Well, I hadn't marked hotels on my little map," he said. "Maybe I should have. But I do know there's a Hyatt a couple miles further up 93 in Medford." He showed her his map. "We're here, and that Hyatt is right about here, just over the river. 93 is the most direct route."

"How far is that?"

"Two, maybe two and a half miles."

"Ugh. I don't want to sound whiny, but that's another hour of walking. I'm already tired. I sure hope the Hyatt has a room on a lower floor — no stairs…and no fighting."

Martin gazed at the upper deck of 93. "I was planning to hitchhike on 93. Traffic is heavy up there, but moving. That's better than the lower deck or the surface roads, which are dead-stop. We could hitchhike on 93 and get a ride for the two miles, or walk down here. Which would you rather do? Your call."

Susan squinted at the traffic moving at a walking pace on the upper deck. "I've never hitchhiked before. Seems risky…"

"It sounds like there's a 'but' coming," Martin interjected.

"Yeah. But my feet really hurt. I suppose, since you're coming too, and it's broad daylight…but if I get the slightest sense of creepy from whoever the driver is, I am not getting in their car. No sketchy vans. No old cars with black windows…"

"Okay, okay. I get it. No risky rides. Agreed. It's not like I'd get into some sketchy van either. Over there is the on-ramp. We'd better get started."

Martin and Susan walked along in the breakdown lane of 93. All four lanes inched along. Sometimes the cars rolled slightly faster than they were walking. Sometimes traffic stopped and the pair got ahead.

"I've been trying to catch the eye of one of these drivers," said Martin. "You know, ask-with-my-eyes? But they're either ignoring us, or we're become invisible." He studied his hand against the skyline to check for transparency.

"These shoes were always so comfortable," Susan said. "...but then, I don't think I've ever walked this much in them before. I'm beat."

Martin spotted a tradesman's pickup slowly catching up with them. *Walsh Bros Remodeling. Manchester, NH*. It was an extended cab pickup, so Martin thought they might have room. The truck's passenger had his window down and elbow on the sill, so it would be harder to ignore him.

"Hey there, " Martin called and waved. The man gave a little wave back. "Think you could give a couple of tired travelers a ride?"

"Ain't no room. Sorry," said the young man. "Bed's full of scrap, and back seat's full of tools n' buckets."

Those were technicalities, not an outright rejection, so Martin kept up his appeal. Maybe tool buckets could be moved. Maybe sitting on scrap metal would not be so bad. He had a fish on the line. He might as well see if he could reel it in.

"Oh, well, it's just that the young lady here is really tired." It was a blatant appeal to a young man's chivalry.

The man shrugged at the impasse. "Sorry. Too much stuff in back."

Martin was not ready to give up on a possible ride. A Plan B flashed through his mind.

"Maybe we could stand on your running boards? Hang onto your pipe rack? We'd settle for that."

"We could what?" Susan was taken by surprise. "Ride on the outside? I've never ridden on the outside of a truck before. That doesn't sound safe."

"You'd rather walk?" Martin said out of the side of his mouth. "Smile at the nice man."

The young man looked skeptical, so Martin tried harder to sell the idea. "Not much can happen at these speeds, right? And we're not going far. Sure would beat walking." He felt his smile was too cheesy, but held it.

The driver and passenger discussed his proposal. Martin and Susan walked faster so as to stay even with the truck and maintain eye contact.

"Yah, come on up." The passenger waved them over.

Chapter 4: A ride to the O.K. Corral

Even catching a metaphorical fish felt great. Martin thanked them over and over as he hefted Susan's roller bag on top of the tangle of bent metal studs in the bed. He helped her onto the passenger side running board, then climbed up in front of her, beside the open window.

"We really appreciate this. I'm Martin, by the way. This is Susan."

"Hey, no problem," said the driver. "I'm Leo Walsh. This is my brother David."

"The Bridge Street Boys!" David added with a wide grin. Leo smiled too. David said it as though Martin should have heard of them, but he had not. Martin smiled and nodded as if impressed.

"So, Martin, if things clear up and traffic speeds up, we'll have to drop you two off," Leo said.

"That's okay. Any progress without walking is a gift. We're only going up as far as that Hyatt in... hey, is that the news on your radio? Could you turn it up? What do they say about all this?"

"Not too much," said Leo, as he fussed with buttons. "Had it on for over two hours, but they just keep repeating the same five minute's worth of info. Power grid's down all over. Phones don't work. Pregnant lady has baby on a train. Airplanes aren't falling from the skies, but all flights are cancelled. Emergency this and emergency that. There's supposed to be a statement by the governor -- any minute now -- for the past hour."

"Turn it up, Leo," said David. "This might be him."

"...has been in close contact with state and local officials...."

"That's not the governor," said David. "That's just some guy..." Leo shushed him.

"...reports of widespread failures in the power grid..."

"Everybody knows that, Einstein..." Leo shushed David again.

"...crews are working to restore power as soon as possible. Residents are being advised to remain calm and stay wherever they are..."

"Stay stuck on 93?" David quipped. Leo backhanded David on the shoulder.

"...The governor's office is working to get essential services restored as quickly as possible. We are asking the people of the greater Boston area to stay off the streets so emergency personnel can do their jobs. In the event that this outage lasts into the night, residents should secure flashlights and blankets, avoid the use of candles or open flames. The governor will be meeting with federal authorities this evening to map out..."

Leo shut the radio off. "That was a total waste of time. They don't know nothin'."

"Yeah, but now it's *official*," David said deadpan.

"Did they say what caused it?" Martin asked.

"Nah. They keep talking, but they don't know," said Leo. "They had some guy on talkin' about solar storms, but said how a solar storm would wipe out computers and cars should stop dead. He couldn't explain why cars and computers and phones still worked. Another one said it was caused by greedy power companies skimping on maintenance."

"Then there was this other guy," David chimed in, "Said it was right-wing militia extremists tryin' to start a revolution or somethin'."

"Bah," scoffed Leo. "That was just NPR. They think anything they don't like is cuz of 'right-wing extremists'."

Martin leaned in a bit more. "I heard reports that lots of other cities were down too. DC, New York, Philly..."

"Yeah, we heard that too. This is a big one, alright. This ain't gettin' fixed very fast."

"Won't get fixed? Susan asked. She gave Martin a worried glance.

She must be thinking about her test. "Why not?" Martin asked Leo.

Leo gestured with both hands like a professor giving a lecture, steering with his knee. "The way I see it, whenever there's been a storm or something, like that last big ice storm, power was out for what, half the state, right? What did they do? They called in crews from other states like Pennsylvania and New York that weren't hit, to help out. Same with our crews going down to help with Katrina or Sandy n' stuff. The extra help came from unaffected areas. See?"

"Uh huh," Martin agreed to keep Leo's point moving.

"So from what they're saying on the radio, there *ain't* no unaffected areas. There won't be fleets of other crews comin' in to help us. They'll all be busy working on their own problems. That means we've only got whatever crews we've got here already. Last big storm, it took 'em a week to get the power back on, right Davy?"

"Yeah. Gram's house was out for five days."

"And that was *with* all those out-of-state crews helping," continued Leo. "You can bet it's gonna take waaay longer if all we've got is just our PSNH guys to get New Hampshire's lights back on."

"Yup. This one's gonna be a long one," nodded David. "Looking at a few weeks without power, minimum."

Susan said, "Weeks? I don't have enough money to stay in a hotel for weeks."

"Yah, well. Money might not be your problem, Missy." Leo pointed ahead. "That's your hotel up there, ain't it? The Hyatt?" The others followed his gaze. "Looks like smoke comin' out from a couple places."

"Oh no, not again!" moaned Susan.

Martin swung his backpack around and fished out his little binoculars.

"You carry binoculars?" Leo asked.

Martin bought them for his Walk Home Plan, but did not want to invite yet more ridicule. Taking a cue from David's hat, Martin said, "Um. Red Sox games?" He had never actually been to Fenway, so felt uneasy with the little-white-lie. He mollified his conscience with the notion that he *could* use them at Fenway, if he ever did go see a game. To his relief, Leo seemed satisfied.

"I don't think fire is the real problem," said Martin. "Only a little smoke. The problem is water. I see people sweeping water out of the sliding doors on the upper floors. It's running down the walls from the sides of the balconies. There's some people wringing out towels over the railings. Up top is a couple hanging wet bedding over the railing. I think the sprinkler system must have gone off, or something."

"Lemme see," said David. He reached for the binoculars. "Oh man. Them people look like wet dogs. Everything inside must be soaked. Good news is: the fire's out. Bad news is: tide's in."

Susan asked for the binoculars. She studied the stricken hotel a long time, as if looking for some hopeful sign, but found none. Her glance at Martin with tragic eyes that said, now what?

"Okay, apparently the Hyatt's out." Martin tried to sound like it was no big deal. "You guys think we could keep riding up to Woburn? There's a Comfort Inn right off 93 there."

"I suppose so," said Leo. "The same deal goes if traffic speeds up, though. But, at this pace, it's gonna be gettin' dark by the time we get to Woburn."

Martin leaned back and spoke to Susan. "Maybe the further out we get from the city, the fewer refugees there will be. Better chances to find you a room."

"But I still can't afford to stay in a hotel for weeks. I've only got a few hundred in my checking account. You said the Holiday Inn was only taking cash. What if this other hotel only takes cash too? I've only got a little cash on me."

Martin scratched his head with his free hand. "I can help you out a little, but yeah, that could be a problem. On the "plus" side, I bet you won't be the only one short on cash. Hotels will be full of people who also got caught with nothing but plastic. Who carries cash anymore? I can't see them just kicking out everybody that can't pay in cash. That would be just about everyone. I bet they'd make some sort of deal."

"That's not a very reassuring plan," Susan frowned.

"I know, but let's cross that bridge when we get to it. First thing is to get you a room, then work on options."

Traffic crept along. Sometimes it got up to jogging speed. Other times, it was dead stop. Martin felt impatient as the afternoon faded into early evening. He had to admit that their pace was a bit faster than walking, it was easier on the feet too. The sun had gone down behind the suburban skyline. The top halves of the trees on the right side of the highway were still radiant reds and yellows with the last of the setting sun.

Their progress was a little steadier. Martin started to think they might make Woburn before it got totally dark. Susan would have her hotel, but where would he sleep? All he could remember of Woburn was dense old suburbs and industrial parks. Perhaps he would have to try hitchhiking in the dark. That seemed a dismal prospect, if not downright dangerous.

As they crested a small rise in Stoneham, traffic slowed to a stop.

"Hey Martin," Leo called. "Use your Fenway glasses to see up ahead. Is it a breakdown or something? Which side's best for getting around it?"

"Sure." Martin looked. He saw movement. His angle was not the best for a clear view. "There's some people walking between the lanes."

Martin continued. "Kinda like those panhandlers that walk between the lanes at traffic lights begging for change."

"Maybe someone ran out of gas and wants to borrow money?" offered David.

"What good would that do, ya dummy?" countered Leo. "It's not like there's a gas station on 93. What are they gonna do with the money?"

"But why are they…Oh hey." Martin stood a little taller to see better. "Some guy got out of his car and he's running this way. One of the panhandlers is chasing him…"

"He just left his car?"

"Ow. Smacked him down. What was THAT all about?

"Road rage or something?" David suggested.

"Maybe. But people in the cars are giving stuff to the walking guys. Looks like...bags, purses, maybe? Hold on. Uh-oh." Martin could see the two men brandishing pistols at the people in the cars. He was momentarily taken aback at witnessing a crime in progress.

It had taken most of the day for the populace to absorb the new reality. Police departments were overwhelmed with the chaotic flood of bewildered civilians. Reaching 911 was iffy at best. Even if successful, any dispatched units would be mired in gridlock. Quick-thinking criminals connected the dots and improvised some bold schemes which, in normal times, would have been ridiculous.

"Both the walker guys have guns."

"Guns?" Susan's eyes got wide.

"What kind of guns? C'mon, what kinda guns?" demanded Leo.

"Pistols. Yeah, it looks like they're robbing people in the stalled traffic between these two rock cliffs. No place to go. They're going down the line from car to car."

"What kind of guns?!" Leo demanded again.

"I don't know." Martin was not so 'into' guns to recognize the subtle differences. "Can't tell from here."

"David, get them glasses. I wanna know what they got."

Martin stepped down so David could open his door and step up on the sill. He stood tall and studied the scene ahead for a few seconds. "Couple of pocket guns, Leo. One's a Kel-Tek for sure. The other guy's got a...Baretta. Looks like both are 9 mils."

"What difference does it make what kind of guns they have? What do we do?" Susan's tone had hints of panic.

"Not to worry, miss," said David. "The Bridge Street Boys got guns too." Leo reached under his seat and pulled out a well-worn traditional 1911. David pulled a newer Glock from under the dash. From a tool bucket behind the center armrest, David pulled out two magazines. He snicked one into the grip of his pistol. Leo fished out a handful of magazines from a box and snapped one in too.

"If them punks want trouble..." began Leo.

"...we don't want to disappoint 'em," finished David. He pulled a little nylon bag from under the dash. He handed Leo several more loaded magazines for the Colt and a box of rounds. He put several other magazines in his own shirt pockets.

Susan stared in shock, as if they were putting rattlesnakes in their pockets.

"Listen, guys," Martin said, "Maybe we ought to be someplace else while you're taking care of business. I think I'd better get Susan out the hot zone."

"Damn straight, skippy," said Leo menacingly. "Get the wimmin folk to safety." He cocked his slide. "We've got us some justice to deliver. Safeties off, Davy boy. This is not a drill."

Martin did not have much of an inner Rambo nature, but his inner John Wayne scowled at him for running away from a fight. His rational side reminded him that he had no weapon. He would be more hindrance than help: a human sandbag, at best. He also felt that his Good Samaritan duty was to get Susan to safety. Martin hefted Susan's bundle out of the back of the truck. She still looked stunned that she had been so close to two actual loaded guns and lived. Martin headed for the guard rail.

"Susan, come on. This way." He returned to pull her by the arm.

"Leo and David. They have guns! Those guys down there, *they* have guns. Oh God, someone's going to get hurt."

"Maybe," said Martin, "Let's make sure it isn't us. We need to put some distance between us and them."

"Where are we going?" Susan hesitated.

"Hopefully, *around* the trouble. Perfect, a gap in the chain link. C'mon. Duck under."

He pointed to the small lake on the other side of the fence. "This here is Spot Pond. That hill to the left is the back side of the rock cliff on 93. See? It's a little peninsula sticking out into the reservoir. We walk around it and we come back up beside 93 on the other side of the rock cliffs."

"Why would we want to do that? There's people out there with guns."

"We'd come back up to 93 *beyond* them. The thieves were in the middle of the cliffs. Ideally, we come back up to the highway well past them. We'll see if we can catch a different ride outta here. The bluff will give us cover if there's shooting."

"Shooting? Oh God." Susan looked over her shoulder nervously.

"Try not to think about it. We'll just go through these woods here as quickly as we can. Hmm. Your roller bag isn't going to be easy through this brush. I'll carry the wheels end. You carry the handle. Follow behind me. If I drop down low, you drop too. Okay?"

"Oh, I don't like this. I've never been anywhere *near* a shooting. I hear about them on the news, but I never thought…I don't even like to see those things on TV."

"That's okay. Being scared is normal. But the idea here is to keep moving away from the trouble. Get it all behind us. Okay?

"Okay." Her tone was doubtful. Her eyes were still wide.

When they were about halfway around the peninsula, Martin said over his shoulder, "I know I'm going kinda fast, but I'm hoping to get back to 93 before…"

Pop pop.

Susan yelped a scream. Martin spun around, wondering if she had been hit by a stray bullet. She did not appear hit, but stood tall and stiff, eyes staring up the hill. Martin squatted down and tugged at her coat to pull her down. He tilted his head to get a better bearing on the sounds. Susan dropped to her knees, eyes darting around like a trapped animal. Martin could hear shouting and banging. Muffled shots? Car doors? Fender-on-fender impact? It was hard to tell.

"We're okay," Martin whispered, trying to reassure her. "We've got the high ground between us and them," He tried to sound reassuring, even if he was not entirely convinced himself.

Pop pop pop. Susan yelped another little scream.

"Okay, I know you're scared, but you really can't keep doing that."

"I can't help it."

"Well, *try* to help it. Screaming only calls attention to yourself."

POW. Susan squeaked with her hand clamped over her mouth.

Martin squatted down a little lower. "That last one sounded like something bigger than a 9mm. Maybe Leo's .45. We'd better find some cover. See those big rocks up ahead there?" Susan nodded, with her hand still over her mouth. "Stay low, and follow me."

Pop pop pop. Bam pop pop. Susan squeaked again, but made apology with her eyes. They stopped and leaned their backs against the boulders.

Geez, it's like the O.K. Corral down there, Martin thought.

"I want to go up ahead and see if it's clear. You stay here behind these rocks. It's a safe place."

"What? You're going out there? People are shooting! They're shooting guns! "

Martin felt the urge to say something snide about pointing out the obvious, but he could see she was sincere and still grappling with a reality she never expected to have to deal with.

"I'll be careful and stay out of sight. Just remember: no screaming."

He ran as best he could, hunched as low as he could and still run. From one tree trunk to the next, he worked his way down nearer the shore and away from the rocky ridge. He could still faintly hear people shouting. A woman was screaming, not hysterically, but more like she was giving orders. There were still occasional pops. They could have been shots, or maybe just slamming of car doors. The rocky canyon reverberated the sounds, making them less clear. Martin worked his way around the shore to where he could see the guardrail and motionless cars up on 93.

Pop POW. *Sounds like Leo is still in it.* Martin moved in closer, one tree at a time, eyes scanning to detect any other movement in the woods. The shore curved close to the embankment of 93 with precious little brush for concealment. Was the way clear?

It was not. Through the gaps in the brush and trees, Martin could see one of the robbers. He sat awkwardly, huddled behind the jagged end of the damaged guardrail. The robber peered over the rail in nervous little one-eyed peeks. Pop pop. He fired back down the highway, periscope style. The guardrail clanged loudly from a bullet strike.

Must be Leo or David who has him pinned down. Martin could almost pity the pinned robber's plight. Almost.

An unseen motorcycle suddenly roared to life far to the right and buzzed up the off-ramp. Martin heard it whine off into the distance. He could hear Leo's voice shouting. The thief behind the guardrail shouted back and fired off a couple wild shots without looking. The standoff continued for what seemed forever, though it may have only been ten or fifteen minutes. Daylight was fading.

The sound of multiple motorcycles grew amid the background of honking and distant sirens. From the sounds of the engines, Martin guessed there were three motorcycles, maybe four. They whined down the off-ramp, stopping several dozen yards from the pinned man. The riders hopped over the guardrail and let fly a few quick shots in what Martin guessed must have been Leo and David's direction. The big .45 answered back with loud clangs on the steel rail.

A long section of the guardrail was still missing. The week before, a tractor-trailer swerved and rolled its load of precast on its side. It took out forty or more feet of guardrail. A few orange cones and yellow tape marked the site where repairs were to begin.

The motorcycle riders were trying to make their way past the gap in the guardrail, to their pinned down cohort. They tried a charge with a volley of covering fire. Pop pop...pop pop pop. Boom. One of the newcomers yelped when a spray of gravel from a near miss raked his legs. They scrambled back to cover behind the bent end of the far guardrail. Leo's field of fire was too close for their comfort. Pointing in different directions, they did not seem to really know where Leo and David were.

The stranded thief yelled to his friends. They yelled back. Did they want him to climb the fence? The lower ground behind the fence would give him cover, if he could get over it. The pinned man shook his head. He either did not want to, or could not. Perhaps he was injured. One of the newcomers threw a bundle to the trapped thief. Spare magazines? One of the other cohorts crouch-ran back the way he came, to higher ground. He ran from the guardrail to the chain-link fence.

Martin felt a sudden rush of fear and worry. He could guess his plan. The reservoir side of the fence was lower than the roadway. The embankment would give him cover to reach his pinned friend. Or, maybe he planned to work his way up the ridge and neutralize the threat with flanking fire on Leo. What if this gunfight started to spill out into the woods? He and Susan might end up in the line of fire or worse, crossfire. With the reservoir behind them, there was no escape route.

Martin's mind was quickly assessing the trees along the ridge, the crook's likely path, his possible line of sight to the rocks Susan was hiding behind. Martin would not be able to get back to Susan unseen if the crook came over the fence and started into the woods. Would Susan stay down? He hoped so. What if she mistook the approaching crook for him? He could not see her from his low position, so he could not gesture to her to stay down. A million possibilities raced through his mind. He did not like any of them.

The crook pointed at the ridge, then the fence. He looked over his shoulder, stuffed his pistol in the back of his pants, grabbed the top pipe and hiked his belly to the top pipe. He was trying to kick a baggy pant leg over. Martin's heart stopped. Trouble was coming their way.

POW. Leaf bits sprinkled down around the man. He tried more urgently to swing his leg over the pipe. Pow-Ting! A shot rang off the fence pipe. The crook dropped back down and shouted what must have been profanities. Apparently the fence was high enough that it exposed a climber to Leo's .45. The fence-climber argued with his buddies. After some animated arm gestures, one of them scrambled back north along the guardrail. The trapped man held his gun over the rail, and fired a couple wild shots as covering fire.

The scrambler vaulted the guardrail and dashed out among the stopped cars. Peeking heads inside the cars ducked down.

Perhaps he was going to try his flanking move from the median side. Maybe he was going for more reinforcements. Neither bode well for bystanders, but Martin was relieved he had gone the other way. The crooks yelled back and forth to each other.

Bam clang. Bam thwack. Leo silenced their yelling with some well-placed shots on the guardrail and a post.

While the crooks were busy behind their cover, Martin took that opportunity to make his way back up to Susan at the rocks, keeping a tree between himself and the thieves. He hoped their attention was more focused on the highway than the darkening woods behind them. The daylight was getting dim, but Martin could still make out the black silhouette of the big rocks against the fragments of dull slate sky that peeked through the leaves.

"Oh! Oh my God, You're okay!" Susan grabbed him in a sudden hug. Since both were kneeling it was awkward and unstable. "Oh my God. There was SO much shooting. I thought you got shot. I didn't know what I'd do. Oh my God you're okay…"

For a few long moments, Martin was a deer in the headlights. His mind had been full of bad guys, movement options and sight lines. A sudden hug was unexpected. He waited for her let go, but she did not.

These things happen, he reassured himself. *Sometimes women go all huggy when they are frightened. It's normal,* he told himself.

He knew Margaret would not be happy at all if she saw this. *It doesn't mean anything*, he told himself as if he were telling Margaret. *She's just scared.* He decided he should disengage from the hug. He started to pull back. Susan's hair smelled faintly of vanilla and some sort of oil. Her neck and shoulder were warm too. The fact that he even noticed these things unsettled him. The warmth did make him realize how cool the evening air had become.

Martin cleared his throat, pulled down her arms and faced her. "Um. Yeah. I'm okay. But I have some bad news. We can't get past them like I'd hoped. The fight moved up the road. Now the bad guys are pinned down behind the guardrail right where we'd have to go."

Susan continued in a half whisper. "I was just sure you had gotten shot. I didn't know what to do. I was going to look for you, but they kept shooting. I screamed. I know I did. I'm sorry. I couldn't help it. I'm just so glad you're okay."

"Thanks, but I was careful. As I was saying, we've got a problem. I think it must be Leo and David that's got the bad guys pinned down, but they're pinned right where we need to go. There might be somebody else helping Leo too. It sounded like something else besides their two .45s shooting back at the baddies. No way to know. Anyhow, one of the bad guys went and got help, but one of them is still trapped and can't get out. I counted maybe three or four bad guys down there now. The thieves are up to something, but I don't know what. Could be they're trying to flank Leo and whoever. Could be they're going for more help. Neither is good news for us.

"What do we do? What if they come down here?" she asked with a gasp of horror. "They could start shooting down here!"

Martin had thought about that very prospect on his way back, but Susan was getting upset. She needed reassurance, not his own worst-case imaginings. "It's possible," he whispered back. He decided not to mention the almost-fence-climber. "But I figure if they do, they'll be moving up along the ridge up there, where they can still see. Maybe trying to get a shot down on the highway. Coming down here into the dark brush doesn't seem likely. But, as long as they're shooting at each other, there could be stray bullets flying around. I think our best course is to stay behind these big rocks and wait."

There was just enough twilight to see the worry lines fade from Susan's face. A wry little smile grew. He realized what he had said.

"I know, I know," said Martin. "But this time waiting is different. It's a safety thing. If it quiets down soon, we can try and get past them and keep going up to Woburn." He was surprised how much her little smile lifted his own spirits.

"And what if it doesn't settle down soon?" Her smile was gone.

"Well, it has to...eventually. Infinite ammunition only happens in the movies and bad novels. For right now, though, it's getting cold. We're not active and generating any body heat. No telling how long we have to wait. We'd better put on a few more layers so we don't get too chilled." He clicked on his little red-beam flashlight.

"I've got a light sweater in my pack, gloves and stocking cap. Here, use my light to get out your sweater and gloves. The red light will be easier on your eyes and won't carry far. I'll go cut off some pine branches for us to use as screening and to sit on."

Martin got out his multi-tool and flipped out the little saw blade. Crouching beside a nearby young pine, he sawed at a lower branch, seemingly with no effect. *Stupid little pretend saw. I could have chewed my way through with my teeth by now if...* The branch broke off. *Okay, maybe it wasn't totally worthless, but still. Next time, I pack a real saw.* He cut several more branches and drug them back.

Pop pop...Bam. Pop. Susan flinched with each report, but did not scream.

"They're still at it," Martin said softly, trying to sound matter of fact. "Wonder if they tried flanking Leo, or what. Part of me wants to know."

"All of me *doesn't* want to know," she whispered back.

"No, I suppose not. Best to just lay low and keep out of it. But that means staying here for who knows how long and it's getting cold. Weather's been nice for mid-October, but still, they were calling for low 40s tonight."

Martin ran his hand over the leaf litter beside him. The leaves are already getting clammy with dew. "We'll lose a lot of body heat sitting on the ground. Here, quietly scrape up a good pile of these leaves to sit on with these pine branches on top. It will help insulate your…insulate you. And we shouldn't lean against the rocks, either. They'll pull heat out of us too."

They gently pulled leaves into piles to sit on. Sometimes a burst of faint yelling would rise up louder than the background medley of distant honking and sirens. Susan carefully sat atop her pile of leaves. She pulled her knees up under her coat and folded her arms over them. She pulled her head down into the tall coat collar. "I just can't believe what a whacked out day this has been," she whispered to herself. "A totally whacked out day."

The woods were becoming a featureless mass of darkness with irregular patches of deep blue sky overhead. The far side of the reservoir would normally be sparkling with street lights and house lights as night fell. Now, it resembled a lake in the far north of Maine.

Around the side of the boulder, Martin could see the tree trunks, leaves and ridge as black silhouettes against the glow from car lights below. A few shouts were followed by a pop, then more shouts.

Geez, thought Martin. *I'd read that gun battles are usually over in seconds, or a couple minutes. This just keeps dragging on and on. I wonder if these guys know they're doing it wrong. They need to read more gun expert blogs. Then again, if both sides were well entrenched and had lots of ammo, this might be more like World*

War One than the O.K. Corral. If that's the case, this could go on all night.

Martin leaned over to Susan to whisper. "I wonder when they run out of ammo."

She jumped slightly. "What?"

"You fell asleep?"

"Oh, I must have. Weird. I'm scared, but I am sooo tired too. Can we rest a little longer? Maybe a half hour? I'll be good to go after that."

"Yeah, you just rest awhile. They're still going at it down there anyhow, so we might as well rest up."

He realized that even when the gunfight was over, it would still not be safe to walk past the highway for awhile. The woods were so dark that he would have to use his flashlight to walk. He could use his little red light, but even that would eventually become visible from the highway. A random flashlight could easily spook a jittery armed man, whether crook or Walsh brother. No. The fight had to be completely over before it was safe to move.

"If we're going to be here awhile, we'd better wrap up in one of these."

"What's this?"

"One of those little mylar reflective blanket things. It'll keep your body heat in while we wait, especially if you fall asleep again. It'll keep the dampness off as well. Pull it up over your head too, like a hood."

"But what about you?"

"I've got two. They're small." Martin winced at all the crinkling the cold stiffened mylar made as they each wrapped themselves. He had them stop periodically to listen. The background honking, sirens and periodic clamor from the highway were easily enough to overpower any of their crinkling noises.

Off his feet, and bundled up, Martin noticed how heavy his arms and legs felt. His feet ached. His shins ached. He welcomed the prospect of a bit of rest himself. He extended the little knife blade of his multi-tool and folded the handles back to make a fat grip. It was a laughably puny weapon: a knife at a gun fight, and a small knife at that. But it felt better to have something clutched in his fist than nothing.

A flickering orange glow mingled with the headlight glow. Whiffs of burning plastic, or rubber drifted through the woods. Martin thought he heard a couple of shots, but they were much fainter. More echo. The background of distant honking and sirens became a rhythmic pattern, like summer cicadas. He could hear Susan's slow, deep breathing in the quieter spells.

Poor thing. Must be totally exhausted.

The shouting seemed further away. *Maybe the fight has moved, but which way? If it moved south, maybe the thieves were gone from the guardrail. If so, we can press on north after our rest.*

Susan gradually slumped over, leaning her shoulder against his back. She was fast asleep.

I guess she IS more tired than she is scared, Martin thought.

Martin was exhausted too. Sitting still, bundled up, felt very good. He wondered how Margaret was handling things at home. He drew some comfort in knowing that she was, most likely, okay. She would have had the house in power-outage mode long before dark. He imagined her grumbling as she lugged the generator up onto the deck, because he had not gotten around to putting wheels on it like she asked him to. She would have a toasty fire going in the wood stove and probably heated up some soup on it for supper.

Martin shook off that line of thought. It only made him feel colder and hungrier. Instead, he pondered their next move after their half hour rest was done. If the battle had moved south, he and Susan could resume their travels north. But, if the fight had migrated north it would still block their way. He rested his eyes and tried to concentrate on sound clues to which way the trouble was moving. He could feel the slow rise and fall of Susan's breathing against his back.

Chapter 5: New dawn, new direction

Martin woke suddenly with sharp pain in his calf. Charlie horse! It was like his toes were trying to curl back the wrong way. He stood up quickly, trying to put pressure on his foot and stretch the tendons.

"What? What's going on?" Susan slumped into the void where Martin had been sitting.

"Charlie horse," Martin said. "Man, this hurts."

"Oo. It's cold." Susan quickly pulled her blanket tightly around herself. "Hey. I slept here all night? The sun's coming up."

"Looks like we needed more than a half hour of rest." Martin took a few steps back and forth. The pain had subsided to a dull ache. Then, remembering why they were still in the woods, he crouched down.

Susan's eyes grew wide. She remembered too. "The shooting! What's going on now? I don't hear anything," she whispered.

"I don't either," he said. "I'd better go see."

Susan protested with her eyes, but said nothing.

"Yeah, things are quiet, but we need to know for sure before we go walking over there." Martin flipped out the knife blade of his multi-tool.

He tried to low-run as he had the night before, but his stiff legs were not making the task easy. His progress was awkward and slow. Leaves, slippery with a heavy dew, did not help. Nearing the fence and embankment, he had the red-orange glow of sunrise behind him. It gave him great light for seeing, but he cast a long shadow in front of himself. He worried the sunrise would silhouette him, if anyone hostile was still down there.

He approached slowly, trying to minimize leaf rustle. He tried to steer his shadow. If he could see all of his shadow, he reasoned that there should be no bright silhouette for anyone else to see. He peered from beside a big oak. Through the brush he could see many cars still sitting motionless down on the dark highway.

Not a good sign, Martin thought. He moved higher on the hill than he had before, to get a better look. The highway to the south was full of motionless cars. Between the rock cliffs, cars were stopped at odd angles. A minivan with burned out hood sat in the middle. The highway was empty further north. Martin noticed that chorus of car horns and sirens was missing. A few chickadees chattered in the trees, making the morning seem like a denial of the night's gunfight.

Is anyone still down there? he wondered. The cars looked abandoned. From the prolonged gunfire, he expected to see bodies scattered in the road. He was relieved that he saw none. He also noted that he did not see a white pickup with a pipe rack.

Looks like Leo and David made it out, he thought. Martin backed up and peered from the other side of the tree. He expected to see no one behind the guardrail. A tingle ran up his spine. Someone was still there.

The figure lay on the ground, face turned away. Had the trapped crook slept under the stars too, or was he dead? Martin stared for a couple of long minutes, looking for movement. He saw none. Thinking that he might be too far away to tell, he moved closer. Through one good hole in the foliage, Martin had a clear view. He stared for several more minutes. There was no rising and falling of the man's back. Martin noticed one of the crook's pant legs was dark, as was the nearby sand. Blood? Was he shot in the leg and bled out overnight? The hairs on Martin's neck stood as he realized he might be seeing his first dead person.

Sure, he had seen his father and mother in their caskets, but something about funeral homes and caskets made them unreal, like wax sculptures on display. The man laying facedown in the roadside gravel was brutally real.

Martin peered up the road at the far guardrail for signs of the other crooks. Nothing. No sign of them on the median side, or behind any of the cars, either. He could see a few passengers in the cars beginning to stir behind fogged up windows. Perhaps the crooks were gone.

Things were clearly dangerous. His eyes studied the saplings on his way back down the hill. A young poplar looked like a perfect candidate for a hefty walking stick. Green wood had more spring, more flex. A deadwood stick was likely to break if he hit someone with it. A walking stick was a pretty scant defense tool too, but it had more reach than a three-inch blade.

He nibbled at the base of the poplar with his little knife, trying to keep the process quiet. He whittled off the few branches as he walked. Susan peeked over the rocks at the sound of his approach.

"Looks like the gunfight is over." Martin tried to force a little cheer into his tone. "I think it's safe to go now." He decided not to mention the dead man.

"I kinda figured that," she said. "It was so quiet out. What did you see? Anything?

Martin chose his words carefully to avoid both a lie and alarm. "Well, I…uh… saw a lot of cars still sitting down there, some abandoned. From the fogged up windows, I'd say some have people in them that spent the night. But no sign of Leo's truck."

"What about…you know…hurt people…on the road?"

Martin winced. Does a dead man count as a hurt person? It seemed not, but that was too far into the gray zone for comfort. "I didn't see anyone hurt on the highway." The shoulder was not technically 'on the road'. Yet, he wondered why he felt so constrained to avoid lying to her.

"It's a miracle then, with all that shooting. I'm glad to hear that. I started trying to pack so we could get going, but I can't get these mylar things to fold down anywhere as small as they were. Is there a trick to this?"

"No. There's no trick. They just don't. But you did pretty good. They'll pack okay like that."

"Man, I'm hungry," Martin said to himself. "I bet you're hungry too. I didn't eat anything yesterday since breakfast."

"Me either. Never really thought about food."

He dug in his bag. "Afraid all I've got is a couple of old bagel halves and water."

"I've got an oatmeal bar in my purse," she said. The two of them gnawed on the stiff bagel, half an oatmeal bar and shared sips from his bottle. Martin turned on his phone to see if there was signal. He had no bars of signal, but his phone chimed with two incoming messages. "*DD:Mon.3.45. Im OK. Going 2 Ivrson farm w/Jake. <3s 4u. L*". The other message was from Margaret. "*Mon-2pm. Got yr msg. Alts working good. B careful. M*".

Martin tried to send a text, but a box flashed up saying that he needed cell service for text messaging.

"Humph. Enough to receive, but not enough to send. Still, at least I got a couple messages. They're pretty old, but I had my phone off. This must mean part of the system is still running on backup power. Did you check your phone?"

Susan rummaged in her purse. "Rats. Mine's dead. I should have turned it off yesterday. I didn't think of it. Who were your messages from? Was there any news about what's going on?"

"No news about the outage. One was from my daughter Lindsey out in Wisconsin. She's okay and going to stay with her boyfriend's family. The other message was from Margaret. One of my messages got through. Don't know which one. She told me to be careful."

Martin pointed to Susan's low-top fashion boots. "We've got a good bit of walking ahead of us. You should change out of those city shoes. Your sneakers would be a lot better for walking in."

"That's okay. These are pretty comfortable."

"Suit yourself." Martin shrugged. "I'll take the wheels end again. You take the handle." He tucked his walking stick under his arm and maneuvered them through the brush, down closer to the water's edge. His legs ached, making his steps unsteady. He hoped that going down nearer the shore would hide the dead man from view. It did not.

Susan dropped the handle of her bag and gasped. "There's a man laying on the ground up there. You said there wasn't anyone hurt out here."

"You asked about 'on the road'."

She shot him a stern glare. His gray-area mincing was not appreciated.

"I saw him when I went to check on things." Martin whispered. "I didn't want to upset you."

"Too late for that! Is he hurt? Or is he…?"

"Yeah, I think he's dead. That's the crook I was telling about who was pinned down last night. Looks like his friends didn't get him out."

"We should go check or something, right?"

"In normal times, I'd say yes. But, these aren't normal times. I'm guessing that's blood beside him and a lot of it. There's nothing we'll be able to do for him. I couldn't call 911…or anyone else. My phone still says there's no cell service. And, we don't know if any of his buddies are still up there."

Susan crouched a bit and looked around. "Oh."

"What we *do* need to do," Martin whispered. "Is to get away from here as quickly and quietly as we can and get you safely up to a hotel so you don't have to spend any more nights in the woods." Martin lifted the handle and put it in her hands.

"I suppose you're right." She continued to stare at the dead man. "I've never seen a dead person before. I feel kinda sick."

"Then it would be best not to look." Martin pulled at his end of the roller bag, and the two continued walking. Susan stumbled a few times since she kept looking back towards the body.

After they had walked far enough around the reservoir that 93 was obscured by trees, Martin stopped. "We're going to have to climb this fence, I'm afraid," he said. "The fence is curving back around and I don't see any breaks. How about I help you over first, then hand over your things?" Susan nodded.

She climbed the fence unsteadily. Martin occasionally flinched as if about to help her, but stopped when he realized where his hands would have to go. Susan rolled over the bar and dropped to the other side. Martin hefted the bundle up and over. It felt twice as heavy as he remembered. He scrambled up and over the fence.

"Well, now we have a choice," he said. "Back down the ramp is 93. We take that north. That's the direct route up to the hotels. Or, we can go up the ramp and take Route 28. The two run parallel-ish, but 28 would be longer. Which would you prefer?"

"28 sounds fine by me," she said. "I've had quite enough of the highway. I want a 'road less traveled' about now."

"Okay, 28 it is. Maybe we'll find a store open or something. We'll be wanting more to eat than a half a bagel and need to get more water too." He shook his empty water bottle.

"And we should tell people about that guy laying back there," she added. "What if there were other hurt people back there?"

Shortly after reentering the old suburb of Stoneham, Martin and Susan came upon a crowded Mobil station. Despite the early hour, long lines of cars were already lined up on both streets. A few engines idled. Here and there, a person stood between the cars with a gas can at their feet. Other people stood in clusters chatting, sometimes laughing.

"They look like they're camped out to buy the latest iPhone or something," Martin said. "From the look of things, they'll be here a long time. Without power, the pumps won't work, but they look like they plan to wait."

"Hope, maybe?"

Martin and Susan threaded through the line to the little station building. Inside, Martin found several people sitting on rust-mottled metal chairs, discussing when the power would come back on. Clearly, they were just waiting for it. Martin interrupted and told them about the gunfight. A couple of the men had heard shots, but did not seem interested in details. Martin tried to tell them about the dead body on 93, and how there might be hurt people out on the highway, but the consensus was that Martin was mistaken and watched too much television. They resumed theorizing about the outage.

Whatever, Martin thought. *So much for doing one's civic duty.*

"I could use a little girls' room," said Susan.

Martin spotted two keys hanging on the wall. They had grease-smeared Mickey and Minnie tags hanging from them. "Here you go. I'm going to look for some water." He found a vending machine, but the door was unlocked and the bins cleaned out.

"Rats. I was hoping for some snacks for the road," he said to himself. A soda vending machine was likewise open and empty. Martin walked around the building and found a garden hose attached to a faucet. There was still pressure. The water tasted strongly of iron, but was better than nothing. He drank his fill then topped off his bottle.

Susan returned with a sour expression. "I should have used the woods like you suggested. That was more disgusting than any woods."

Martin suppressed his I-told-you-so urges. "Here, drink deep from this. I'll refill it for the road." The iron water only deepened her sour expression. "I know, I know," Martin said. "But we need to be drinking more water. We'll see if we can find better, but for now, at least we'll have this."

While she drank, Martin continued. "I tried to tell the guys inside about the fight on 93 last night, and the dead guy, but they didn't care. I don't think they believed me."

Susan pointed across the street. "Hey. People are going in that Friendly's Restaurant. It must be open."

"Great." Martin said. "Let's go see if they have anything to eat. I'll tell them about the dead guy."

The inside of the restaurant was lit only by the daylight coming through the many windows. All of the booths and tables were full of people. Most sat quietly. A few carried on hushed conversations. No one had plates in front of them, only red cups.

A large-boned woman in a brown apron stood behind the counter. Her face clearly had a go-away expression, but Martin approached her anyway.

"Hi, excuse me. There was a shooting last night on 93, back there by Spot Pond. You probably heard the shots, right?" The woman's eyes turned to fix on Martin, but her expression remained unchanged.

"There was a *lot* of shooting last night on 93. We were okay behind some rocks, but there's a guy laying out there beside the guardrail, dead, we think. Our phones don't work, or we would have called 911. So we thought that we should…" Martin's voice trailed off. His civic duty was falling on stony ground again.

"Our phones don't work either," the large-boned woman said.

"I suppose not, I mean, it doesn't seem like anyone's phones are, but we just thought we should tell someone. There could be others up there, hurt…"

"That's the police's job, not mine. Is there anything else?" Her tone suggested that there should be nothing else and that Martin should move along.

Martin stepped back, frustrated at the woman's indifference. He shifted to more immediate needs. "You wouldn't happen to have…"

The large woman preempted Martin's question with a canned statement that she was clearly tired of making. "No, we don't got any food. Power's out. Everything's spoiled. Sorry." Her last word was anything but apologetic.

"Oh. Not even some…"

"Nope." She took a breath then launched into her second canned statement. "No bread, no muffins, no buns. That stuff was gone yesterday. All I got now is rotten meat, melted ice cream and spoiled diary."

"What about water?" asked Susan.

The woman was taken aback for a moment. "Yeah, I guess I got water, but there ain't no ice or anything, and you'll have to share a cup 'cuz I'm running low."

"That's okay," said Susan cheerily. The woman shuffled slowly into the kitchen.

"Weird that no one seems to care if anyone's hurt back there," said Martin.

"Maybe shootings aren't all that rare here," Susan offered. "Boston certainly isn't like Chicago or anything. I could never live in a place like *that*, but even here, they happen. People get used to them, I suppose."

"I don't think I could get used to that," Martin said, mostly to himself.

The large woman returned with a red plastic cup. Instead of offering the cup to Susan's outstretched hand, she kept the cup close to her apron.

"That'll be five bucks."

"What?" Susan's voice had a tinge of outrage.

"Sounds perfectly reasonable, ma'am. Thank you." Martin stepped up to the woman and pulled a bill from his wallet. Susan looked dismayed at both of them. "I assume this is for the cup." The woman nodded. "So we could get a refill?" The woman glowered, but nodded.

Martin gestured towards the far end of the counter. "Let's go stand over there and enjoy our water, shall we?"

"Five dollars for a glass of water?" Susan said in a scolding whisper. "And you just paid it?"

"I know, I know, but we needed more water. And it tastes better than the gas station water, doesn't it?"

"Yeah, but still…"

"We needed water more than I needed the five bucks."

The angry furrows in Susan's face disappeared. "Huh. The water-and-diamonds paradox."

"The what?"

"It was one of those things Mr. Skinner used to talk about. One is useless, yet expensive. The other is vital, yet cheap. Value systems. I always thought it was sort of silly and abstract when he was talking about it, but I just experienced it. Weird."

"Hmm. Water and diamonds, eh? I'm going to guess that water will be treated like diamonds down here when the pumps run out of backup power. Drink up. I'll see if I can get our 'free' refill before our charming hostess changes her mind. We can take it with us."

Outside of the restaurant, Susan kept looking back. "Did you notice? All those people just sitting in a restaurant that had no food."

"I thought it was odd too. Since this outage looks like a major one, you'd think they would be home getting things squared away, or something."

"Hmm," Susan mused. "I didn't do all that much in that last outage. I lit a few candles. Ate cold food. But it never occurred to me to go sit in a restaurant that also had no power or food."

"This is only the second day, so maybe they're still in that denial stage," guessed Martin. "Biding time with familiar routines, waiting for somebody somewhere to flip the switch and make everything go back to normal."

The walk up Route 28 seemed ploddingly slow. Martin's legs still ached. Block after block seemed the same. Martin had time to study the patterns of the houses around them. Here and there were the occasional big old farmhouse from the 1800s, back when the area was mostly farms growing food for the city folks. Between the big farm houses were bungalows from the 1930s, little capes from the post-war 40s, and ranches from the 50s. A few splits from the 60s must have filled in the last of the old fields and forests. Land that had grown food a hundred years ago had become a continuous mat of houses and tiny yards.

Toys lay strewn in those yards. Minivans were parked in driveways. The scene could have been any autumn Sunday morning, except for it being Tuesday. The sameness of all the little yards, hedges and homes made it feel like they were making no progress at all. The gray day gave the neighborhoods an air of bleak uniformity. Now and then, a car would turn onto 28 and travel north. The sound of a generator could be heard humming somewhere a block or two away.

Martin and Susan did not talk much. Martin was lost in his own thoughts. How far had they traveled? It felt like many miles, but probably wasn't. His plan to walk home had not counted on delays from helping someone else. Part of him wanted to resent Susan for slowing him down, but resentment was a fire that would not light. He had a cozy home to get to. She did not. He had his comfy chair and books to look forward to. All she had was trundling along behind her in a roller bag. The least he could do was to get her set up in a hotel for the night.

He tried to focus on the future. After his good deed was completed, he could make better time. He had a golf course marked on his map as a way point. From Google Earth, it looked like it had a fair amount of woods and a pond. Could he get that far before nightfall? Such a gray day would turn dark sooner than usual. Would twilight find him anywhere suitable for an overnight camp if he did not reach the golf course? He did not relish the idea of traveling after dark through an unfamiliar area.

"Hey," Susan called from behind him. "Could we take a break? I'm getting kinda tired."

Martin snapped out of his million-questions trance. "Oh sure. Sorry." He pointed to a low concrete retaining wall along the sidewalk at the next house. Susan nodded.

She sat down heavily then flopped onto her back over the brown stubbly yard. "Oh, this feels good."

Martin sat down, blew out a long sigh. They had not been traveling long, so he felt embarrassed to admit that it did feel good to rest. He was certainly no triathlete. He consoled himself that they were both still tired from the previous day's adventures and the cold night sleeping in the woods, sitting up, afforded little good rest.

Whether those were reasons or excuses, Martin resolved to make better time by pulling Susan's load and his backpack. She could probably walk faster if unencumbered.

Perhaps, he thought, if he refreshed his feet, he would feel more perky. He took off his shoes and socks.

"What are you doing?" she asked.

"Changing socks. I've found that on long hikes, it helps to let my feet air out now and then. Happy feet are...um...no...that's not how it starts. Never mind. I forget how that goes. Anyhow, I probably should have done this before we started out this morning, but it felt way too cold for bare feet. What about you? Even if you don't want to change shoes, it would do your feet some good to…"

Susan sat up quickly. "No no. I just need a rest. That's all." She tucked her feet behind her.

Martin shrugged. "Whatever." He realized that she only had few miles left to go, so perhaps it was not all that necessary. He put on fresh socks and clipped his old ones to the side of his bag.

"How about I pull your load for awhile. Give you break," Martin offered.

"Okay, but only for a little while."

As they walked further up 28, more cars passed by. A few people walked in from side streets to trudge up or down the street. Ahead, Martin could see more activity. The gas station on the far side of the intersection had lines of cars and people like the Mobil station had. The convenience store parking lot on the near side had a dozen people clustered around between parked cars. An imposing figure of a man with a gray crewcut stood in front of the store.

Susan read the sign out loud. "Andrew's Market. Looks like they're open."

"Cool. Maybe *they* some food," Martin suggested. They moved in closer. The tall man glowered, arms folded high across his barrel chest. He blocked the convenience store's door. His posture alone told Martin that something was not right. Seeing the grip of pistol sticking out of his waistband confirmed it.

A fleshy little man in pajama pants and slippers was pleading with the gray-haired man. Several roundish women, also in pajama pants or sweats stood behind pajama man, urging him on.

"Aw c'mon Andrew. We're outta food. The wife's hungry. Stop n' Shop is way too far to walk."

"Cash only," said Andrew with a vague accent.

"I already told ya, we don't got cash. My EBT balance is good, I swear. Same as cash! You always took my card before, remember?"

"That was then. No power now. No card reader. Cash only." It was a slavic accent: Russian maybe.

Several in the crowd, apparently in the same predicament as pajama man, murmured amongst themselves.

"You could write down how much we buy," said one of the round women. "And when the power comes back on…"

"No writing down. Cash."

Martin stepped up beside pajama man. "I've got cash." He showed the corner of a $20 bill folded in his hand. Pajama man scowled at Martin. The women behind him were more vocal in their disapproval.

"Okay," said Andrew. "You go in." He pulled open the door, but took a quick step in front of pajama man who made a move towards the open door. After Martin and Susan had gone through and the door closed behind them, Andrew resumed his Black Knight pose. Martin could not make out the more heated exchanges through the glass, but it was clear the pajama folk were upset.

"I don't know if you'll find much in here to spend your 20 bucks on," said Susan. She pointed to the rows of low shelf units, mostly empty.

"Whoa. Looks like the locusts have been here, " said Martin. Colorful signs advertised for chips and candy, but the racks were empty. Helpful labels identified where canned soups, crackers, cookies and snacks would be, but the shelves were bare.

"Locusts don't like artichoke hearts…" Susan held up two jars. "…or olives." What remained on the shelves were inedible goods: cat litter, laundry soap, sandwich bags and air fresheners. "Not much in here to make a meal out of. There's some ketchup and mayonnaise here, and a bottle of vinegar."

The woman behind the counter watched them carefully. She looked apprehensive, so Martin approached casually, smiling broadly.

"Business has been pretty good, I see." He pointed to the empty candy racks beside her.

"Yes, people buy many things yesterday." She too spoke with the remnants of a Russian accent. "We only take cash now. Andrei told you, yes?"

"Yes, he did. We have cash. We wanted to buy some food, but you don't have much."

"Food sell fast yesterday. What kind food you are looking?"

Martin guessed that she must have some unseen inventory. "Nothing fancy. Do you have any bread? Rolls? Hotdog buns? Something more filling than…olives?"

The woman looked out towards Andrei, who was impassively resisting the protests of the pajama crowd, which had grown in number. "You wait here. I be back." She sidled out from behind the counter and disappeared through a door in the back.

While the woman was away, Martin noticed that she had a portable radio on the counter. The volume was turned down too low to hear well. Hoping for some news on the outage, he turned it up.

"...boro, Sudbury and Westford relay stations. Workers told me they do not have spares for the burned out units, which are manufactured in Germany or Asia. Crews say they can't work around these problems. Power is going to be out for very long..." The report stopped abruptly. A crackly silence filled several long seconds. Martin reached for the volume knob, thinking that the batteries might be getting low.

Before Martin touched the radio, a suave new voice came on the air. *"The governor wants to assure the citizens of the Commonwealth that essential services will be restored as soon as possible. There is no cause for alarm. Citizens should remain in their homes if they can. Temporary shelters are being set up in and around the greater Boston area for those in need. These will be available soon. Shelters will have heat, hot showers and meals. These are being set up at Soldier's Field, Moakley Park..."*

The woman returned and set a cardboard box on the counter. She turned off the radio. "Bah, more lies."

"You don't believe them, I take it?" Martin made conversation while peering into the box.

"No. Even little child can see things not okay. Maybe not okay for long time. State, she just say things be okay soon to keep peoples calm." She waggled a finger in the air. "Is the same all over. States afraid of riot and lose control. Always worry about control. Will say anything to keep peoples calm. Easier to control. But enough about State. You look through box of food. See what you like. You buy for cash." She pushed the box forward proudly, as if it were a fresh birthday cake.

"Andrei and me had store in old country. We learn not to put all things on shelf all times. When people get scared, they run in, buy like crazy, store has nothing left to sell. Not good for business."

Martin could not decide if Andrei and his wife were shrewd business owners for staggering inventory, or opportunist scalpers looking to reserve some goods to sell at higher prices. Regardless, he and Susan were hungry. The box was full of small bags of chips, chocolaty snack cakes and candy bars: all typical convenience store wares, but too salty or sweet to subsist on. Martin thought they could find more substantial food in another store, so did not want the candy or chips. He did find a box of wheat crackers on the bottom. It wasn't much, but it was some longer-lasting carbs. He thought it might tide them over until they found a different store. After all, this little store was open. That bode well that others might be open too.

"How about these crackers?" Martin asked.

"Oh. For those…um…five dollars," said the woman.

Martin sighed. The orange sticker said $2.39. *Is everything going to cost five dollars now?* He pulled five ones from his wallet. The woman tried not to be obvious about peering into Martin's wallet.

She leaned closer to semi-whisper. "We have beer and wine in back. Perhaps you and your pretty wife will like some beer or wine, yes?"

Susan glanced at Martin, blushed, then looked away quickly. Martin could feel his own face getting warm.

The woman looked back and forth from Martin to Susan. Her expression was a mixture of embarrassed hostess and curious gossip.

"No, thank you," said Martin. "The crackers will do."

"Oh, So sorry. You two looked so…"

"That's okay. The crackers are all we want. No beer or wine, thanks."

A commotion from the parking lot was a welcome distraction. Andrei had pushed away a more zealous pajama person. Things had escalated to where Andrei kept one hand on the grip of his pistol that was still in his waistband. The other hand was pointing accusations at the pajama person on the pavement.

Susan motioned towards the tumult outside. "Do you worry about staying open when people are...like that?"

"Oh no," the woman said reassuringly. "Andrei is strong man. I not worry."

"But there are so many of them," Susan persisted. "And only the two of you."

The women took a half step back and motioned with her eyes for Susan to look behind the counter. The woman pulled a gun halfway out of its hiding place. From the brief glimpse Martin got, it looked like a short-barreled AK without a stock. In the close confines behind the counter, it looked huge.

"We had small store in Tverskoy many years, you see. Rough part of town. Learn quick proper tools for to stay in business."

Susan shrank away slowly and with a nervous smile. Again, she was closer to a gun than she liked. Martin had to admit, it was a serious looking gun — the kind terrorists or radical insurgents wave in the air.

"Could we use your back door?" Martin asked. "I'd rather not go back out through all that."

"Da," said the woman, after locking her secret hatch. She led the way past the empty coolers to a heavily scuffed door marked "Employees Only". She pushed it open and pointed to the far wall of the dimly lit room. "You see yellow door? Go to outside. You sure you no want maybe couple bottles beer? I give you good price."

Martin smiled. "No. Still no beer, but thank you for the crackers." The two of them maneuvered past stacks of boxes in the dim back room. The yellow door pushed open with a loud metal-on-metal scraping sound.

They both squinted in the sudden daylight. The noise of an agitated crowd around across the street at the gas station caught Martin's ear. He peered over the top of the dumpsters.

"I wonder what's got those people in a huff."

"Sounds like maybe someone was cutting in line, or moved something they shouldn't have," Susan said.

Martin quickly studied the two crowds. The pajama people were confronting Andrei with harsh words and flailing arms. A few dozen people at the gas station were embroiled in loud exchanges, animated with pointing fingers.

"I don't like the idea of walking between two angry crowds. What do you say we take a block around and reconnect with 28 a bit further up?"

"Definitely."

The mature suburban street was lined with tall trees in full autumn color. Children played in the crunchy leaves, enjoying the unscheduled school vacation. Parents sat on front steps watching their children and chatting together.

"That first guy on the radio must have been talking about power relays and substations," Martin said. "This thing must be a system-wide problem with the equipment of the grid. Clearly not just a regional glitch."

"So what did Asia have to do with that?"

"He said that they don't have spares," said Martin. "Apparently, those would have to come from Asia. That's gonna be a problem, or at least part of the problem. Do you remember hearing about that sniper attack on a substation out in San Jose awhile back?"

"No. When was that?"

"Right after the Marathon bombings, so it didn't get much media attention. Some snipers shot out a bunch of transformers at a substation."

"Do you think that's what happened here? Snipers?" Susan asked.

"Not really. It's too widespread for guys with rifles. That would take tens of thousands of snipers — all at once."

"Okay, that does sound unlikely. So if it wasn't snipers, what then?" she asked.

"Beats me," Martin shrugged. "Some people think it was an EMP or a solar flare."

Susan looked puzzled.

"Which is where some big flash of energy causes electrical things to overload and burn out."

"That sounds like a good fit." She started nodding her head, but stopped and shook it a couple times. "But I gather you don't think so."

"I'm no expert on EMPs," Martin said. "Brian talks about them, sometimes. That's most of what I know. From what he said, a big surge of energy — whether it came from a solar flare or a nuclear bomb — would affect our little delicate electronics first. You know, fry our phones and iPods and stuff. Heck, they still warn you not to have static electricity on you when you open up a computer to install more RAM. Doesn't take much to fry 'em."

"But our phones were fine…well, until I let my battery die," Susan said.

"Exactly," Martin said. "The little stuff is fine, and it's the big industrial stuff that seems to have been hit. That's where this all seems backwards."

"So you're back to snipers?"

"No, but that was where I was going about San Jose. Back then it took the power company a *month* to get that substation back online. Big parts aren't quick to come by. And that was with only the one substation to repair and while everything else was working fine so they could route power around it. Add in what Leo was saying about there being no extra crews to call in, and it kinda backs up what the first radio guy was saying. Power could stay out for a long time."

Susan walked along, lost in her own thoughts. Martin fell into a mental hole of conspiracy theories.

Would greedy power companies fabricate a crisis? Was the equipment all still intact and they just lied about massive failures? Why would they do that? Perhaps as a sort of corporate-utility "strike" to extort more government money. Could anyone get all those utility people to agree to that scheme? That seemed unlikely. Too many people would have to be in on it. How would they prevent some middle-level minion from blabbing? Thousands of minions would remain quiet? That seemed even less likely.

"The second guy mentioned emergency shelters," said Susan. "I wondered when they'd start opening shelters."

"I'm sure a lot of people will end up in them," Martin said.

"Well, I don't want to. A shelter is the *last* place I want to be. I much prefer the hotel idea."

"Can't say I blame you there. Oh sure, officials start out with great intentions and all, but things get chaotic pretty fast. Kinda like that old maxim about battle plans not surviving first contact with the enemy. Bureaucratic plans don't survive first contact with an emergency."

"So government should do *nothing*? People need help," Susan protested.

"Sure they do, but bureaucrats and their staff tend to be faithful rule followers. Rules become a substitute for thinking. Following proper procedure is what gets them promoted, so they tend to be good at doing just that. Free-thinking gets you nowhere in agencies. Real crises need free-thinking and adaptation."

"It's easier to adapt and respond on a smaller scale," continued Martin. "Back in our last local outage, we put some people up in our church. We had to improvise quite a few things, like cooking, but we could change our plans and adapt. We weren't stuck with bureaucratic rules. I'll grant you that the church wasn't just-like-home, of course, but at least everyone was fed, comfortable and had some privacy in the classrooms. Do you remember seeing photos from inside the Superdome after Katrina? No privacy there."

Susan shuddered. "Oh yeah. I remember the photos. They brought back bad memories."

"You were in the Superdome after Katrina?" Martin was prepared to be impressed.

"No, not that one. I was in one of my own. When I was little — maybe 5 — my family had to stay in a shelter for almost a week. A train derailed. It was carrying gas or something. I don't remember what it was. Houses all around were evacuated just to be safe. Hundreds of us were in the high school gym. I don't remember a lot from back then, but I do remember that it was never quiet, even in the middle of the night. People were talking, babies crying. I don't think I slept the whole time. The part I remember clearest, was that it seemed like there was always someone looking right at me. It really creeped me out. That was my Superdome."

"I can imagine the noise. With all the people, I bet there were dozens of babies and little kids too. Probably at least one kid crying around the clock."

"Yeah, there was. Mom said I never cried, although mom said I always looked like I was about to. Truth was, I was too terrified to make any sound. I was afraid that if I did, even more people would be looking at me. I was never so happy as to get out of there and back into my own little room. Sure, I'm an adult now, but I still don't want anything to do with living in a shelter if I can possibly help it."

"I hear ya," said Martin. "If I stayed in town, I'd end up in one of those shelters. To be honest, I'd rather walk home and sleep in the cold woods."

"I'd rather have a hotel room, if it's all the same. Even if it's way out by 128 and doesn't have power. That's okay. All I want is a room with a door."

"That's the plan," Martin said. They walked in the street, as the narrow sidewalk was in use by kids on skateboards and scooters.

Groups of adults chatted over hedges or fences between the houses. Some sat in their cars listening to the radio. The neighborhood had an air of being all dressed up, but nowhere to go. Snarled traffic and The T being out of action were part of it, no doubt, but even if they could get into the city, what would they do?

"All these people," Susan said. "Just standing around."

"They've probably heard what the roads are like, so they stayed home."

"Sure, but what will they do later?" she persisted. "If the power is going to be out for a long time, what happens to all these peoples' jobs? I was thinking about my job at the bank. We could open the branch without power, I suppose. Things would be cash only, and we'd have to work on paper. It would be clumsy and slow, but we could do it."

"How many people really use cash anymore?" he asked.

"The little sandwich shops do a lot in cash. The pizza guy, the chotchkies gift shops: they deposit lots of small bills. Where I was going with that, was that even their cash-based jobs use electricity. If they can't make sandwiches, or cook pizzas, they don't have jobs. There would be no one coming into the branch with cash anyhow. What about all these people?" She waved discretely at a knot of adults chatting in a front yard. "What about their jobs?"

"A couple days off are nice, but what will they do after that? Without power, who would still have a job to make the money to pay the five bucks for water?"

Martin tried to think of some profession unaffected by the grid going down. He finally thought of something. A music teacher for an acoustic instrument like a violin might qualify, if they were teaching in a building that did not require power for lights or heat, etc. Even though he thought of a non-powered job, if things were grid-down, why would anyone bother taking violin lessons? There would be a lot more serious chores to tend to just to survive. Learning to play the violin would be pretty low on the priority list.

Martin's musing took a more personal turn. What would *he* do in an extended outage? His job not only required power for the internet, it relied on clients who required power. Those clients, in turn, relied on customers carrying on normal lives — which required power.

What if Brian did not reopen the office for a month? He and Margaret had enough in savings to cover the basic bills for a month. Could they pay bills? Most of their money was in the bank, accessed electronically. Could he get cash from the local branch? Would there be any employees working there? Would there be any employees working at the companies that send out his bills? The outage could mean no incoming bills and no outgoing payments. He would have to see how that stalemate worked out.

What if Brian never reopened the office? Martin felt a cold shudder down his back. What if he had to start over completely from scratch? He felt his own house of cards was collapsing.

Chapter 6: For lack of easy options

Martin and Susan emerged from the tree-lined cocoon of suburban Stoneham, back to the stark landscape of small stores, garish signs, and parking lots.

"Ah. Here we are. Route 28 again. Do you want to rest?" Martin was hoping she would say no, so they could make better time. The chances of his making it to that golf course before dark were looking slim.

"That would nice. Thanks," she said.

That was not what he wanted to hear. Martin tried not to let out an exasperated sigh, but he must have.

"Only a short one," Susan quickly added. "I'm sorry I'm slowing you down. I know you're eager to get going to home."

Martin winced. Why was being a jerk so easy? Yes, he was eager to get home, but at least he had one. She did not.

He turned to look her in the eye. "Hey, I don't mean to sound impatient or walk too fast. Sure, I want to get home as soon as I can, but that's not important. I said I would help you find a place. If I said it, I'll do it. I won't just take off and leave you without someplace safe to stay."

She looked away, but he moved over to catch her eye again. "Getting *you* situated comes first, understand? I'll get home eventually. I'm not worried about that. So, don't go feeling bad about slowing me down. Okay?"

Susan did not say anything. She continued looking at him with sad puzzled eyes, which made him uncomfortable.

"Ahem, well. How about we have a snack while we rest, eh? We can enjoy some of our five-dollar crackers. At that price, they've got to be good, right?" His attempt at levity did not erase his jerk damage as he had hoped. She still looked sad and puzzled. The crackers being stale did not help. Neither did washing them down with the iron water.

They walked up 28 in silence longer than Martin felt comfortable. Normally, he was fond of silence, but unredeemed-jerk silence was hard to take. He tried again to restart a conversation.

"Have you noticed all these shops we pass are for a service of some kind? Nail salon, hair stylist, gourmet coffee, travel agent, custom curtains."

"So?" she said. It was just a monosyllable, but it was better than silence.

"Back to your point about jobs. I suppose someone could paint nails or cut hair without electricity." He pointed to a pair of store signs: Cuts 4 Less and Nails by Nina. "But would they have any customers? If food gets scarce and water costs five bucks a glass, are you going spend what little cash you might have for someone to paint your nails or style your hair?"

"Probably not," said Susan. "Speaking of food, There's a Stop n' Shop up ahead there. See the sign?" Susan pointed to a distant sign on the left. "Hopefully, they'll have more than olives and artichoke hearts."

"Or just one box of crackers."

As they walked across the parking lot, they could see a long line of people along the front of the building. A man with a bullhorn was addressing the line, although he was talking too close to the mic.

All Martin could hear was inarticulate buzzing. He turned to comment on this to Susan.

"I can't make out what he's…" Martin began, but stopped. "You're limping. Are you okay?"

"Oh, it's nothing. Just a little tired."

Martin raised one skeptical eyebrow.

Susan pointed towards the store. "What's that guy saying? I caught something about letting in only five people at a time, and something about cash only. The rest was gibberish."

"You caught more than I did," said Martin. "I didn't make out anything."

As they neared the store, two employees with flashlights opened the doors. Five women came out, blinking in the bright gray morning. The carts they pushed contained only a few boxes or a bag. *Were the shelves already picked clean,* Martin wondered? *Was that all they could find, or had prices gone up so much that a few things were all they could afford?*

Bullhorn man began his spiel again. His words were still buzzy, but decipherable. "For safety reasons, only five shoppers are allowed in the store at a time. Please wait your turn. Everybody gets a turn. Remember everyone, we are setting a fifty dollar limit for each shopper. This is to ensure that everyone will get some groceries. We are accepting cash only. Cash only, ladies and gentlemen. We have no way to process credit or debit cards."

"I guess we should get in line," said Martin. "Just in case they have anything left on the shelves. From the length of the line, we could be here for an hour or more."

"But, this is slowing you down even more," said Susan.

"True, but you'll need something to eat in your hotel room. I'll need something for the road. It's a calculated trade-off. I'm kind of regretting not getting some of that candy at Andrew's now."

Martin and Susan took their places at the end of the line. Martin did not like the delay. He would have to make extra-good time to reach his golf course woods before dark. He comforted himself that the prospect of some more substantial food would be worth it. Knowing that Susan would have some supplies was a consolation too.

The manager continued. "Okay. Next five, step up to the door. You in the blue. Yes, you. Step on up, please. Have your IDs out, ladies and gentlemen. It will speed things along."

"IDs?" Susan asked.

"Stoneham residents only," the manager said. "You must have a photo ID with a Stoneham address. No exceptions, I'm afraid. Stoneham residents only please."

"Well, that stinks," said Martin. "That leaves both of us out." A few other people grumbled loudly and slowly pulled out of line. They drifted out to join the Kuiper Belt of have-nots beyond the orbits of the 'haves'.

"Can they do that?" Susan's voice had a hint of outrage. "How can they sell to some people and not others?"

"On a certain level, it kind of makes sense."

"Sense?" Susan was clearly miffed.

"Kinda. The store managers here are probably trying to head off panic buying and make sure their local community gets what there is before it runs out."

"Runs out? It's a huge store."

"True, but even so, what they have in there now won't last long without trucks bringing more. A couple years ago, we did an inventory app for Atlantic Grocers to help them coordinate orders from the warehouses. The suits at AG wanted to trim what they called 'excess stalled capital' and 'excess elasticity.' Products sitting in warehouses were a bad thing, apparently. Our little app worked nicely for them. Order in the evening and have it come on a truck the next day. From working on the app, I learned how the most conservative stores keep about three days worth on the shelves, mostly as a cushion for demand spikes. That's assuming normal demand. Smaller stores don't even keep that much on hand. It's often hand to mouth — or truck to shelf — every day. No one ever sees empty shelves because trucks keep coming. But, if trucks don't come, this place will be picked bare in a few days or less. Probably won't even find a jar of olives."

"Well, I still don't think it's fair."

Martin steered the frowning Susan beyond the semi-circle of disappointed onlookers who either had no cash or no proper ID. They watched the five in, five out routine for another cycle. Susan maintained her scowl of disapproval, arms folded tightly across her chest.

Leaning on his walking stick, he glanced around. Martin noticed the wide band of pavement that went around behind the building. "Hey. I've got an idea I'd like to check out. Come on. No point in standing here anyway, right?"

"What idea?"

They rounded the corner of the building. Martin pointed to the dumpsters beyond the loading docks. "Dumpsters!"

"That's your idea? Trash?"

"Not trash, treasure!…maybe. It's worth checking out, anyhow." Martin said with a sparkle in his eye. "Back when I was in college, my roommate and I had a very lean winter one year. I was washing dishes only part time. Doug got laid off from the logging crew that winter. So, we had to get creative. We would dumpster dive at the supermarket across the highway. Sometimes it was pretty rancid, like slimy lettuce day. But, Sunday nights were usually good. That's when they'd throw away the out-of-date stuff before the big truck came on Monday mornings. One of us would stand watch, the other would dive. Some nights it was 'woohoo mama' and we'd be set for a week. Other times, nothing but cardboard."

"You ate out of dumpsters?" Susan stuck out her tongue as if she had swallowed a bug. Martin walked briskly past the big green dumpster container.

"Of course not. We took it home to eat it. Ah ha!" Martin said louder than he expected. "Just like I thought." He softened his tone to be more stealthy. "We hated it when stores started using these compactor dumpsters. Couldn't get in, and it just crushed everything into mush. But, the compactor on this bad boy is electric too, so they couldn't squash all the discards as they usually would."

A big pile of white trash bags lay piled up against the side of the dumpster. Martin waded into them, rolling them over with his stick.

"Doug had this amazing sixth sense for which bags had good stuff inside. I wasn't as good…Not this one. Squishy produce." Martin carefully turned over bag after bag, eyes darting from bulge to bulge.

"Keep a look out, okay? Let me know if you see anyone coming. Managers get kinda testy about people rummaging through their trash." Susan looked around nervously, uncomfortable with her sudden role as trash accomplice. Martin continued to pull over bags, studying the shapes beneath the white plastic.

"Ah. This one." Martin cut a small slit in the trash bag. "Dairy case. Looks promising. Yogurts. Shoot. They're all broke open. Sour creams, dips too. What, did they stomp on this bag? Ha!

Cheese." He thrust in his hand and pulled out several small yellow bricks and stuffed them in his coat pocket.

He peered deeper into the bag. "That's all?" he said to the bag, then cast it aside.

He pulled at a nearby bag. "I would have thought there was more. Oh well, a couple for me, a couple for you. It's something anyhow." The next bag was obviously heavy. "Ooo, milk case!" He held up a half gallon jug as if it were a trophy trout.

Susan made a sour face. "It sat out all day yesterday and today. It's bad."

"Maybe. Maybe not." Martin twisted off the cap. He took a big gulp. His throat flinched closed at the tart flavor, but he forced the swallow down. "Okay, it's on the edge, I'll admit, but I've drunk worse and lived to tell the tale." He took another long swig and forced it down too. Then he turned it over and poured out the rest.

"What are you doing?" Susan could not make sense of his actions.

"I would have offered you some, but I was sensing that you didn't want any." He smiled impishly.

"Of course not."

"Actually, I just wanted the container. Bottles of water are scarce, but milk bottles, on the other hand…" He emptied a second bottle and climbed out of the debris field of trash bags. "One for me. One for you. Now we need to find a… Ah, there, a hose faucet."

He rinsed out the jugs several times before filling them. Voices arose from the corner of the building. Some of the crowd had followed them and discovered the trash pile.

"We'd better move along," said Martin. "Now that others know about the trash, it won't take long before a manager comes back here and makes a stink…so to speak." He chuckled at his accidental wit. Susan did not look amused.

They walked out from behind the building and out the parking lot exit. The buzzing bullhorn was still engaged in crowd control.

Martin studied his map. "This should be Williams Street. Only a mile or so to go." His feelings brightened. His protracted good-deed was almost done. He could start making faster time. Soon, Susan would have her room with a door and she would not have to spend the night in the woods again.

He looked back at Susan to share that tidbit of optimism, but his smile dropped away. "Okay, you're limping badly now."

"It's nothing. I'll be fine."

"Uh huh, I don't think so." Martin stopped to face her. "Is this why you keep falling back?"

"Really. It's no big deal. See?" She tried to stride past him with an even pace, but grimaced sharply with each left foot step.

"No big deal," Martin grumbled. "You've got a blister and probably a big one. Come on. Sit over here on this grass. I'd better take a look at it."

Susan took a step back. "No no. It will be okay. If I just rest a little, it will get better."

"Rest a little? If you've got as bad a blister as I'm thinking you've got, you'd have to rest for *days* before it 'got better'."

"I'm sure it's not as bad as all that."

"If it's burst already, and you keep rubbing it around in there, it'll get infected and become an even bigger sore. Do you want that?"

Martin's hopeful plans for covering many miles yet that day were fading fast.

Susan frowned at the ground.

Martin tried to dial back his irritated tone. "I don't mean to sound all pushy. It's just that you should take care of little problems, like blisters, before they turn into really big problems." He slung his backpack onto the grass and dug in the front pocket. "I've got some first aid things here. Come on. Come sit on the grass over here." He patted the ground.

Slowly, Susan sat where he indicated, but kept both feet close together and nearly tucked under her.

"Um. I'll need your foot for this." Martin held his hand out. In his mind, he began to replay earlier events. She had been standoffish about changing shoes. Now she was in blister denial. He wondered why.

A sudden rush of awkward feelings engulfed him. *What if she had a deformity? What if she had lost toes due to frostbite from a skiing accident? What would that look like? Or, what if she had webbed toes from birth? What would that look like?* A deformity would explain her avoidance. Embarrassing her felt like a huge breach of chivalry. Yet, there he was insisting that she take her shoe off.

Still, it was obvious that she needed some medical attention. Martin vowed that he would be considerate and understanding. She had a blister. It needed tending. Even after she was safely in the hotel, she would have to walk everywhere she had to go. He would not be there then, so the least he could do now was to patch up her blister before they parted ways. He decided to steel himself for whatever her deformity was. He would not show any surprise or shock -- just a dispassionate doctor face. At least, he hoped so.

"It will be okay, Susan. I just need to treat your blister. You'll feel better afterward." He tried to sound like doctors he had seen on television.

She extended her left foot, but turned her head away.

Was it so bad that even she could not bear to look at it? Martin gently lifted her foot and laid her calf across his lap. Carefully, he unzipped the short boot and worked the opening wide so it would not rub as he pulled the shoe off. The boot slid off easily. Her sock was wet along the instep. Little patches of blood spotted through the white sock just behind her big toe.

"Just what I thought. " Martin said, in his best dispassionate doctor voice. "A burst blister, and it looks like it was a big one. I'll...um...have to take your sock off."

Susan's eyes flared wide and tragic.

"I'll have to." Martin temporarily fell out of character, but recovered his doctor voice. "I have to put a bandage on it. It's the only way to help it heal."

She bit her lip and closed both eyes tight. He took that as approval, of a sorts, so started to slowly roll down the sock. He determined, that no matter what was wrong with her foot, he would say nothing. He was going to focus on the blister and treating that.

His imagination would not leave him alone. *What if her father ran over her foot with a lawnmower when she was little, and the doctors sewed the chopped off parts back on? Would she have big Frankenstein scars?* He would say nothing. Focus on the blister.

As he rolled the sock over her heel, and down to the toes, he was careful not to let it pull or rub on the sore. Susan squeezed her eyes shut tighter and turned her face away. Martin paused and took a breath. He would not comment on whatever it was. He would be a seasoned battlefield medic. He rolled the sock off.

"Oh for crying out loud!" Martin half-shouted.

Susan cracked open one eye. "What?"

"There is NOTHING wrong with your foot! I mean, yeah, you've got a nasty burst blister, but your foot is normal. Normal!" His tone was accusing.

"Huh?"

"Geez wheeze," he ranted. "The way you were carrying on, I was beginning to think you had hooves or Franken…something."

She looked confused.

"Oh for God's sake. This is just a plain foot." he said. "You had me all worked up thinking that you…oh, never mind. Why were you making such a big deal?"

"I don't like my feet."

"Don't like your feet? Wha…you're attached to them. What has liking got to do with it?" He held her foot up as if selling it to her. "This is a perfectly fine, normal foot. What's not to like?"

"I just don't like feet, especially mine."

Martin rolled his eyes and muttered to himself. "Oh, that's just weird."

To Susan he said, "Hand me that little towelette pack there. Let me get this area cleaned up." Under his breath he muttered, "Pfft. Don't like your feet."

"Now hand me that other long packet. The Mycitracin." He applied it to a small gauze circle and gently laid it on the raw pink skin. He cut a hole in a square of moleskin and stuck it around the gauze. "Okay, now the tape." He taped it all down snuggly, but not tight. He put a strip of duct tape over it all.

"There. This should help. It'll keep your shoe from rubbing on the sore. Dig out some fresh socks and your sneakers. She pulled her bundle over closer and rummaged through the duffle bag. He rolled the clean sock on as gently as he could.

He worked her sneaker open wide. "You'd better put it on yourself. You can tell better than I can if it hurts. Go slow, and don't cinch it too tight or... " His words trailed off when he realized she was staring at him with that same sad-puzzled look. He felt like a bug under a magnifying glass.

"What."

She did not answer. The furrows remained on her forehead while she pulled her shoe on slowly.

"Does it hurt a lot?"

"No."

"Oh, well, you look like it still hurts."

"The pain isn't gone, but it's better."

"That's good. Now stand up," Martin encouraged. "Put some pressure on it."

Susan took a few steps. She still limped, but less. She sat down on the wall and looked at him with sad eyes, which Martin interpreted as her wanting to apologize for being weird about feet, but having a hard time finding words. He certainly knew how it felt to be at a loss for words. He sought to save her the trouble by accepting in advance.

"I'm just glad you're feeling better."

Apology accepted, Martin studied his map. "Well, if you're feeling good enough to get going again, this here is Williams Street, like I said. We go down that way. It crosses under 93, and then we'll be in Woburn. Go up Washington Street and there's four hotels up there that I know of -- probably more." He stood up and offered Susan his hand to help her up.

Susan kept her hands in her lap. "Um, about that. I've been thinking."

"Thinking?"

"Maybe I've been a little too focused on finding a hotel."

"Too focused? You need a place to stay. You want a room with a door."

"I know, I know, but now I'm not so sure. I feel bad that I slowed you down all this time for nothing. I really do. It's just...I think I've been so dead-set against going into a shelter that I think I got hotel tunnel vision. I didn't think of anything else. But now I'm thinking that was a mistake and that I should, maybe..." Her voice trailed off.

Martin sat back down on the wall. "I don't understand. Now you don't want to find a hotel?"

"I don't know. Maybe not? I'm all conflicted. What if I finally do find a hotel with a room left? That makes tonight more comfortable than sleeping in the woods. But what about after that? Even if the money thing wasn't a problem, this outage sounds like it will last a lot longer than just a couple nights or even a week. Will *any* hotel be such a great place to be in a week? Two weeks?"

Martin scratched the top of his head under his cap. "Hmmm. probably not." Now that she mentioned it, he too had been so focused getting her to a hotel that he had not thought much about the longer-term fate of hotels themselves.

"Oh sure," Susan continued, as if trying to convince herself. "Hotels have beds and doors, but they aren't food warehouses. What will people in hotels eat? What would I eat? Vending machine snacks? Those are probably gone already." Susan pointed back to the Stop n' Shop. "They won't be getting food from places like that, either, from what you were saying. In a week, they'll be picked over worse than that Andrew's Market was."

"Probably."

"And that's why I'm rethinking the whole hotel thing," she said. "Will people be fighting over the last of the food? What if my hotel turns out like La Quinta? I'm no fighter. I won't last long in that."

Martin leaned back on his hands. "Well, Geez. You don't have anyone in the area to stay with and you don't want to go to a shelter. Now you don't want a hotel?"

"Exactly. So I'm thinking that maybe I don't have the luxury of rejecting the shelter option as quickly as I did. Remember that second guy on the radio back there? He said shelters would have food and showers and stuff, right?" She could see Martin wincing.

"I know you don't like shelters," she leaned forward, chin in her hands. "I don't either, but what choice do I have? I guess I'd rather have people staring at me than fighting me for a jar of olives. I suppose I should find a policeman or something, and ask where the nearest shelter is."

A thought flashed through Martin's mind -- *Lindsey's room is empty.*

He sat up, startled by the thought. He glanced at Susan, as if expecting that she heard his thoughts. Apparently she had not. She was still staring across the street. He shook his head to expel the idea.

It was a terrible idea. Martin was shocked that it had occurred to him at all. He recalled the long stony silences last summer when

Dustin and his new wife Judy stayed with them after graduation. One woman should never rearrange the cupboards of another. That ought to be a rule. Then there was the summer before that and Margaret's barely concealed irritation with that young missionary woman who stayed with them: Kathy-something. One woman should never refold another woman's linens. Who cares quarters or thirds? That should be a rule too.

Two hens in a nest are nothing but trouble.

Partially to veto his bad idea and partially to try and comfort Susan, he tried to talk up the idea of staying in a shelter. "You know, maybe I was being too hard on FEMA shelters too. The government *has* to have learned a few things since Katrina, right? They probably have lots of supplies and fuel stockpiled like that guy said. Maybe they'll have armed guards to prevent fighting. Might not be so bad." Martin did not think he sounded as sincere as he hoped.

Susan turned to look him square in the eye. "Do you really believe that?"

Again, it was a prime opportunity to lie. He tried to suppress a hard swallow. He did not think the shelters would be good at all. Armed guards are a two-edged sword, but who was he to criticize? If she was warming up to the idea, who was he to be Mr. Negative? After all, FEMA probably did have stockpiles of food. Maybe they had those lame MREs, but it would be better than discarded cheese and stale crackers.

MREs. Margaret despised processed, pre-cooked food. She had always been a little fanatical about cooking. She always kept a couple months of ingredients on hand so she would never come up short on some recipe. Cooking from scratch was "real" cooking and she took pride in it. She sneered at frozen dinners, MREs or any other "factory food" as she called it. 'Fake food is for losers,' she sometimes said.

Of course, Martin thought, a third person in the house would use up their supply of food faster. He could help stretch supplies if he scaled back on his portions. It would do him some good to cut back on his portions anyhow. Three people would not require any more firewood than two did. An oil lamp can light a room for three as well as two. Water would be different, though. Three people would require more frequent trips to the well, but with three people, the water-hauling chores could be spread out, so that was actually a net gain.

What am I doing? I'm figuring out ways to fit her in. Am I nuts? Margaret would be furious!

Martin shuddered at the prospect of long, stony silences when everything was 'fine,' but most assuredly *not* fine.

He suddenly realized Susan still stared at him with a piercing gaze, waiting for an answer. *What did she ask? Something about the FEMA camps?*

She could tell she had to repeat her question. "Do you *honestly* believe the shelters will be okay?"

Why did her eyes have to be so big? He had to look away from her. "No, I don't really believe that."

She sat back with a heavy sigh. "I didn't think so. I had my mind half made up to go if you thought it was a good move. But now I'm right back where I was -- no place worth going to. Maybe I'll just have to take my chances at a hotel after all. Maybe it will be okay. I just don't know."

As a Good Samaritan, Martin felt duty bound to complete the mission he had volunteered for. He could not simply abandon her to the streets or some gulag of a FEMA camp. The hotels probably would devolve into La Quintas eventually. An angry Margaret would be bad, but leaving Susan, or anyone, to face the food brawls would be far worse. To abandon her to such a fate felt cowardly. He could feel John Wayne glaring at him already. Better to endure the silence of 'fine' than take the coward's way out.

He resolved that he would invite her to stay at his house. He pulled in a breath to speak, but stopped.

He was about to invite a woman who hardly knew him to come stay with him. How does one ask such a thing? No matter *how* he chose his words, it sounded incredibly creepy.

Was he any different than that sweaty opportunist at Holiday Inn? This thought pushed him into a deep hole of introspection. What if he actually *was* a closet creep who had, up until this point, simply lacked opportunity? Do creeps realize that they are creeps?

No, he decided. His intent was only to offer shelter -- nothing more. He cleared his throat.

"Look, I feel really awkward saying this, so please don't misunderstand, but we have room at our house, since the kids are gone, and well..."

"What?"

Martin rushed in the fine print disclaimers. "Don't feel like you have to...I mean, it's totally up to you. And only until things settle down here and you can come back. It's not like I...or that I think you..."

"You're blushing."

Martin rubbed his face with both hands. "Aw man. No matter how I try to say it, I sound like that guy at Holiday Inn..."

"What guy at Holiday Inn?" Susan interrupted. "The one you pushed?"

"Yes. Him."

Her eyes narrowed. "What about him?"

Martin did not want to talk about the seedy side of events she had avoided. She had enough on her plate without adding worry about sleazy creeps trying to jump her bones. Yet, no matter how he tried to phrase things in his mind, it always came down to some guy trying to jump her bones. He had already talked himself into a corner, so he continued, hoping gentler words would come to mind.

"There was this sweaty guy in the lobby. He heard me telling the clerk that you had no place else to stay. You were sort of in shock or something over your house burning down and all. So this sweaty guy figured to...he was offering for you to stay in his room...um...with him."

"What?" Susan sat up tall and peered as if she could see the Holiday Inn from where she sat. "He did? I don't remember any of that."

"I didn't think so. You were pretty shook up, thoughts all jumbled." Martin's jaw muscles tightened and his eyes narrowed. "He could see that, and was hoping to smooth talk his way into... Ooo, that really burned me up."

"Why? What did he say?"

"It doesn't matter. A guy can tell when... He walked fast and got up to you first and..."

"Then you pushed him? And rushed me out the door? That much, I remember."

Martin's hands formed fists. "Oh, I wanted to do a whole lot more than push him, I can tell you."

"It all happened so fast. I had no idea all that went on."

They sat in silence for what seemed a long time. Martin wondered why he had such a knack for painting himself into corners. Why was he so tongue-tied? He had spoken before scowling boards of directors and kept his cool. He had given conference lectures before dozens of people and never broken a sweat. Why was he all of a sudden so flustered? Susan looked off into the distance.

"That's like something from a movie," she said, mostly to herself. "Where the hero rushes in and rescues the girl from…"

"Rescued?" Martin was shocked out of his dark thoughts. "Geez, I don't know about 'rescued'. I was just…I mean, he had no right to think that he…I'm sure you would have seen through his scheme before he… I couldn't just *leave* you there."

"You're blushing again."

Martin turned away and waved his arms in the air, attempting to erase the topic. "Never mind about all that. What I'm trying to say is. You're welcome to stay at our house until this mess gets sorted out. A couple weeks. Whatever. That's all. You can leave whenever you want to. I don't want you to think I'm some sort of creep like him. I'm not trying to…I'm not…" Martin slumped, head in hands. He gave up talking. If there were gentler words for a ravaging, he could not think of them.

"If it helps," she said softly, "I don't think that."

Martin blew out a long sigh. "Thanks. It helps…a little. But I still feel all kinds of awkward. I couldn't think of any other good options for you either. I think shelters will be bad. Hotels might be bad too. Then I thought, hey, I have an empty room. But that's as far as it goes, I swear. Nothing more."

"Don't worry about it. I believe you only mean well. If I didn't, I wouldn't have accepted."

"You what?" Martin thought she was in the preamble of politely declining. Part of him had hoped she *would* decline so he would not have to deal with an upset Margaret. Another part of him could not imagine why any woman in her right mind would agree to such an outlandish offer.

"You'll come to my house?" It still did not compute.

"Yes."

"But, why?"

"Why? We just got done agreeing that hotels and shelters were bad options. Are you changing your mind?" she asked.

"No. You're still welcome if you want to, but I expected you to say no. Why *didn't* you say no? I mean, how can you be so sure I'm not actually a sleazy weirdo?"

"You're not a weirdo. A girl can tell. These past two days have been totally bizarre. People are getting rude and downright violent, but you've been…well, you haven't been like everyone else. You've been the one stable thing I've seen in all this. I feel that I'm better off going with you than staying here."

"Yeah, but still…"

"I'm sure you'll be a proper gentleman." She leveled a stern gaze at him that must come from maternal instinct. He felt like a kid picking up his date for the freshman dance.

"Of course, but, gentlemanly behavior aside, walking to New Hampshire won't be easy. It's a long way to go and probably means sleeping in the woods again. Are you sure you're okay with that?"

"YOU were planning to do it." Her tone was both statement and challenge.

"Yes I am, but you said it was crazy."

"Yeah, I guess I did. Sorry. I think I understand better now. And, not to sound all 'liberated', (She made air quotes.) but if you figured you could walk it, I think I can too — even with a blister."

Martin chuckled. He had to admire her attitude. It took spunk to agree to venture off into the vast unknown with her few worldly possessions trailing behind her. There must have been a bit of pioneer blood in her.

"Keep in mind that it'll be kind of simple up there without power. At least you'll have a room with a door. You're welcome to stay until they get things back to normal down here."

Susan smiled a little smile and touched his arm. "Thanks Martin."

He could feel his face getting hot again, so stood up and put on his backpack. "Yeah, um. You're welcome. We'd better get going. Need to get as far north as we can before dark."

Chapter 7: Thugs and Doom People

As they walked up Route 28, Martin tried not to be obvious about sneaking glimpses at Susan's foot for signs of discomfort. During one of those glances, he noticed that she was looking at his face as much as he was looking at her foot.

"I was just seeing if your foot was doing okay. Is it okay?"

"Not too bad."

"You look like you want to say something," he said.

"I guess so." Her eyes glanced around while she seemed to be gathering resolve. "I've just been wondering..."

"Wonder out loud. We've got a long stretch of road ahead of us. We might as well make conversation. What have you been wondering?"

"You didn't look...grossed out. I mean, when you were holding my foot."

Martin laughed. "Well, It's hard to put a bandage on your blister without touching your foot."

"Yeah, but still, weren't you..."

"You have plain ordinary feet, Susan. It was no big deal. How about we talk about something other than feet?"

Susan nodded, though she did not look satisfied.

Up the block, they passed a Walgreen's pharmacy on the opposite side of the street. People milled around between the cars in the parking lot. A police car was parked very close to the front of the building, blue lights flashing. A somewhat portly older policeman stood in front of the door. A few dozen people stood in an orderly line, waiting their turn to be let in, one at a time.

Susan gestured towards the policeman. "People picking up their heart pills requires a cop?"

Martin shrugged. "Probably not. Could be they're worried there will be rush of people 'off their meds' or desperate addicts. Some of them ran out of their stash yesterday and can't get more by their usual sources."

In his mind, he was connecting dots. Pharmaceuticals come by truck. Even illegal drugs are driven in from somewhere. Local stashes would dry up quickly. Home-brewed meth would fare little better. Meth also required ingredients made elsewhere and trucked in. Would addicts attack pharmacies when their dealers' stockpile ran out? Perhaps that explained the policeman.

Would meth-makers start raiding people's homes looking for drain cleaner and cold medicine? The average thief, looking to steal TVs or laptops, might flee at the sound of a warning shot, but would a desperate addict? Martin wondered what the local policeman-to-addict ratio might be. It was probably not good.

A pair of thin and nervous-looking young men, and a heavy-set woman with purple hair caught Martin's eye. They semi-crouched behind a car across the street from the pharmacy. Maybe it was nothing, or maybe it was trouble looking for opportunity.

Martin gestured with a tip of his head, towards the trio. "That doesn't look good. I don't want to get caught in another O.K. Corral. Think you feel up to a bit faster pace?"

Susan nodded. She walked a little faster, leaning more heavily on Martin's walking stick as she limped. They heard shouting behind them, but no gunshots. Something was going on in front of that Walgreens. Maybe it was simply people getting impatient and not an attack of some kind. Martin was glad to have put a little distance between them. After getting trapped in the shootout on 93, he was taking no chances.

Once well past the pharmacy, Susan spoke up. "Can we slow down now? My foot feels a little hot again. Maybe we could take another break?"

"Sure. Going faster probably didn't help. Sorry. Maybe that was nothing back there, but I didn't want to take the chance. Over there's a good little wall."

It felt great to get off his feet. Martin's shins were getting sore and his feet felt hot too. He took off his shoes to help cool them.

"It might help if you took off your shoes too," he said, cautiously.

"No, no, I'm fine..."

"Susan. You just said your foot felt hot. It's okay. You don't have weird feet."

She frowned.

"Your foot will feel better if you let it cool off and dry out some. You don't have to take your sock off or anything, if that helps."

She looked from her shoe to his face and back several times, as if trying to make up her mind.

"Tell you what," he said. "How about if I turn and face this other way? That way, I won't see a thing." He turned, somewhat theatrically, facing up the road. He thought her squeamishness about her feet was silly, but decided that she deserved some slack.

Susan quietly took off her sneaker. "Ooo. That does feel better."

"So, do I get a turn at wondering?" Martin asked over his shoulder.

"I suppose."

"I know I said I didn't want to talk about feet anymore, but now I've gotten curious. If it's not too personal or anything, could I ask *why* you don't like your feet? I just don't get that."

Susan let out a long slow sigh. "I've never liked my feet, even as a kid."

Martin shrugged. "Hmm. I'll be the first to admit I was an air-head as a kid, but I don't think I ever once thought about my feet, let alone liking them or not. I was too busy getting them dirty to care. Why did you care?"

"I don't really know for sure. I just thought they were all wrong. I'd look at pictures in catalogs, you know, sandals and flip-flop ads and such. I didn't have toes like they did. Theirs were pretty. Mine were ugly."

"I suppose everyone is entitled to their own opinion, but..."

"Oh, it wasn't just me. Other people said so too."

"No way. That was just kids being cruel. You know how kids can be."

"It wasn't just kids. Mark, my EX-boyfriend, he said so too. He insisted that I wear socks at all times. If I forgot, he used to make little jokes about my 'freaky toes' to remind me."

"Wha?" Martin spun around. He could tell his mouth was hanging open. "Why *on earth* would anyone say such a thing?"

Susan quickly tucked her left foot behind her right. "I don't know. I never thought about it. I thought he was right."

"Oh Geez." Martin turned away again. "I hope I'm not talking out of bounds, but this Mark guy sounds like a major league jerk." Martin could feel his face getting hot.

Susan put on her shoe. "We'd better get going," she said flatly. She took her bag by the handle and started walking. Martin quickly put his shoes on and caught up to her.

She walked with her head down, brow furrowed. Martin was certain he had just insulted her. She liked this Mark enough to have him as a boyfriend, at least at first. Was calling Mark a jerk also calling her foolish for liking him? How was he any different? A pot calling the kettle black.

To take his mind off of feet and jerks, and hopefully take Susan's mind off the same topics, Martin suggested they drink more water. He cut off hunks of cheese for both of them.

Susan slowly chewed her cheese without saying anything. Again, she had her sad and puzzled expression. The awkward silence was more than Martin could stand.

"You know," he said. "It seems like I'm always being a jerk to you and having to apologize."

Susan looked over at him.

"I'm sorry I spouted off back there," he continued. "I really don't know this Mark guy, so I had no right to call him a jerk. I mean, you liked him. After all, it's not like I can talk."

She continued to look at him with her sad-puzzled look. Perhaps he had been a jerk once too often and the damage could not be repaired with an apology.

"That's okay," she finally said. "You were right. Mark *is* a jerk."

Martin was not prepared for agreement. "But, he was your…"

"I know, but not anymore. Oh, he was all charming in the beginning. He opened doors for me and sent me flowers. It was really nice."

"Look, if you'd rather not talk about this…"

"No, it's okay. I think it helps, actually." She leaned out to look up the long stretch of Route 28 ahead of them. "It will help pass the time, like you said."

They gave a gas station and its cloud of would-be buyers a wide berth. People stood in line with gas cans, or leaned against their cars. Very few of them were conversing. Most stood with arms folded and frowns. The scene had the tense air of forced peace, like a school yard brawl broken up by teachers before the kids had settled the score.

"Mark was really nice at first. At least, he seemed nice. I was fairly new in the area, didn't know many people. He took me to plays and the symphony. We went out to eat in cute little cafés and even did some museums. We went to gallery opening parties, on harbor cruises. City life was really glittery and exciting. Looking back now, I wonder if I was more taken by the glitter than him."

Martin felt like he was eaves dropping on a phone call.

"Anyhow, after we got serious, I moved in with him. You know, why pay rent on two apartments?"

Martin squirmed. This was far more information than he was entitled to. "You know," he interrupted. "You really don't owe me any explanations."

"Oh, sorry. I'm rambling. What I was trying to get at, was that his true colors came out after I moved in. He started to change. It was little things at first. I thought I was doing stuff wrong to make him upset with me, but it got worse, no matter what I did. You know how sometimes people can seem nice, but really they're self-centered, impatient and actually kind of mean?"

Martin cringed. Guilty as charged. "I know I've been pushing the pace and…"

Susan looked up suddenly. "No wait. I didn't mean it that way."

"That's okay. Seems like I'm always…"

"Oh shoot no! It's just that every hotel you picked out turned out to be a failure…"

Martin winced.

"Agh!" She covered her mouth with both hands. "That came out all wrong! I meant that even though every time you tried to help, things went really wrong. No no no. That sounded worse. I only wanted to explain how…that you…that I was…I never meant to say that you were…ughh." Her arms dropped to her side in surrender. She heaved a sigh of resignation.

"I should just shut up. Nothing is coming out right," she said.

"I know exactly how you feel," he replied.

They stood in awkward silence. Martin wanted to promise he would not say insensitive things anymore, but realized he seemed to have no control over that.

Susan squared up her shoulders. "What I was trying to explain — and not very well — was that you were right about Mark being a jerk. He is. And, with everything going wrong around us — and none of it your fault — you have always been…well, thoughtful and going out of your way. In fact, I'm the one who's been the jerk. Here you've been trying to get home and I've been this huge burden, slowing you down."

She looked aside and said, mostly to herself, "Why couldn't I have said it that way the first time?"

Martin took a breath to speak, but Susan raised her hand. "Hold on. I wasn't quite done. Ahem. For the record, I never once thought you were being a jerk. There. Now I'm done."

"For the record," Martin matched her formal tone. "I never once thought you were a burden."

A small smile eased Susan's worried expression.

Martin held up one finger. "No wait. There was that one time."

Susan's smile evaporated.

"That time you made me carry you over that raging river of crocodiles."

"What?!"

"That was SOOO unfair."

"Oh stop it." She smacked him on the shoulder in mock rage. She had a sparkle in her eyes that Martin liked much better than her sad-puzzled look.

"Next time we come to a raging river of crocodiles," she said. "I'm going to push you in."

Martin pretended to write on an invisible note pad. "Note to self: Avoid rivers of crocodiles."

Susan snatched away his invisible note pad and pretended to tear it up. "That's just dumb. Why would anyone have to write down something like *that*?"

"My note pad!" Martin acted shocked.

"Oh, stop whining," Susan retorted. "Here, you can use mine." She slapped an invisible pad into his hands.

Martin stared at his hands while they resumed walking. "But…It's pink."

Susan pushed him on the shoulder. "Whiner."

Both of them chuckled.

The sidewalks had more people on them: some had bundles. Martin wondered if they were also refugees from downtown, or local traffic. If they were refugees, were they on their way to outlying hotels? Perhaps they had friends or relatives living nearby? Had they started out in a car, but ran out of gas? He wondered where they were all going.

The traffic along Route 28 had picked up considerably, both in volume and speed. From the way people revved their engines to accelerate in from side streets, there was an air of urgency and impatience. Where were they all coming from, or going to, in such a hurry, Martin wondered. It was rush hour on steroids, but in the middle of the day – and a day in which no one was going to work anyhow.

"You think your wife, Margaret, will be okay with me staying awhile?"

"Oh sure, she loves having company," Martin said, but he was thinking, *Two hens in a nest. Everything will be painfully 'fine'. One of Dante's levels of hell must have been labeled "Fine".*

"Just promise me you won't rearrange the cupboards. Okay?"

"What? Why would I do that?"

"I have no idea, but it's against the rules. Just sayin'."

Martin kept their pace slower than he would have liked. They had a lot of ground to cover but he did not want Susan's blister to get worse, or for either of them to develop any new ones. Letting her use his walking stick helped, but she still had a noticeable limp. Slow and steady would trump a faster pace and downtime for more repairs.

"What if this outage does last for a month or more? Won't I be a burden on you…and Margaret? I mean, the stores up your way will run out too, and trucks not delivering, same as down here?"

"I expect you're right, but don't worry about it," he said. "We'll all be okay."

"You say that so quickly. I mean, a room with a door is nice and all, but the power's out and it's October. It's getting colder and fuel won't be delivered. Aren't you worried?"

"Not too worried, no."

"I hope you don't mind my asking all these questions."

"Nah, go ahead," said Martin.

"Okay. *Why* aren't you worried? I'd like to understand. This whole outage thing has me kind of freaked out inside."

"You don't look freaked out," Martin said.

"Alright, maybe not wild eyes and flailing arms freaked out. More like really worried and stressed: that kind of freaked out. Most of the people we've come across, like at La Quinta or Andrew's or the gas stations, they seem freaked out too. So, why aren't you?"

"Well, a big reason is that we've got the house pretty well set up. That takes a big load of worry off. Margaret likes to keep a deep pantry, and even some boxes of canned goods downstairs, so we easily have three or four months worth of food on hand."

"Canned goods?" Susan sounded surprised. "In the basement?"

"Sure. Can't keep it all upstairs. No room. My point was that we'll be set for food for a good while, so I don't worry about it. We'll make it work."

"Oh…"

Susan did not look as relieved as he thought she would. He wondered if she had an aversion to canned food. Some people are food-fussy that way. This was not a good time to be fussy. They walked awhile in silence. She looked at the ground with little frown wrinkles between her eyebrows. Her pace was slowing down. Martin thought maybe she needed more reassurance.

"It'll be okay. Really." Martin said. "Margaret is quite a good cook. You'd never know some of it came from a can."

Susan did not look reassured. Martin thought a change of topic would help.

"Like I said, our house will be comfortable enough, even with the power out. It'll just be a little rustic."

"What? Rustic?" Now Susan looked almost upset.

"Well, yeah, but it won't be like living in a cave or sleeping in the woods or anything. I just meant that we won't have all the usual conveniences of on-grid living. But we'll be okay. We've got the wood stove for heat, oil lamps for light. A generator if we need it. I've got a hand pump on the well, so water's no problem."

His attempts to reassure her were clearly not working very well. Susan walked slower and with her head down. She had more frown wrinkles. He wondered if his own misgivings about how far their food supplies could be stretched, or his growing pessimism about how slowly the grid might be repaired, were somehow leaking out in his tone, or mannerisms. Was he talking peace-and-plenty, but telegraphing worry-and-woe?

After a long quiet stretch, Susan asked slowly, "What about…guns?" Her face had a sort of pleading look as if to silently say, *please tell me you don't have any guns.*

"Guns?" The question caught Martin off guard. Based on her reactions to guns thus far, it was about the last question he expected. Given his apparent total lack of skill at reassurance thus far, he fished for some hints to what she meant.

"What do you mean, 'guns'?"

"You know, like Mrs. Andrew had behind her counter?" she added.

"Oh no. Nothing like that." He wondered where her line of questioning was leading.

Is she suddenly worried I might be some gun-crazed psycho who fantasizes that he's secretly a Special Forces Rambo? Did that just occur to her? Now she's worried that she had agreed to stay with one of those nut jobs who has an arsenal in his closet, snaps a gasket, drives to a shopping mall and starts shooting random strangers? What a mess she must think she's in — having to chose between a Government Gulag, Hotel FistFight or Mr. Mall Shooter. Poor thing.

He was certainly not the trigger-happy soldier-wannabe type. He wanted to reassure her that he was not some gun nut, but listing off his firearms did not seem like the best way to make that case.

Perhaps a little truth is better than too much truth for the moment, he thought.

"We do keep a small pistol in the nightstand, but just for protection around the house, for like when I'm away on business. That way, Margaret isn't home alone without some protection." This part was true, if only a half-truth. He thought that including Margaret would soften the gun ownership image. The little revolver in the nightstand was hardly the bristling black "assault weapon" so infamous in gun-control press conferences. It seemed prudent not to mention his other pistols or long guns just yet.

"Oh."

Susan still had her look of concentration and worry as she walked slower still. She did not look reassured in the slightest. Martin decided that he should never try a career as a diplomat or hostage negotiator. He would starve and people might die.

They walked in silence for another block. Martin's mind replayed as much as he could remember, but could not find an obvious faux pas. How could he be so utterly bad at being reassuring?

After a long silence, Susan asked with a careful, deliberate tone, "Martin? Do you think that a comet will strike the Earth sometime soon?"

The absurdity of her question made Martin snort and laugh, but he quickly stifled it. Her expression was gravely serious, like a mother asking a doctor if her son would ever walk again.

"No. I do not think a comet is going to strike the Earth soon. Where did *that* question come from?"

She stopped and faced him. "Really? You don't think about comets, even a little bit?"

He squirmed slightly at the pop quiz. Should he be worried about comets? He could not think of a reason why. "Um…No? Should I?"

Susan stared skeptically into his eyes for a long moment, as if waiting for him to admit that he really did think about comets. Finally, her skeptical expression melted into a look of relief. She let out a long sigh. She took a deep breath and launched into an avalanche of words.

"No, you shouldn't and I can't tell you how relieved I am to hear you say that. Of course I was all happy, at first, that you offered to take me in. I mean, sure, it's a long walk, but it had to be better than hotels or shelters, I figured. But then you started telling me about your house being rustic (air quotes) and canned goods stored away and then you said you had a gun, and I started to wonder if you might be one of those Doom People."

"Doom people?" They resumed walking.

After a deep breath, another verbal avalanche followed. "Yeah. That's what I call them. I've heard about them on NPR: crazy people who think a comet is going to strike the earth, so they plan to hike out into the woods with a backpack full of stuff, to live in 'rustic' (again, with air quotes) log cabins and make sausage out of bears or something. They're convinced that a comet is going to turn everything into chaos, so they plan to stay locked in their cabins, eating canned goods from their basements and shooting zombies from their rooftops."

"What?" Martin felt bizarreness overload.

"It's true! I saw this show on TV awhile back, about this weird guy and his weird wife. Oh, they were sooo weird. They had a basement full of canned goods and an attic full of machine guns like that lady had back at Andrews and…"

"Oh, you mean Preppers?"

"Yes. That's the word. Doom Preppers. Doom People. They were so totally nuts. Underground bunkers. Barbed wire. Hidden cameras. Running around in army outfits like they were Special Rangers with machine guns. Afraid of comets, or volcanos, or something, and zombies. What is it with them and zombies? I don't get that. They gave me the creeps just seeing them on TV. I never ever dreamed that I would actually…someday…"

She lowered her head and avoided eye contact. "…then you said how you had lots of canned goods in your basement, and your house was rustic…and had a gun…so, naturally, I started wondering if you thought…you know, that a comet was…"

"No no no." Martin stopped to face her. He stooped a bit to look in her downcast eyes. "It's nothing like that all. We are *not* 'doom people.' I am *not* worried about any comets. I do not have machine guns in the attic and I certainly do not believe in zombies. We just have our house set up to comfortably withstand winter power outages. They happen almost every year, so we try to be ready. That's all."

"But, Doom People have backpacks full of stuff. And you have your bag." She pointed at his bag with her eyes. "And it's full of that kind of stuff."

"Well, yeah, for walking home, not for zombies. Besides, my little first aid things were pretty handy for your blister, weren't they?"

She responded with a long, reluctant "yeah."

"Nothing to do with comets or zombies. It's just stuff for…um…a fifty mile walk home from…" His voice trailed off. He was not helping his own case. Martin also resolved to never try to be his own lawyer. He would get himself Life without parole for a parking ticket.

The worry lines disappeared from her forehead as she smiled slightly. "You think walking fifty miles is kinda crazy too, don't you."

He hung his head. "Yeah, to be honest, I kinda do."

"That's good," she said with a wider smile.

"Why is that good?"

"It means I wasn't wrong after all. What a relief!"

"Wrong about what?"

She started walking again. Her tone was more perky. "Wrong about *you*. I much prefer *not* being wrong, of course. I suppose that's pretty typical, huh? Who wants to be wrong?"

"But you thought I was a Doom People and I'm not. Isn't that being wrong?"

"Well, yes, but that's not what I meant. It's kind of a long story. You see, working at the bank, I came to realize that I could read people pretty well. You know, by the way they moved, or their eyes, or the little things they said. I could tell whether they were honest, or stuck-up, or if their 'friendly' was only an act because they wanted something."

"Like, there was this one guy who was giving off all kinds of bad vibes every week. Shifty eyes, evasive, secretive. I trusted my feelings and told Mr. Skinner. They did a little digging and they found that he was using his employer's account to make payments to a fake company that was really just him. Turned out I was right about him. I was thinking, hey, this would be a good skill when I became an Associate. You know, for loan pre-screening and things like that."

"And this relates to comets and zombies by…" Martin could not see where her topic was headed.

"I'm getting there. Even from the little samples I got at my teller window, I could tell that deep down inside, lots of people were truly mean-spirited, or full of themselves, and even a few weird ones who, I think, really believed zombies were after them. See? There's the zombies. Anyhow, over the months of you making your EdLogix deposits, my read on you was that you were one of the nice ones. You know, normal."

"Normal. That's a relief to know," Martin smiled.

"Well, nowadays, yeah. Normal is kinda rare. Like with this outage, for instance. It's like peoples' real selves are coming out fast, and it ain't pretty. Most people are totally selfish; just looking to get what they can for themselves and don't care who they step on. For some, their mean-streak…Man, it is running wild. Like those drivers yesterday, or the fighting at La Quinta, all that shooting on 93? Those people were probably always mean and pushy, but this outage has scraped off whatever thin coat of social politeness they might have had. But you, you were going waaay out of your way to help someone you barely knew."

She paused, talking to the ground more than to Martin. "That was really nice."

Martin felt awkward again.

Susan resumed. "I mean, who does that anymore, right? Everyone is just out for themselves. So, I figured I was right — you were nice. But then, when you started talking about your house being rustic and all, and I remembered those wacky Doom People. I began to doubt myself."

"I mean, what if I had been so upset over my apartment fire and staying in shelters and such, that I was accepting help from one of *them*? I knew you weren't some lecherous creep like the Holiday Inn guy, but what if you were a Doom People? I don't think I could handle that. They are sooo weird. I decided that I had to ask you while we were still inside of 128. If you were one of *them*, I could still politely decline, go my own way and go look for a hotel or something."

Martin smiled. "Now you don't think I'm a Doom People…person? Whatever."

"Nope."

Martin slowed his pace. He subtly held out his hand to catch Susan's arm.

"What? Why did you slow down?" she asked.

"I'm not liking the scene ahead of us." He pointed with a tip of his head. Several long plain brick apartment buildings sat very close to the sidewalk. On the front steps of the first building were a half dozen young men and women. A pair of young men, one in a black do-rag, the other wearing bright orange shoes, leaned on the low chain link fence at the sidewalk edge, watching the street.

"What does your people-reading sense tell you about them?" Martin asked quietly.

She squinted at them. The women leaned against the porch columns in carefully crafted "casual" poses. The men leaned on the fence along the sidewalk, looking up and down street like raptors.

"They look like trouble," she said softly.

"That's how I read it too." He slowly took the walking stick from Susan's hand. He felt better with it in his hand, but he wondered what he was going to do with it if the porch people made a move on them.

Am I going to try to go all bojitsu on them? he wondered. Would the six of them stand obligingly in a ring around him, attacking one at a time like they do in cheap action films? It seemed more likely that he might hurt one or two of them with his stick, but they would eventually overwhelm him, or they would grab Susan. Neither sounded good.

"I think we need to be on the other side of the street now, even if it means dealing with this traffic."

As they stepped off the curb to cross, the railing raptor with the orange shoes stood up tall and called out.

"Hey, you guys there. Whachu got in dat bag?"

The young woman with big hair stood beside him. "Got any food in der? We've got, like, starving kids in here. Could ya help da kids?" The rest of the young women stood up too, to see what their friends had spotted.

Martin glanced at the fast flowing traffic and back at the young men. He and Susan were between a rock and a hard place. Orange shoes and Do-rag began moving towards them.

"Hey. Where ya goin'? We jus wanna talk," called out Do-rag.

Martin grabbed the handle of Susan's bag. "C'mon. We've gotta play Frogger again."

He dashed through a gap in the first lane. Susan was right behind him. The driver honked, but did not slow down. The young men fanned out, also looking for suitable gaps in the fast traffic.

Martin's heart pounded. No good gaps were coming in the traffic flow. They were between lanes, cars whizzing by just inches away. The young men were just on the other side of the first lane, eyeing gaps to get through.

"There," he shouted to Susan. "Behind the white minivan. One. Two. Three!" They jumped in so near the minivan's rear bumper that Martin was certain they would smack into it. But, since the van was traveling away from them, they did not hit it. The gap got wider. The pickup behind the minivan swerved a bit to avoid them, but did not slow down. Martin pulled the roller bag up just in time to avoid it being clipped.

Standing on the narrow median, the oncoming traffic seemed to be going twice as fast. The young men found gaps. Both were through the first lane, maneuvering for gaps in the second lane.

Judging gaps in the oncoming traffic was scarier. Martin spotted what might be a big enough gap, ahead of little gray Chevy. He glanced at Susan, to tell her, but she was looking back at the young men working the gaps.

No time. Martin grabbed Susan's wrist and leapt off the median.

Chapter 8: Roadblocks

Martin leapt into the gap in traffic, between the little gray Chevy and the generic SUV. He had Susan by the wrist with his left hand, and the roller bag handle in his right. The Chevy driver looked horrified but otherwise did nothing. No swerving, no honking, no braking. She drove straight at them.

Martin saw that the gap in the far lane, between the black Accord and the Rav4 was not large, but would align with their path IF they kept running. There was no time to swallow hard or hesitate. As he ran, he pulled Susan up beside him, intending to slingshot her ahead of him, in case he misjudged the gaps. He might get hit, but she would be clear or would get hit by him instead of a car. He fixed his eyes on the Rav4's headlight and ran.

Susan had regained her footing and her stride, she did surge beside him. They both made it to the other side. The roller bag, however, was not so lucky.

The corner of the Rav4's bumper clipped the end of the roller bag, spinning it around and twisting Martin with it. He made a full turn and lost his footing. He went down on his left side and skidded up to the curb. The Rav4 driver honked long and loud, but did not brake. It was a good thing he did not slow down. People were tailgating each other so close that a sudden stop from any of them would have caused a massive pile-up.

"Oh my God! Martin!" Susan ran to where Martin lay.

He laid still, in a daze for a few seconds, going through a personal reboot. He looked around to see where the voice was coming from. He raised himself up on one elbow, which hurt.

Another loud honk from the far side of the street caught his attention. The honk was followed by a sickening sound — part thud, part moan, like someone hitting the ground after falling off a roof. Screams. The screech of tires. More honking. More screaming. Martin could not see anything beyond the steady stream of tires and bumpers in the lane near him. He became aware of Susan's voice again.

She stared across the street, her hand over her mouth. "Oh my God. One of those guys just got hit. Oh, that sounded awful." She turned back to Martin.

"Oh no. You get hit too? Oh my God, what do I do?

"It's okay. It's okay. I don't think I'm hurt too bad," said Martin. He rolled onto all fours then sat down. A quick mental assessment suggested no broken bones. He saw no bleeding. His jacket sleeve was ripped open from the left shoulder down to the elbow. His shirt was too. He had a bad case of road rash on his upper arm, but it was not bleeding much.

Susan gasped when she saw his arm. "Your *arm*. Oh this is terrible."

Martin slowly stood up. "I think we need to get out of here in case those people try to come after us again."

"Oh, I don't think you're supposed to stand up. You should lie down maybe? And tip your head back, or something?" She began looking around, as if she expected to see paramedics that she would call over to the scene. There were no paramedics. The few people there were on the sidewalk were fixated on the scene across the street.

"I'm okay," Martin said. "A bit beat up, but nothing serious."

"Are you sure? Are you sure you should get up?"

"No, I'm not sure, but I'm getting up anyway."

She helped him stand. "Oh, look at your arm. Oh dear."

"Yeah, I've got a nasty rash. Let's get over behind those cars for now, okay?" Martin took some hobbling steps across the sidewalk. His knee hurt. The palm of his hand had serious abrasions too.

"Where's my bag?" he asked.

"It's still on your back," she said, with a worried look, as if suspecting that he might have brain damage too.

"Oh, so it is. Let's go up against that wall there." He pointed to a section of wall between overhead doors of a tire shop. He leaned his back against the wall. With his good hand, he fished out his first aid kit. He tore open an alcohol wipe packet with his teeth and rubbed it across his palm. He winced at the sting.

"Where's your roller bag?" he asked.

"What? Who cares? You're hurt. I need to help."

"I think I'll be okay in a few minutes. But seriously, what happened to your bag? That's everything you have. I had ahold of it when we ran through, but I lost it."

Susan looked up and around. "Oh. There it is. It's over by the curb. Your walking stick is still out by the median."

"While I dab at my hand, why don't you go get your roller bag and see how bad it is?"

She looked from him to the bag then ran over to pick up her roller bag. The duffle and canvas bag were knocked loose. One of the wheels had been knocked loose, but other than that the roller bag itself seemed to have only suffered scuffs and dirt.

"We need to put some distance between us and those people over there," Martin said. "I'll try to clean up a bit when we're clear."

The scene across the street spoke of injuries worse than Martin endured. Orange shoes was still lying face-down on the street. His friends were ringed around him. Big-hair was shouting and flailing her arms. Do-rag knelt down beside him, dabbing at his head. For the time being, the pack had forgotten all about Martin and Susan.

Martin limped for a while. His knee felt stiff. "Let's go around the corner of this store. We should be far enough from those apartments, and out of sight. Martin wanted to pour some water on his upper arm, but his abraded right hand trembled and would not close enough to hold the jug.

"Here, maybe you better do this," he said.

"Me?"

"Yeah. Could you pour a little water on my scrape. Need to get the dirt off. I can't hold this jug worth beans. Then, if you could use one of these alcohol wipes too? Need to clean out the scratches, so it doesn't get infected. Who knows what's been on those streets, eh? What if they had a circus parade yesterday — with elephants — and swept the poop to the curb…"

"Don't joke at a time like this. You're hurt."

Susan took the wipe and dabbed ineffectually at the edges of the scratches.

"Don't worry," Martin assured her. "Just wipe gently along, in the same direction as the scratches. It'll be okay."

She did as he asked, but the alcohol stung worse than he expected. He flinched and grimaced.

"Oh sorry. I'm hurting you. Sorry. I don't know how to do nurse stuff."

"No, no. You're doing fine. It's the alcohol, not you."

She reluctantly dabbed and wiped more.

"Okay, now rub some of the ointment on and rub it into the scratches."

She frowned the whole while. His right hand was trembling less, so he was able to assist. He rubbed some ointment into his palm scrape too.

"Shouldn't we put a big bandage over your arm? It looks awful."

"I don't have anything big enough for that. I'll just have to leave it covered with my clean shirt, I guess. I think it'll be okay just getting some air. What are they doing over there?"

Susan peeked around the corner. "Two of them are still with the guy on the street. The others are running back to the apartment building."

Martin fished in his backpack with his left hand and tugged out his old flannel shirt. He pulled off his jacket with some difficulty, as his left arm did not want to flex much. He started to unbutton his torn shirt, then noticed Susan was watching.

"Um. Could you turn around?"

"Oh. Sorry, sorry." She blushed and quickly turned away.

"I'll let you be all shy about your feet. If you'll let me be all shy about my unimpressive physique, okay?"

"I'm sorry. I didn't mean to…"

"That's okay. I'm mostly kidding."

Trying to pull the shirt on with one hand and a claw was awkward, but he managed. Buttons with one hand was a challenge, but also managed.

"Okay. I'm decent again. What's going on across the street?"

Susan peeked around the corner of the building again. "They're still standing around the guy on the road. I think I saw him move. Why aren't any of these drivers stopping to help? Where is everyone going in such a hurry?"

"Beats me, but I want us to get moving before that group starts looking around for us again. They could be really angry at us."

"Why? We didn't do anything to them? They were trying to get to us," she protested.

"Won't matter to them. These days. society teaches people that they're all victims of something. Injuries demand vengeance. I'm sure they won't see themselves as responsible for anything. It'll be all our fault, somehow."

Martin pointed to her roller bag. "Looks like we need to tie up your bundle again, but I'm afraid you'll have to do most of it. I think I can salvage my jacket, for the most part, with a bit of duct tape. But this shirt is toast."

Susan stuffed the stray socks and pant legs back into the duffle and tugged on the cord to tie new knots. Martin pulled off a strip of duct tape to secure his torn jacket sleeve to the shoulder. Putting on the jacket was as awkward as the shirt had been, but his arm was feeling less stiff.

"There we go. Looks like I've got a unit patch now, doesn't it? Duct Tape Brigade." He smiled. She was not amused. He shrugged. Apparently, he was as good at humor as he was at reassurance.

"Ahem, well. How about you help me stick this square bandage on my hand, then give me a hand tying my old shirt's sleeve around it? It will look a bit hobo, but it will help keep the bandage on."

Once they had their things in order, Martin peeked around the corner of the store. The apartment gang was still gathered around the young man who was now leaning up on one elbow. Cars continued to stream by quickly.

"They're still occupied with the guy who got hit. He's conscious at least. Let's go back around this hedge and come out a bit further up the street. I got that loose wheel to snap back in, but it's in bad shape."

Around the hedge, they emerged into the parking lot of a CVS pharmacy. Like Walgreens before it, the parking lot was full of cars and people. Some stood upon the parking lot's retaining wall so they could look across the street at the injured man. Most had their attention focused on the line to the door. Martin steered between the groups, trying to keep low, without looking obvious. He tried not to limp as much as he could manage in order to not attract any attention.

The parking lot sat lower than the street, so they would be harder to see if the apartment gang started looking for them. Martin tried to stay mingled among the parked cars: more difficult to see.

"I wonder if that guy will be alright," Susan said.

Feeling battered and sore from trying to escape the apartment predators did not encourage sympathy in Martin. The whole group of them was intent to take whatever they wanted from him and Susan. The fact that they had been waiting for a target of opportunity to walk near them contradicted the hungry-kids story. What mother of hungry children strikes poses, waiting for food to come to her?

As for the young man lying in the street, he chose to dodge into traffic to chase them. Martin felt very little compassion for the man. In his mind, he paraphrased a Bible verse, *Those who expect to gain by violence can expect to die by violence.*

"They had no business chasing us," was Martin's condensed thought.

"I know, but still…"

"I don't think they would have shown us any sympathy if they caught us. I'm just glad we got away." Martin was not in the mood for conversation about the would-be muggers.

As they cleared the big strip mall's parking lot, the damaged wheel on Susan's roller bag popped out. "Oops! Hold on. I got it," Martin said as he hobbled after the little wheel.

"Got it, but now my hand bandage is coming loose. Need to tighten up and see if we can fix this wheel again."

"How about in the shade back there by those dumpsters?" Susan pointed at the back of a store's shallow parking lot. "We should be pretty much out of easy sight back there."

Martin tried to sit on the pavement beside the stockade fence, but his sore knee did not want to bend. Sitting down looked more like a ship capsizing.

Susan pulled his hand up for a closer look. "Hmm. Give me your bag," she said. "The gauze is okay, but that strip of shirt will have to be redone. Maybe some tape to hold it better."

While Susan rewound the bandage, Martin stared at the junk people left around the dumpster stockade: a CRT television, a bent folding chair, a very tired air conditioner. *This must be the locals' equivalent to the Cheshire transfer station*, he thought. Then something caught his eye. It looked like a baby buggy wheel sticking up between two crushed cardboard boxes.

"Hold still," Susan scolded. "I'm almost finished."

"Sorry," Martin said. "I want to go check out that junk over there." Standing up looked like a barn raising, with him as the barn. When he pulled on the spoked rubber wheel, a tangle of chrome wires came with it, and a matching wheel.

"What was that?" Susan's tone was appropriate for roadkill.

"I think it was one of those little two-wheel carts that old ladies use to carry home their groceries."

"It looks like someone ran over it."

"It does, but look at the wheels. They're okay. The axle is a little bent, but…"

"Are you thinking we can put those wheels on my roller bag?"

"I am. Here. Hold this. We need to break off these mangled wires." Martin bent the wires until the tack welds broke. The remainder looked like a battered cookie cooling rack, with wheels. "Now let's push the axle against….that post over there and see if we can straighten it enough."

The axle bent as metals often do — anywhere but where you want them to. The result was a mild zigzag, but the two wheels were roughly parallel. Martin capsized down onto the pavement again and started lashing the little wire rack to the bottom of her roller bag. The broken welds made workable stops for paracord knots.

"There you go," Martin beamed. "You've got wheels again, and more off-road than the little plastic ones. Try it out!"

Susan walked a few paces, pulling her bag. "Hey. This is way better than before."

"Cool. This will be easier on both of us. Let's get going again."

After a few blocks of walking, Martin noticed his stiff knee was loosening up. He also noticed the sound of honking and revving engines grew louder as they approached the intersection of North Street and Route 28. The traffic lights were out, so all the drivers were fending for themselves. The steady northbound flow up 28 backed up against the muddle at the intersection. Most drivers ended up turning east or west. No one was getting any further north.

No policeman had been dispatched to direct traffic. It was a wonder that anyone actually made it through the intersection. North Street was normally a two-lane road, but people were making it as an impromptu four-lane road with an occasional fifth lane on the sidewalk, or in the grass. Fender scrapes and bumper taps were common, but no one was getting out to swap insurance information.

One driver in a line of cars on North Street made a sudden lunge for an open space, then changed his mind and hit the brakes. The man behind him surged to follow him, but smacked into the rear of the first car. The second car did not fare well. The plastic grill was mangled. Green coolant poured out onto the street. His engine would not restart. A heated argument flared up between the stalled driver and those stuck behind him.

"This might be a good time for us to cross the road," said Martin. He and Susan threaded through the stalled outer eastbound lane, then through the slower inner line of cars. The westbound lanes were sporadic enough that gaps appeared as needed.

The drivers blocked behind the damaged car gathered around the disabled vehicle to push it out of the way. At first, the driver thanked them for their help, but the group went beyond getting the stalled car out of the lane. They gave his car an extra push so it rolled into the brick wall of the corner bakery. When it hit with a dull crunch, they cheered as if they had scored a goal. The driver of the damaged car flailed his arms and shouted. Martin could not make out what he was shouting, other than, 'are you all crazy?' The other drivers pointed at him and laughed as they got back into their cars to resume creeping up to the intersection.

Martin and Susan walked north on the far side of 28, along the sidewalk of the southbound lanes.

"Kinda strange," Susan commented. "So much traffic trying to head north, but nothing coming south."

The northbound lanes were full of motionless cars, lined up in three long lines. A state police cruiser was parked across both lanes, lights flashing. The trooper waved his arms impatiently at the drivers lined up in front of him. He wanted everyone to turn around. No one seemed to understand, or intended to turn back. Some drivers were out of their cars shouting at him. Others honked. The few near the back tried to back up or make three-point turns in too little space, and go back to the intersection.

Martin got out his little binoculars. "Hmm. There's another state cruiser on the other side of the interchange, blocking the southbound side too. Wonder what's up?"

"I don't know, but it's sure causing a mess," said Susan. "Good thing we're walking."

As they approached the off-ramp from 128, a different state trooper stopped his chore of placing orange cones across the off-ramp. He stepped in front of them, with his arms outstretched as if shooing away chickens.

"No access here, people. Go back. Go back," said the trooper.

"We just want to walk through," said Martin.

"Do you two live in Reading, Middleton or Andover?" the trooper asked.

"Um. No, but we just want to…"

"Then, it doesn't matter," interrupted the trooper. "Only residents are allowed in. You gotta turn around and go back to wherever you stayed last night."

"The woods!? Why can't we walk through here? We're just trying to get to…"

"Only residents. Nobody else is allowed in here. Now go back." The trooper sounded impatient and resumed his chicken-shooing gestures.

"Why can't we walk through?" Martin insisted.

"Look Jack. You just can't. This area is…closed. Nobody else is allowed through. Now Go Back. Do what I tell ya."

The trooper took what Martin perceived to be an alpha-dog gesture of a menacing step forward. Martin did not oblige with the lesser-dog response, but stared hard at the scowling trooper. Susan must have seen him change his footing and draw in a big breath. She pulled at his arm.

"Never mind, Martin. Let's go back, like he says."

Martin could feel his heart rate rising and his face feeling hot. He knew it was a fool's errand to argue with bull-shaped trooper — with a gun — but after his injuries, he was in no mood for authority figures being vague and throwing their weight around. He did not want to give the bull the satisfaction of seeing him comply with arbitrary tyranny.

"Come on, Martin," she insisted. "Please?"

Martin broke off his stare at the trooper. *Why did her eyes have to be so big?* Big eyes were an unfair tool. Martin grumbled, turned and stomp-limped off down the sidewalk. The trooper turned and strutted back toward his car beyond the overpass.

"Where do they get the idea they can just close a public road to everyone?" Martin ranted to himself. "We'll just find some other way through without violating his precious stinking forbidden-zone."

"That's right," she tried sounding upbeat. "We'll find another way through."

As they walked back past the northbound roadblock, they could see the first trooper telling everyone that the roads were closed to allow emergency vehicles to get through.

A woman stepped out of the crowd, pleading loudly at the trooper. She wailed with anguish, not anger, complete with flailing her arms as if she were on fire. The trooper was yelling at her to get back, but she kept coming closer. Others in the crowd were inching forward too, in her wake. The trooper shouted at them all to keep back. They kept advancing slowly. He drew his sidearm and held it high. The crowd shrank back with a few screams. The hysterical woman alone kept coming towards him.

"She's speaking Spanish," Susan said. "I don't think he understands her. She's saying something about her babies."

"You speak Spanish?"

"A little."

"I don't think that woman understands him either. This is going bad fast." Without thinking enough, Martin rushed across the road to the median. He dropped the handle of the roller bag so he could have both hands open wide and held high as he straddled over the guardrail. As he entered the trooper's field of view, the trooper pointed his pistol at Martin.

There was something in the trooper's eyes that looked more frightened than menacing. Martin was worried, but felt strangely calm. Certainly the trooper must see that the frantic little hispanic woman was no threat. Martin thought he might be afraid he was on the brink of losing control of the crowd. If the lady could get too close, so might the others.

"Hey. Easy now." Martin half-shouted. "Don't shoot. Take it easy. I have no weapons. See?"

The trooper was young and looked like he had played football in high school. His eyes were wide. This was fear, not rage.

"She doesn't understand what you're saying to her," Martin said. "She's no threat." Martin said as soothingly as one might with a Glock aimed at their head.

"Back off. All of you. Just. Back. Off."

The hispanic lady did not back off, but continued to slowly advance on the trooper, pleading her unintelligible case. She continued to wail a torrent of Spanish. The trooper put his sights back on her. The bull trooper was jogging awkwardly down the road towards the scene.

Susan had come up behind Martin. "She's worried about her babies," she called out to the trooper.

"I don't care. She has to back off or I'm going to drop her." His last few words did not sound like a threat, but more like the woman was dangling over a cliff and slipping out of his grasp.

Martin looked back over his shoulder to Susan. "Can you tell her she has to back off?"

"I think so." Susan kept her hands in the air as much as climbing a guardrail allowed. She came up behind the wailing woman, gently pulled her arms down and began talking with her. Martin could not hear what they were saying, but it would not have mattered, since he knew virtually no Spanish.

Susan turned the woman slowly away from the trooper. He still looked upset, but visibly relieved. He held his gun at low ready, which made Martin blow out a sigh of relief. The bull trooper arrived, panting, sidearm drawn, but too late to be of any help.

Those of the crowd that had not scurried for cover behind cars, looked on in silence. The woman repeatedly turned towards the trooper and raised her voice, but Susan kept turning her back, talking soothingly and walking her away.

Martin backed along behind them, keeping himself between the women and the nervous trooper.

"No one passes this point!" the young trooper shouted, regaining his in-charge voice. "All you people. Just turn around and return to wherever you were last night. No one is allowed through here."

The crowd was regaining its nerve. A few resumed hurling questions at the trooper. The fact that he had not re-holstered his Glock, and that there were now two troopers, kept the questioners less assertive than before.

As they walked back between the cars, Martin began to breathe easier. His heart still raced, and his legs felt weak, even though the danger of the moment was past.

What's with me and rescuing strange women? Martin wondered. *Do I have Compulsive Rescue Disorder, or something? CRD is going to get me killed one of these times.*

His mind still tried to make sense of the situation. Maybe closing the interstates to civilian traffic was necessary so emergency vehicles could get around. The clog of 93 proved how quickly the masses could shut down a major highway. But why would foot traffic not be allowed to pass? The first trooper asked where they lived. What did residency have to do with anything? That made no sense to him either.

The woman's ranting grew loud enough to break Martin's train of thought. "What does she keep yammering about?"

"She's talking too fast. I can't make out much. I got that her name is Isabel. She's trying to get home, to Lawrence, I think."

"Oh si, Lorenz."

"Where's her car?" Martin asked. "We should get her back to her car and get her calmed down."

Susan asked. The woman pointed to an old red Civic back in the line of cars. The driver's door was still open. She also burst into a rapid-fire string of words, flailing her arms in the direction of the trooper.

"Hable lentamente, por favor," said Susan. "Lentamente." The woman took some deep breaths then repeated her volley only slightly slower.

"She said she's been trying to get home all morning," Susan relayed. "She says there are no roads."

"No roads? What does that mean?"

"I'm not sure," said Susan. She held the Civic's door and urged Isabel to sit and rest. Susan asked her more questions. Isabel picked up her GPS, tapped on it and pointed. All the while, a river of words flowed. She showed Susan the screen several times, getting more agitated at each display. Susan tried to calm her down.

"She means that all the roads are blocked, like this one."

"With state troopers?"

"It's hard to tell. Policemen of some kind, I guess. When the power went out, she went to check on her mother in Malden. She left her two boys with her sister back up in Lawrence."

"Sí sí, meesbebays...Deboconsekorahlorenz."

Martin could only offer a half-smile apology. He had no idea what she said. He gestured for the GPS. Isabel pointed out the roads she had tried, all the while babbling something. From the screens and her pointing, however, he understood that anything that crossed 93, 128 or Route 1, was blocked.

Is that why everyone is driving so fast now? Martin wondered. Everyone's hurrying to find a way past the road blocks? But why the roadblocks? Was the emergency vehicles story a smoke screen? They had not seen any. There hasn't been much for sirens all morning. Was the goal simply to keep people from moving around? Why do that?

As Isabel was pointing out her failed routes, Martin's eye was caught by an apparent dead end road near 128. It did not look right.

He dug out his paper map for comparison. On his map, the road was an overpass, not a dead end. He had drawn one of his faint red pencil lines along that street when he made his maps a couple years ago.

He could not read the GPS's Spanish text and labels, but navigated by icons and guesswork.

"My map says this road crosses 128," Martin said. "But her GPS doesn't, so it never would plan a route that way."

"Do you think the road does connect?"

"Maybe. I haven't ever driven on it, so I'm not positive. It's worth a try. Maybe we can help Isabel and she can help us too at the same time. Ask her if she'll give us a ride to up to Lawrence if we help her get there."

Susan translated in fits and starts as her mind scrounged for appropriate words. Isabel nodded enthusiastically with many "Si, Si, Si" bursts in Susan's pauses.

Isabel fired up the Civic. Susan got into the passenger seat. Martin climbed into the back with the roller bag. He slid in amid scattered plastic zoo animals and toy cars. Martin held the GPS between the front seat backs. "We need to get back to the intersection and then go east on North Street."

Susan translated. Isabel executed a hasty three-point turn, tapping a couple of the other cars' bumpers in the process. Their drivers yelled at her, but she ignored them.

"Tell her to go around behind this restaurant" Martin said. "The back of the parking lot connects up to North Street."

Isabel powered her little red Honda through gaps between cars that Martin was not sure they would fit through. He and the toys were getting tossed from side to side with the sudden maneuvers.

"Whoa. Ouch! I don't know if she's a great driver or a crazy driver," Martin said, bracing himself on the door post.

"A little of both," Susan had one hand on the dash, the other around the headrest. "She's very worried that she won't get home to her kids. It's kind of making her crazy."

"I noticed."

As they came up to North Street, the solid line of west-bound cars would not let Isabel make a left turn, despite her frantic honking, flailing arms and a torrent of Spanish out the window.

"No one is going to let us in," said Susan.

"I wonder about this brick office building on the left," said Martin. "It has parking in the back, see? Maybe there's an exit on the other side."

Isabel either understood more English than she spoke, or must have figured out what Martin was saying from his gestures. She gunned the engine and threaded her Honda between a cedar fence and a telephone pole. They bumped down off a tall curb. She cranked a hard left turn, bouncing off the far curb of the driveway in the process. Martin was tossed onto the roller bag.

"Oof. I guess we'll find out."

The parking lot did loop back to North Street, but the westbound lane was no more cooperative than before. Having already embraced "alternative routes", Isabel bumped up onto the sidewalk to create her own lane. A fire hydrant, some pedestrians, and a parked car were some of the challenges Isabel encountered. She usually found "green lanes" to get around them.

"It's just as well that Isabel keeps finding ways to keep going on this side," Martin noted. "The way traffic is on North Street, I doubt we could ever get back across. We'd have to turn left again."

"She keeps asking if this is the right way to get to Lawrence," Susan said. "I keep telling her yes. We are going the right way, right?'"

"Yes." Martin studied the GPS and his paper map. "Tell her our road is coming up soon on the left. Turn left."

Several cars were peeling off the North Street west-bound traffic to take the narrow suburban side street. The gaps between cars were car-length or better. Isabel merged into the line with only a little tire squeal.

Few cars were coming the opposite way. Compared to the vigorous off-road experience of getting there, on-roading the winding suburban street felt as smooth as glass. The line of cars moved along at a jogger's pace, but began to slow.

"Ha! The road does connect!" Martin pointed. "There's a bridge up ahead."

He stared closely at the GPS. "Hehe. Check it out. Her GPS thinks we're off-roading now, or flying, maybe."

"Why is everyone going so slow here?" Susan asked.

As they inched across the bridge, Martin could see below them that 128 was empty except for a dozen or so abandoned cars scattered randomly across the six lanes. It had a ghost town feel to it.

Near the end of the bridge, the line of cars had slowed and snaked to the right. A very young policeman was trying to set up a second blue sawhorse with "Reading PD" stenciled on it. He was trying to erect a simple barricade in the middle of the road, but the line of cars was not giving him enough room. He got the fallen sawhorse set up, and stood behind it with his arm outstretched in a "halt" gesture.

Chapter 9: Evasion and camping in the rain

The driver of the little Ford Focus in front of Isabel was not inclined to halt at the sawhorse roadblock. Instead, she veered sharply left, bumped one wheel up on the sidewalk and drove around the blue sawhorses. Almost. Her fender pushed one of the sawhorses over, unleashing a flurry of shouts from the upset young officer. Isabel and the cars behind her, quickly followed the Focus.

"What is he trying to do?" Susan looked back.

"They must not have enough cruisers to block off all the streets," Martin guessed. "So this poor rookie was dropped off out here with a couple sawhorses. Still, I bet he will eventually get it blocked. All he needs is one overly-obedient citizen to stop on the bridge and it's all clogged up."

"Yeah, but why block the streets?" Susan persisted. "That makes no sense."

"I don't get it either. That trooper back there said only people who lived in Reading could come in. Maybe there's some sort of order about local traffic only? I don't know. That doesn't make any sense to me either. But I am glad we got past him."

"Tell Isabel that we're almost back to Route 28," said Martin. "Right turn."

The line of traffic traveling north on 28 was moving slowly, with little space between cars. "Isabel says she knows this road now," said Susan. "She knows which way to go now."

With no hesitation, Isabel pushed out, inserting the corner of her hood between a minivan and a pale yellow pickup. The pickup driver honked long and loudly, but made the tactical error of braking slightly too. That was all Isabel needed to enlarge her foothold and enter the stream.

"We're not going much faster than a walk," said Martin. "But I'm glad we're riding instead of walking it. My knee is enjoying the break."

"Isabel has been thanking us profusely for helping her past that roadblock. She is one happy momma," said Susan.

"I'm glad she's happy, but we're not there yet," said Martin. "I'm still wondering what's up with these roadblocks. Hey. Maybe there's some news on that'll make some sense of all this. Ask her if she'll turn on her radio."

Susan relayed the request. Isabel popped the radio on. The announcer rattled off Spanish commentary at warp speed. Martin felt naive for expecting the announcer to be speaking English. It was a 'duh' moment he kept to himself.

"So," he asked. "What do they say?"

"Got me," Susan said. "I thought Isabel spoke fast. I'll see if she can summarize for me."

The two women began a long string of back and forth exchanges. Martin used the time to survey the traffic. The north-bound lanes were moving slowly, but there was little coming southbound. Was this a general outward migration? There seemed to be few side streets. If traffic stopped, would they be stuck? The yellow pickup behind them was riding their bumper. He was obviously in a bigger hurry than traffic would allow.

"Isabel said the governor has declared a state of emergency. I guess there have been some violent protests in Dorchester and Roxbury. A food protest in Mattapan got bad and several policemen were injured. So, the governor has called up the National Guard to help keep the peace. She said they're telling everyone to stay home and not be on the streets."

"I'd love to comply," said Martin.

"I sure wish I'd paid more attention in my Spanish classes," said Susan.

"Heck," said Martin. "I wish I would have paid more attention to Sesame Street when the kids were watching it. Besides the numbers, I think I only learned one other word."

"What was that?"

"Oh sure. Now that I said that, I can't think of it. Not like I ever used it." Martin wracked his brain for the old memories. "There was this big bird — a flamingo. Yeah. That was it. Doing a play or a skit. No, it was an opera. The bird was called…Placio Flamingo. Yeah, yeah, and he was singing about danger as he wrecked the stage set." Martin laughed. "I loved that bit. Now I remember. The word was Peligro!" Martin announced triumphantly.

"Peligro?" gasped Isabel. She slammed on her brakes. Martin was thrown against Susan's seat back.

The yellow pickup squealed to a stop just inches behind Isabel's Honda. The angry driver gunned his engine and veered around Isabel's Honda. Out his window, he hurled insults, drowned out by the V8's roar.

"Dondayestael Peligro?" she demanded, glancing around nervously.

"Danger?" said Susan, brushing her hair out of her eyes. "That's your word?"

"Oh jeez," Martin said. "Yeah. That had to be the only word I know."

Susan tried to explain to Isabel about Martin's Sesame Street memories, but Martin interrupted.

"Whoa. Hold on. What's going on up there?"

He pointed ahead of them. A policeman in full riot gear was talking to a driver in a gray sedan. The yellow pickup tried to pass them on the right, which brought out a swam of other policemen in black gear, with ARs aimed at the driver. They ordered the yellow pickup driver to turn into the adjacent parking lot where many other detained drivers stood beside their cars, or sat inside them.

The gray sedan driver took advantage of the distraction to execute a hasty u-turn. He was temporarily blocked by another car making a sloppy three point turn.

Martin stepped out and waved down the gray sedan driver.

"Hey. What's going on up there?" he asked.

"They're checking ID. If you don't live in Reading, you have to go to that lot over there."

"Then what?"

"No idea, I ain't gonna find out." The gray sedan sped away.

Martin got back in Isabel's Honda. "They're stopping people without local ID."

"Why?"

"No clue. That's all the guy said. None of this makes any sense. But if they're using guns, it can't be good. We need to turn back and find a way around this."

More impatient drivers drove around Isabel's stopped Honda. They, too, got pulled over by the SWAT team.

"Have her turn into this side lot here. I need a sec to look at my map."

"Are there riots or something up ahead?" Susan asked. "Is that why they're stopping non-locals?"

"Who knows. Have Isabel keep listening for news. We need to know what's going on out there. We've had power outages before that lasted longer than two days without riots breaking out. Must be something else too."

Martin's finger traced along the map. "We need to take some side streets and get around the center of Reading. We passed a little side street back there."

Susan relayed what Martin said. Isabel veered around a fence, into the next parking lot.

"This is good," Martin said. "I think these parking lots connect. Keep going."

They eventually bumped out onto a narrow side street. It ended in a T at another street.

"She's asking which way now?" Susan said.

"Give me a minute." Martin studied his map. It was clear that all the main roads converged on Reading center. If the authorities were out to stop traffic, that would be the place to block.

"Wait. What's that over there?" Martin pointed at a narrower road on the right. "It's not on my map or her GPS, but it looks like it goes behind these commercial buildings. Tell her to try that way."

Isabel kicked up a swirl of dry leaves as she sped down the narrow commercial driveway. Vast parking lots stretched out behind the low brick buildings.

Isabel drove around parked cars and concrete dividers. The last parking lot ended, however, at a landscaped berm. Separating the parking lots was a bark mulched ridge, perhaps three feet high with a line of yew bushes atop it.

"Shoot," Martin said. "So close. That's the road we need, right over there. It connects back to a main road." He pointed between two of the ragged bushes.

Isabel sat up tall in her seat to see where Martin pointed. She said something to Susan, then backed up a few feet. She aimed her car's nose at a wider gap between two of the bushes.

Susan braced herself. "Hang on back there. She's going for it."

Martin started to ask what she was going for, but grabbed the door handle and the seat back. The little Honda bounced up, then down the other side and onto the pavement. Martin's head hit the headliner. Toys landed in his lap. Isabel quickly found the exit, crossed some railroad tracks and sped up the little side road.

"Ow man. She's clearly not babying this car," said Martin.

"Which way now?" asked Susan.

Martin uncrumpled his map. "Left at the next intersection, then another right. Tell her not to get too crazy. We don't want to be attracting attention."

After several turns and side roads, the three had found their way back to Route 28 north. Traffic was not as thick and moving at a better pace.

"Isabel said the radio reported that they're calling for a curfew in lots of towns because of some riots. Something about some policemen killed by a mob. She didn't hear where."

"Things are getting nasty kinda fast," said Martin. "Tell her to turn right up ahead here."

The radio station had been fading out steadily. Isabel messed with the buttons, but there was mostly just dead air or static. She dialed past an english-speaking station. The signal was weak and scratchy, but at least Martin could understand what they said.

"Wait, wait. Tell her to go back to that one," Martin said.

...reported a dozen people injured...I've been told that the protest started with a large crowd demanding that city officials seize...of the supermarket and distribute the food to hungry residents. Supposedly someone in the crowd fired upon the police, injuring two officers. I say 'supposedly' because when I traveled to Stoneham, to try and interview the injured, I was unable to locate any of them.

"Stoneham?" said Susan. "We were just there. Do you think he was talking about the Stop n' Shop we were at?"

"I don't know," replied Martin. "Maybe there's other supermarkets."

...unable to reach the Stop n' Shop building either ...the area cordoned off and roadblocks set up...prevent more looters from...cannot confirm...but there are...fts...

The station finally faded out.

"Wow. It *was* the Stop n' Shop we were at," Susan exclaimed. "Sounds like we got out of there just in time, huh?"

Martin grunted an agreement, but his mind was already down a rabbit trail. The crowd around that Stop n' Shop were not the least bit rowdy. Even the people who had to step out of line, for lack of a local ID, were well behaved. No one was shouting or chanting slogans. Had a fight broken out over the trash pile? Martin could not even recall seeing any police officers. Walgreens and CVS each had one, but none at Stop n' Shop. Maybe things escalated very quickly after they left. Or maybe they had not.

This last thought was the edge of a black hole that Martin was reluctant to enter.

"Isabel is so grateful for us helping her," said Susan. "She's offering to drive us up into New Hampshire."

"Oh, that would be great," Martin said. "Tell her thanks. We might get home before dark after all!"

"That would be so nice," Susan added. "I really didn't want to sleep in the woods again."

As they approached the interchange for 495, traffic grew thick and finally slowed to a crawl. When it stopped, Martin got out and looked up ahead with his little binoculars.

"There's a trooper up there. A black SUV with the blue lights. A couple lines of those orange barrels too."

"Esayohtra Baracada?"

"Uh, a barricade?" Martin asked. "Yes. uh, Si. Baracada. This one is different, though. They're turning some people away, but letting others through. Maybe it's that residency thing."

Susan spoke to Isabel, who then dug in her purse. She showed her driver's license to Susan.

"Isabel has her ID," Susan said. "It has a Lawrence address. That might get us through this roadblock, right?"

"Maybe." Martin was hopeful.

"She asked if it would be okay if she checked on her boys before she drives us up into New Hampshire," Susan relayed.

"Of course," Martin said. "Even if she just drives us up into Salem or maybe Windham, it will save us hours of walking. Tell her thanks again."

Martin peered at his map for the shortest route to his house from southern Windham. He imagined sitting in his own comfy chair again, in front of his warm wood stove, instead of sleeping in the cold woods. The mental images cheered him up. Walking home had been more tiring and spartan than he imagined.

The trooper waved Isabel ahead and motioned to her to roll down her window.

"License please," the trooper said in weary monotone. Isabel just smiled.

"Lye-sens-ia Poor fuh-vor." His spanish could not have been more gringo. He squinted at her driver's license, as if trying to decide if it were counterfeit, but handed it back to her.

"Your license too, ma'am," he said to Susan. "And yours too, sir."

"But why?" Susan asked.

"We're with her," Martin said, pointing to Isabel.

"Doesn't matter. I need to see your ID too." The trooper recited a prepared statement that he was obviously tired of reciting. "As of this morning, Governor Baylach has officially declared a state of emergency for the entire Commonwealth of Massachusetts and ordered the implementation of Mass Emergency Situation Function Plans. Per MESF codes, only legal residents will be allowed to enter an emergency zone. This area has been declared an emergency zone. Lemme see your IDs."

Martin fished for his wallet. Susan dug through her purse. "We're not trying to stay in Lawrence, officer. We're just trying to get up to New Hampshire." He handed his drivers license to the trooper. Susan did too.

"Doesn't matter," said the trooper. "Only residents allowed past this point."

"But..."

"Hey. Didn't you hear me?" The trooper was losing his patience. "Only residents. Either all three of you turn this heap around, or you two get out of the car and she goes in. Make up your minds right now."

Susan explained to Isabel what the trooper said. Isabel shook her head vehemently, speaking very fast.

"Look," Martin said to Susan. "We should just get out. Better that she gets in to her kids than gets stuck out here because of us."

"I agree," said Susan. She told Isabel, who continued to protest. The trooper yelled at Isabel to get moving.

Susan waved as Isabel drove under the bridge. "Poor thing. She felt really bad. I told her we would be okay and to take good care of her boys."

"This state of emergency thing is getting kinda nuts." Martin wondered if there had been riots in Lawrence. Were they worried that car-loads of outside instigators would stream in and enflame things? Like local residents could not cause trouble?

Martin walked slowly ahead of Susan while he studied his map. "Thanks to Isabel, we got a lot farther than we would have on foot. Now we'll have to see how far we can get before dark."

He showed Susan the map. "If we back track to this road here, we can go up this way towards Haverhill. We need to get across the river somehow, and there aren't all that many bridges."

"Won't they just be blocked off for residents only too?"

"Maybe, but I'm thinking this bridge here might be better." He tapped the map with his finger. "495 crosses this loop in the river here, see? There's an exit there, but it's an industrial park."

"So?"

"So there might not be a big line of traffic there. Maybe even light coverage with troopers or police, since it's not a route to anyone's home. I'm thinking that maybe we could cut through some woods and sneak across one of those bridges."

"And then what?"

"Um. I'm not sure. That's as much plan as I have right now. We'll just have to see what our options are if and when we get there."

While they walked the narrow back streets of North Andover, Martin was juggling more mental balls than he liked. People seemed so calm yesterday: annoyed but relatively calm. That fight at La Quinta seemed like the statistical outlier rather than a trend. This morning, they saw more of the same complacency: people waiting for their usual routines to resume. There was some tension at Andrew's Market, and those gas stations, but by and large, people still acting pretty typical. Not all that good, he thought, but typical.

Had things suddenly gone nuts in just two days? Protesters demanding food and clashing with police? Riots? This was only the third day without power. Part of Martin did not want to believe that civility could collapse so quickly. Maybe there *had* been riots in those inner city neighborhoods. It did not take but a day or two for the Fergusson trouble to boil over into riots. Was that happening here?

A vague third option danced around the edges of his thinking like a persistent gnat. Were the reports fake? That seemed impossible to pull off. Even if they could, why would they?

He had no warm feelings towards Massachusetts government, but neither was he one of those twichy-eyed old coots in tinfoil hats, bristling with paranoia about 'The Gubmint.' He had a hard time picturing Mass government as the diabolical Beast from the book of Revelation. A pack of 400 pound Keystone Cops seemed more fitting. They did not seem competent enough to be evil.

Trying to rationalize what he had seen and knew, he wondered if the governor knew the outage was going to be a long one. Food and fuel shipments would be virtually halted. Trouble could brew up. Were they trying to get everyone "locked down" before riots — real riots — could break out? Were the riot stories to scare people into complying with their stern emergency protocols? Authoritarian control via the smoke screen of public safety?

"Hey, could we take a break?" Susan called out.

"Huh? Oh sure. Sorry. I've been lost in thought."

"Noticed. You haven't said a word for blocks. I thought you were really angry or something."

"No, not angry, just thinking."

"I guess. You walked across that busy road back there without even looking. Good thing those people slowed down for you."

Martin felt embarrassed. He did not remember crossing any busy roads. Nor had he noticed that the tree-lined suburb had morphed into a low scrabble retail zone. He certainly scored no points for situational awareness.

No more deep thinking, he resolved. *Not until I'm safely at home in my comfy chair again.*

He pointed up ahead. "How about that planter around that sign over there?"

"Sounds good," she said. "I just need to sit for awhile."

Martin coaxed Susan into checking her blister bandaging. The gauze did need to be replaced. He insisted on checking her other foot for any blisters-in-the-making. She reluctantly agreed. Martin noted that she did not close her eyes or look away this time. She did, however, resume her sad-puzzled look.

Without looking up from applying fresh tape, Martin said. "Your feet still aren't weird, by the way."

When she did not answer, he looked over at her. She was not looking at her feet, but at him. He was a bug under the magnifying glass again.

"What?" He sounded more annoyed than he was.

"Nothing?" She answered slowly, like a kid who had a frog in her pocket at church.

"Uh huh." Martin was not buying it, but had a feeling he was better off not knowing.

They were at Sutton Street. It was not as wide as Route 125, but seemed just as full of traffic. Martin noticed more abandoned cars along the sides of the roads: hoods open, doors ajar. People must have used up whatever gas they had in their tanks while trying to get around the roadblocks. More people walked the sidewalks too.

Perhaps the gas-less drivers. From their frowns, they seemed like a cranky bunch.

"Okay," Susan said. "Ready." She had her socks and shoes on, and her bag poised to roll.

"Alright then." Martin stood and stretched. He felt dog-tired.

He stopped in mid-stretch. Across the street, a railroad crossing sign caught his eye. He looked at his map again. Tracks came out of Lawrence and followed the river before turning up into Haverhill.

"What do you say we take the tracks up to the bridges? It will be a little trickier walking, but to tell you the truth, melding into all these other walkers doesn't seem like a good idea. Maybe I'm just spooked by those apartment people back there, but being in a crowd seems like a bad idea right now."

"I know what you mean. Let's take the tracks."

Martin carried the wheels end of Susan's roller bag. She carried the handle. They looked like hobo stretcher-bearers. In the distance, an occasional siren wailed into earshot, then faded out. Sporadic car horns were proof that frustrated drivers were still trying to get around. It was all muffled, like a television playing in another room. It was someone else's reality. Alone, on the quiet tracks, between the red, yellow and brown trees, it was a world removed.

Walking single file did not encourage conversation. Despite his resolution to not get lost in thought again, he did. Would there be policemen blocking the roads to the bridge? Would they be *on* the bridge? They seemed to be trying to cordon off the areas between interstates. Perhaps this was easier, since fewer roads crossed interstates, there was less to block. Even still, were there enough policemen in the state to block all those roads? That seemed unlikely.

Given the modern commuter lifestyle, few people work near home. What would all those out-of-area people do for housing? Assuming everyone settled down within the cordons, what did the authorities plan to do after that? Did they expect that all the non-residents would get put up in the homes of area residents? How long could *that* last?

Perhaps that was where the FEMA camps would come in. Maybe that is what the SWAT teams were doing in the middle of Reading. The pretense could be that the authorities are just trying to "help" all those displaced people. Why not just let them all get home? Being "helped" at the point of a carbine was not all that comforting.

Without houses, intersections or landmarks, it was hard to gauge their progress. The sky had been overcast all day, but was getting darker: subtle proof that time was not as frozen as it seemed.

About the time Martin spotted the overpass in the distance, he began to feel drops on his cheeks. He hoped it was just a passing sprinkle, but it picked up.

"It's starting to rain," Susan said from behind him.

Martin set down the roller bag. "I was hoping it would stop, but the sky seems pretty dark, so I don't think it will."

"I didn't grab my raincoat," she said. "Or an umbrella."

"Well, I've got one of us covered." Martin rummaged in his backpack.

"I've got one of these dollar-store plastic ponchos. Here." He handed it to her.

"You don't have two? I can't take your only one." She handed it back to him.

"No. Take it. I'll be okay. My jacket is water resistant-ish, and I've got my cap. Go ahead, put it on before you get too wet."

When they got to the overpass, Martin had Susan wait beneath the bridge while he scrambled up the brushy embankment. He wanted to see if the police had the road blocked off.

They did. A black Suburban, with blue lights flashing, blocked one side of the divided roadway. A fire chief's big red sedan blocked the other side. A large state trooper stood nearer 125, in an impressive none-shall-pass posture. The traffic coming and going along 125 was taking the hint.

Martin could not see far up the road towards 495. He scrambled back down.

"They have the access road blocked off," he reported. "There could be others up near the interchange, but I couldn't see that from here. I think we should go back to that little road that crossed the tracks back there. I don't think it goes far enough, but it will get us close."

"Looks like you might be right about this little road." Susan pointed to a pair of sawhorses and a half dozen cones where the road met the highway. "The police didn't think it was worth guarding."

The sprinkle developed into a light rain. Drips fell from the bill of Martin's cap. The shoulders of his jacket were starting to get wet. The heavy sky promised more rain.

Through a break in the trees, Martin could see the side of a large commercial building. Two police cars and a handful of officers stood in a loose line, weapons at flat stock, or low ready.

"There's a BJs over there." Martin pointed. "Looks like they're expecting trouble."

"Looters maybe?" Susan offered.

"Maybe. Guess that's why they only left sawhorses back there. More men to guard BJs."

Maybe there really were riots and lootings, thought Martin. *Why would they waste manpower guarding a BJs if the stories were fake? Of course, this only proves that these cops believe the stories were true, not that they are true. Perhaps the State House isn't sharing all their plans with the locals. What if the cops weren't guarding the BJs but taking control of it?*

"Looks like the end of our road," Susan said. The pavement ended in a parking lot beside a commercial building.

"It's getting dark," she added. "And the rain isn't letting up. We need to find someplace to get out of the rain, at least."

"I know. I know. 495 must be just beyond those tall trees," said Martin. I bet we can find a dry spot under one of the bridges."

He found a section of chain link fence mashed down by a fallen tree. They crossed over into the woods. Martin led the way to the left, along the base of the embankment, towards the river. The structure of the bridge loomed over the trees and brush.

The land under the bridge sloped down gently, from the riprap abutment to the river, roughly thirty yards away. Those thirty yards were covered in bushes, weeds and brambles.

"At least it's dry under here," Martin said.

"That's great." Susan did not sound all that pleased. "What do we do now?

"Hmm. The day is pretty well spent," he said. "And the rain doesn't sound like it's going to let up anytime soon. We should probably stay here for the night, or until the rain stops."

"I don't want to sound like a whiny princess, but I'm wet and cold and very tired. You wouldn't happen to have a collapsible clothes drier in your magical bag, would you?"

"Sorry to disappoint," Martin said.

"Figured, but it didn't hurt to ask. When I was still living at home and felt a chill I just couldn't shake, I would put my heavy flannel pajamas in the drier for 10 minutes. Oh, that felt good."

Martin looked around on the ground. "No collapsable driers, but maybe I can get us a little fire going. Not as cozy as hot flannel jammies, but it'll help.

"Make a fire out of what? Everything is wet?"

"Maybe not everything. Why don't you scour around in the brush under this bridge and the other one. Whatever's under here should still be dry. Gather up all the dry twigs, dead branches and anything else that looks like firewood."

"Okay."

"I'll go back into the woods and see what I can find."

Susan began searching the ground between the scrubby bushes. Martin headed back out into the light rain. The canopy of leaves was still shedding the early rain, so beneath the trees was still relatively dry. He found several good low-hanging dead branches that were still dry. He broke off what he could, sometimes using his puny multi-tool saw to score the bigger ones for easier breaking.

Martin gasped. "Jackpot!" He dropped his armful of branches. A tall slender tree, dead for a few years, had fallen over, but gotten hung up in the branches of two medium sized oaks. From the pattern of the branching, it appeared to have been a maple. Good hardwood. The twigs and bark were gone from the upper half. The base of it was pithy from rot.

"Now, how to get you down, my pretty," Martin said in his Witch of the West voice.

He tried shaking and bouncing the maple, but the branches were too interlocked. Martin squatted down at the rotten base of the maple to see if he could yank it loose from the oaks. He was more successful than he expected.

The butt of the maple was not attached, but simply sitting on the ground. His tug released the power of gravity. The dead maple lunged forward, knocking Martin to the ground. Several sharp cracks rang out from overhead as branches broke. The maple fell.

Martin stood up, laughing as he brushed the wet leaves off himself. "Now to make you more portable," he said to the tree. The upper branches broke off easily enough. More good medium wood for the fire. What they needed were some thicker logs that would last longer.

He positioned the maple between the two oak trunks and pushed. A strong push broke off the barkless top. He wanted one more break to give him three manageable pieces. He positioned the trunk between the oaks again and pushed. Nothing, not even a crack.

He flung himself at the maple trunk. He bounced off.

"Martin?" Susan called out. "Are you out there?"

"Yes. Over here."

"I heard a lot of crashing and cracking. Are you okay?"

"Pretty much. I found some good big-wood, but I could use your help." He showed her the maple trunk between the two oaks. His plan was for her to pull and him to push at the far end for best leverage. They would use bounces to create some peak stresses and break the maple.

The first few tries yielded a few encouraging cracking sounds, but no break.

"Hold on," Martin said. "Let me shift it over. All these little mushrooms on the bark could mean a weaker spot. Okay. This time for sure. On three."

Martin braced himself and started the bounce. "One. Two…"

The maple broke with a dull crunch on the second bounce. The sudden release sent Susan onto her back. The log was going to fall on her, so with the last of his shaky footing, Martin tried to toss the log upwards like a volleyball player's diving save.

The log did arc up over Susan's head, but Martin fell partially on top of her.

It took him a moment to get his bearings. He pushed himself up on his arms. The log had landed ahead of him. That was good.

Susan? She was looking up at him with wide eyes. It was a startled expression, but there was also animal fear in her eyes. She had her arms tight up on her chest, fists up by her neck.

"Don't," she gasped.

"Huh? Are you okay?" He asked.

She did not answer. Her eyes shifted back and forth from looking into his right eye or his left.

Martin realized he was looking into her eyes. He had no business looking into her eyes. His face felt hot. He rolled left and scrambled to his feet.

"I'm really sorry," he stammered. He felt like he had dented a friend's car or a fireman that had dropped the cat.

"I really didn't think it would break like that." He offered his hand to help her up, but she ignored it and got up on her own. "Are you hurt?"

She backed up a step as she stood. She kept looking at Martin as she brushed the leaves off her pants. Her expression morphed from worry to sadness. This made Martin squirm inside. He had put a big dent in his friend's car, or maybe ran over their cat.

"I feel awful about this," Martin said. "We needed some bigger wood, see, to make a fire last and…"

"It's okay," she said flatly.

Nothing about her body language agreed with her words. Rain drizzling down Martin's collar reminded him of his goal of making a fire.

"Well, um. I'm going to take this wood under the bridge so it…um…" Martin rushed to gather up the sections of maple in his arms. Action always felt better than searching for words which would not come.

He returned to get his pile of dead branches. Susan still stood, looking at the ground. "I'm going to make that fire now," he said. "You should at least come stand under the bridge…out of the rain."

Martin dropped his armload at the base of the bridge abutment's heavy stone riprap. He set about pulling up the weeds and scrawny bushes around his pile of logs to make a small clearing. He set the pulled brush atop the edge bushes to improve the visual screen. A few of the stones were small enough that he could muscle them down the embankment and set up a back wall for their fire. He did not want their little campfire to be seen far and wide, especially from the deck of the southbound bridge.

He pulled two of the maple logs up to his rock screen then built up a criss-cross of broken branch sticks. He tore a half a page of his Spare Change News and wadded it into a ball. Around that paper ball he made a teepee of the little twigs Susan had gathered.

Out of the corner of his eye, he could see Susan walking slowly towards his little camp. He made no sign that he had seen her, but went on with building his fire lay.

A click of his disposable lighter had yellow licks eagerly consuming the twigs. The warmth from even that little fire felt surprisingly good. He slowly fed on a few bigger sticks, to avoid choking the fire and making more smoke.

The flickering yellow light reflected on Susan, standing nearby.

"It's a small fire," he said. "It won't throw heat very far."

She squatted down on the opposite side of the fire. She had her folded arms atop her knees and her nose behind her arms. She was a little ball. The fire glinted off of moisture in her eyes.

"Are you alright?" Martin asked.

"I'm fine," she said quietly.

Fine. There was that word again. Martin was not fluent in woman-speak, but he knew that 'fine' meant just about anything *but* fine.

"I don't mean to be all pushy," he began. "But you don't look 'fine'. Are you sure you didn't get hurt in the fall?"

"No." She kept her eyes fixed on the little yellow flame.

"Something is bothering you." He wanted to sound reassuring, but had no confidence that he did. "I'd really rather you talked about it. It's going to be a long night."

She turned just her eyes to look at him. "That's just it."

"What's just it?"

"Last night, we were only resting. But fell asleep. Then it was over. I know I said I was okay with walking to your house, but that was during the day, and…it sometimes seemed like we'd be there before dark, so I really didn't think about it. But now…"

Martin felt a cold shiver as he realized what she was afraid of.

"…you're a woman alone in a dark remote woods," Martin finished her sentence. He also felt stupid and insensitive for not realizing it sooner. "with a guy you barely know."

She kept her eyes on him as she gave a little nod.

Martin realized that his falling on her was uncomfortably similar to an assault, even if purely accidental. For all he knew, she had bad past experiences with assault that he triggered. He hated the thought that something terrible like that might have happened to her in the past.

Oh God. Now what have I done? He thought. *Now I'm not just insensitive, I'm cruelly insensitive.*

In the past two days, he had seen in her eyes: rage, sorrow, worry, even some laughter. When she was on her back, he had seen paralyzing fear. He felt horrible being the cause of such a look.

"I'm really sorry about that…back there," he tried to sound gentle and as unthreatening as possible. "Probably nothing I can say will ever be reassuring enough. Heck, I really stink at being reassuring, but for what it's worth, I would never ever…" Again, no gentle synonyms for rape came to mind. "…do anything to hurt you."

She continued to stare at him with her sad-puzzled look. The moisture in her eyes grew.

"I tell you what," Martin said as he rummaged in his pocket. "Words are inadequate, but maybe this will help." He unfolded his multi-tool so that the knife blade was out. He set it on the ground at her feet.

"How about if I give you the knife for tonight?"

She looked at the multi-tool and then back to Martin. Her sad-puzzled look got more puzzled. She reached out and took the tool, then refolded her arms. She clutched the little blade in her fist.

Martin heaved a sigh. It was all he could think to do, but it felt woefully inadequate.

He fed the fire a few more branches. He needed to get them better set up for the cold night ahead. Setting up a little campsite was a welcome escape from her sad-puzzled look.

"We'll need to gather up some of these dry leaves to make us some insulation, like last night. And I'd like to set up a little lean-to, to help keep some of the fire heat closer."

She did not move, but watched his actions with her eyes. He walked out into the brush. The air was quite a bit cooler. The little fire did make a difference. He found the sort of saplings he was looking for and broke them off. On the way back to the campfire, he stripped off the leaves and twigs.

"Here." He put the long sticks in front of her. "You've got the knife, so could you whittle the ends of these two poles into points? I want to push them into the ground."

Without waiting to see if she would whittle the sticks, he dug in his bag. He pulled out one of the mylar blankets and a roll of paracord. He smiled when he turned back. She was finishing the point on the second stick.

"Okay, while I work with these sticks, you should round up a few more armfuls of leaves."

She returned after a few minutes with an armful as he had finished lashing together the frame. He draped the mylar over the little ridge pole stick.

"Put the leaves under here. The mylar will reflect the heat from the fire"

"That looks kinda small," she said, cautiously.

"It'll be enough for one — you."

"But what about you? Are you going to set up a shelter for you too?"

"No. One of us has to stay awake to tend the fire and keep watch. While I was out looking for sticks, I checked out how visible we were. We're good as long as we keep the fire low. Little fires need to be fed more often."

"But…"

"No buts. You curl up in there as best you can. I'll sit over here on the other side of the fire. You'll have the knife. You'll be okay."

Martin sat on his pile of leaves and leaned back against the backrest of pine branches he had propped against a large stone. He could reach his pile of firewood without having to lean forward. He reasoned that he could get a bit of rest and still keep something of a watch. He hoped that anyone approaching would make noise moving through the tangled brush. Susan had curled up on her side, facing the fire.

"I'm going to set up a rain catcher," he said to her. "We'll need more water tomorrow and it's abundant right now."

He draped the poncho between some bushes to form a shallow V. He clipped his pen to the bottom edge of the plastic to provide a weight and a path for the dripping water. Beneath the pen, he positioned one of their half-gallon milk jugs. It would take a good while for the light rain to fill it, but they had all night.

Martin took the long way back, rechecking how visible their fire might be from various angles. With power out, any light at night would be sure to attract attention. Being far from any roads, other than 495 overhead, worked in their favor. With the rain, it was less likely they would have random night walkers stumbling upon their camp. He felt some reassurance that the little flame was well hidden by the mylar and brush pile.

When Martin got back to their camp, Susan was turned on her other side, facing away from the fire. She had her overcoat draped over her as a blanket. Remembering how quickly she fell asleep the night before, he tried to quietly wad up pages of his newspaper. He stuffed them in his sleeves and under his jacket to provide more insulation. He was certain he looked like an absurd Michelin Man, but he did feel warmer.

He reached down to move a half-burned branch further onto the fire. Beside his leg sat the multi-tool, all folded up.

Chapter 10: Kevin and the carjackers

Martin nodded himself awake again. Sleeping sitting up was annoying that way, but it was useful. Rather than grumble, he appreciated the periodic wake-ups to keep the little fire going and listen carefully. The night had been oddly quiet. After the rain stopped, around 1:30, there was a stifling silence that seemed to absorb all sound. At other times, a faint car honk or a tire squeal acted like distant sonar pings from civilization. The world was still out there, even at 4:15 in the morning.

The dampness gave the night's cold a sharp edge. He added a few little sticks to the coals and blew on them. Cheerful flames sprang up, but he felt light-headed. Fatigue and lack of decent sleep were starting to take its toll.

I could sure go for a cup of coffee about now, he thought.

Coffee. He remembered having packed away one of those little tubes of instant coffee. He reached in his backpack and felt his way into the little pen pockets inside the front zipper section.

"Ha!" he said out loud, then shushed himself. "Now for some hot water," he whispered.

He tossed a few more sticks onto the fire. He poured some of the rainwater he had collected into his aluminum water bottle. He raked the burning sticks and coals level and balanced the bottle on top of them, then raked a few more around it.

After several minutes, steam was rising from the bottle neck. With his gloved hand, he moved the bottle to the ground and poured in the little packet of powder. He held the bottle under his nose and swirled it in circles to speed the mixing. It smelled heavenly.

Susan stirred under her overcoat. "Coffee?" she said in a hoarse voice. She sat up and wrapped her coat around herself. She scooted forward to sit very near the fire and warm her hands. "Is that coffee?"

"Yeah. I forgot I had one of those little instant packets. I'm not a big fan of Starbucks, but they do make a good instant." He took a long, loud sip, trying not to burn his tongue. Hot coffee on a cool, damp night, was magical.

"Here," he offered her the bottle. "Use a glove though. It's kinda hot."

Susan savored the smell for awhile, then sipped. "Oh that tastes good."

The gnawing emptiness in Martin's stomach twisted a little tighter.

"I'm really hungry this morning," he said. "I didn't notice so much yesterday. Maybe we were too busy."

"Me too. Is there any of that cheese left?"

"There's a little left. We might as well finish it off now. Martin pulled out the plastic bag and cut the little square in half.

Seeing the multi-tool knife made Susan cringe. "Um, Martin?"

He looked up, chewing his little square of cheese. He handed her the other half.

"About last night…" she turned her cheese over and over in her fingers and stared at the fire. "There's something I need to say…"

Martin could feel his shoulders slump. He had hoped that her returning the multi-tool was a sign that all was forgiven. Apparently not. His stupidity was not water-under-the-bridge.

"Look," he said. "I didn't mean for that to happen. I would never…"

Her sad-puzzled expression shut him down. That look was becoming kyrptonite. It made him feel powerless. What did it mean? Was she still frightened? Was she still upset at him? How does a guy go about repairing such damage?

A faint crunching sound interrupted his jumbled thoughts. He held a finger up to his lips. Silence. Susan was about to speak when a faint scraping sound came from the direction of the river. She turned her head quickly.

"You heard it too?" Martin whispered.

She nodded. "It came from up there." The two of them sat motionless, concentrating on the velvet silence for anything else.

"I think its footsteps," Martin whispered. "Someone is walking across the bridge."

Martin gently scooped handfuls of soil and poured them on the fire. Inky blackness joined the silence. Amid the faint crunches and scrapes, was the murmur of voices being kept low.

Martin reached out to touch Susan. She jumped. "I'm going to go up to check it out," he whispered softly. "As quietly as you can, get ready to go. We might have to leave fast."

"Be careful," she whispered back.

Martin's several trips to check on his rain gatherer had made him familiar with the bushes and trees along the abutment. He moved steadily, but careful to avoid making noise. He had grumbled about the rain yesterday, but was thankful for it now. The rain softened up the fallen leaves. Even he could move with Indian-like stealth on a carpet of damp leaves.

He felt his way up the embankment. The night was still too black to see. There was no distant orange glow on the horizon from nearby towns and cities. He could feel the slope of the embankment getting shallower, so he knew he was getting near the shoulder of the road. The air was cold. He pulled his coat collar up and his stocking cap down. When the leafy scrub gave way to grasses, he stopped to listen.

The murmuring and occasional crunching was, perhaps, twenty yards to his left and coming closer. Martin pulled back into the scrub and slowly laid on the ground. The voices were getting clearer.

"When we were in Kunar, we covered ten times this much territory in, like, half an hour. This is total fubar," said one voice in a slightly vocalized whisper.

"I know, but they don't want us going black on fuel. So…we walk," said the second.

The first voice grumbled. Their quiet footsteps had steady, if casual, cadence.

Martin was puzzled that the two were walking at such a normal gait in pitch blackness. He could see no flashlight beams, not even red ones. Then harsh chill ran up his spine. Night vision. They could see him, even if he could not see anything. If they had heat-sensing equipment, there would be no hiding. He would glow like a man-shaped ember among the bushes.

His eyes had been away from the fire long enough that he could make out a faint tree line across the highway. The sky was still overcast, but there must have been a moon above it. Out of the corner of his eye he glimpsed movement. Two shapes loomed up above the tree line. Every muscle in his body was tense.

"It is freakin' cold out here, man," said voice one.

"I hear ya. I want a hot cup of coffee so bad, I can smell it. Can you believe that?"

Martin's heart sank. They smelled his coffee.

He could just make out faint slivers of green glow in the moving dark shapes, like momentary crescent moons. They *did* have night vision goggles. The glow leaked around the eye-cups as they walked. Martin's body tensed to flee. Maybe he could rush down the hill faster than they could. Then what? He told himself to freeze completely.

"Don't you go complaining when we get back," chided voice two. "This assignment is pretty sweet, actually."

"Yeah," conceded voice one. "Better to be keeping this stupid highway empty than breaking heads in town."

The dark shapes floated past Martin. He still dared not move, but felt some relief. Apparently, they had Gen 2 or Gen 3 devices but not FLIR. He was glad, but stayed frozen, only allowing himself the shallowest of breaths. The last thing he needed was a gasp or a twig to snap.

"Ah. Only a couple hundred yards and we'll be out of this cold," said the first voice. "I can see my Sweet Tina up ahead."

"Man, that is *such* a lame name for a humvee. Should be like somethin' cool like, Rasputin or Spartacus."

Voice one grumbled something Martin could not make it out.

"Whatever," conceded voice two. "We'll take some sips and check the area again at dawn," said voice two. The voices grew faint and inarticulate as they walked farther away.

Martin slowly shrank back down the embankment, making sure he snapped no twigs. Beneath the bridge, everything was a solid mass of blackness.

"Susan?" Martin whispered.

"Over here," she whispered back. "Who was it?"

"A couple of soldiers, I think," he whispered and squatted down near where her voice came from. "They said they'd be back at dawn, so we'd better pack up and go."

"I tried to pack," she said. "But it's too dark."

Martin fished for his little red LED flashlight. The soft red glow was just enough to see, but not carry any distance. Susan held the light while Martin dismantled the lean-to.

A flash of reflected white glow from above lit up the foliage around them. They both froze. A search light slowly swept across the southbound bridge, then the northbound. It winked off. Total blackness returned.

"That must have been the soldiers," Martin whispered. "Sounds like they have a humvee parked up the road, probably near the interchange."

Susan resumed tightening up her bundles. Martin stuffed the mylar and paracord into his bag. He stomped on the earth-covered fire pit.

"You ready?" he asked.

Before she could answer, they heard cracking and rustling coming from the woods.

"The soldiers?" Susan whispered very softly.

"I don't think so." The sounds were too clumsy and loud to have been soldiers. Martin worried that it could be rogue criminal type, or a desperate scavenger. "I'd better go check it out. But, you should quietly take your bag over to the far bridge. Come up the embankment, but wait behind the guardrail. If I don't come back…"

"What do you mean, if you don't come back?" Her voice sounded scared. "You're coming back."

"It could be nothing," he said. "Then I'll be back, but maybe it *is* something. If you hear me shout anything – anything at all – get across the bridge as fast as you can."

"I won't go without you," she protested.

"If I shout, you'll have to," he said. "That'll mean it's bad and I don't want you anywhere near it."

"But…"

"No buts. Here's the map. Go right on the road just on the other side of the river. The 495 bridge goes over it. Follow it up to the streets with the red lines. That'll take you up through Salem. Keep following the red lines to my house."

Susan was about to protest again when more cracking of branches interrupted.

"Okay," Martin whispered. "Go." He turned and threaded his way through the brush. He had his little multi-tool knife in his hand.

The cracking and snapping of twigs came from deeper into the woods beside the embankment. Whatever it was, it was moving towards the highway. Martin wondered if a deer or a moose would make that much noise. Martin moved to within ten yards of the noise maker, then followed it in parallel. Occasional grumbles and swearing accompanied louder cracks. It was a man. It sounded like he tripped a few times.

Martin could just make out the dark mass of the man pushing through the brush up the embankment. Figuring the clumsy man was no threat, Martin was content parallel his course as far as the edge of the highway shoulder and let him go his way. He might have, had Martin not backed into a bush and broke a branch.

"What! Who's there?" the man demanded in a hoarse whisper. Martin did not respond.

"I heard you. I know you're there. Don't bother mugging me. I've been hit already. I have nothing left."

Martin still did not respond.

"I'm warning you," said the man. "I'll fight back."

Just then, the search light flashed on. The beam started on the southbound bridge and began sweeping towards them. The backlit glow silhouetted the clumsy man. He was tall, heavy set and disheveled. He had a hunk of tree branch in his hand as a club.

"Get down!" said Martin.

The man crouched and backed into the brush before the beam swept past them.

"What was that?" the big man asked.

"National Guard, I think," Martin half-whispered. "They're supposed to keep people off the highway."

"Who are YOU?" demanded the man.

"Name's Martin. I'm not a mugger. Just a guy trying to get home."

The light swung around and scanned across the two bridges on the other side of the river loop.

"If you're not a mugger, why are you hiding from them?" Kevin said in an accusing tone.

"Because I've heard there's a curfew and I don't want to get stuck in some detention camp while they sort things out."

"Curfew? National Guard? What the heck is going on around here?"

"Not sure. Governor Baylach is implementing some emergency procedures or something. I don't want any part of it. I just want to get home."

"Me too," said the man. "Kevin Dixon's the name. I've been trying to get home to Salem for two days."

"We're headed up through Salem too, but going further up." Martin was not about to be specific.

"Great! I got kinda turned around tonight. I thought I was getting close to Lawrence when I saw that light, but this isn't Lawrence. Where are we?"

"We're on 495 between Lawrence and Haverhill."

"So you know which way to go?"

"I've got a map, yes."

"Could I come with you? I'm really lost without my GPS, said Kevin. "Safety in numbers too, and all that, you know?"

Martin was reluctant. Kevin was a total stranger. He could be a mugger himself, though there was sincere fear in is voice when he thought Martin was an attacker.

"I don't blame you for being careful," Kevin said. "Can't be too careful, these days."

Martin agreed with him there. If it were just himself, alone, he might travel with a stranger and stay wary, but what about Susan? Martin was feeling protective. Still, these were dangerous times. He and Susan had already seen some of the ugly side of humanity. Perhaps a larger group would help.

"Okay," said Kevin. "I can tell you're not keen on it, but I really don't want to keep traveling alone. Tell ya what. What if I promise to give you a ride up to wherever you're going? Huh? My wife's car will be at my house. I'll drive you home. What do you say?"

A ride the rest of the way was tempting. Their progress had been frustratingly slow. Yet, this could just become a variation on foxhole conversions: easily promised, seldom delivered. Martin had no contractual leverage.

"Aw cummon," pleaded Kevin.

The prospect of saving many hours of walking was too hard to pass up. Martin knew he would have to be wary of this Kevin, keeping an eye on him at all times.

"Alright. We're leaving now. You can travel with us, if you want" Martin whispered. "Follow me."

Martin moved quietly down the embankment, slipping past bushes and saplings. Kevin followed noisily, breaking branches and cursing under his breath. Martin led him to the southbound bridge, where he hoped Susan was waiting.

He turned to Kevin. "Stay here while I go up and explain that you'll be coming with us." Kevin agreed.

Martin moved under the bridges and up the far embankment, a bit less silently than before. "Susan?" he whispered.

"I'm here," she replied. "Who's with you? They make a lot of noise."

"It's just one guy. Name is Kevin, and yes, he's noisy. He said he's traveling up to his home in Salem. Said he would give us a ride home once we get to his house."

She did not reply for a long time. Martin guessed that she was thinking the same things he had.

"I don't like it very much," she said. "But a ride is tempting."

"Agreed. One of us should keep an eye on him at all times, though. We have to be careful. I'll go get him."

The three of them squatted in the brush near the edge of the bridge railing. Dawn was coming slowly. The tree line was a distinct black edge against the dark gray sky. The humvee's searchlight split the darkness again. This was what Martin was waiting for. The light swept the southbound bridge, then the northbound. It swung 180 degrees, to scan the other two bridges leading toward Haverhill.

"Now!" Martin burst out of the brush and over the guardrail. He ran hunched over, staying close to the concrete side rail, pulling the roller bag. Susan followed, with his backpack. Kevin lumbered along behind them awkwardly with his tree branch.

Martin had driven across those bridges many times in the past. It took only a few seconds. Running across them seemed to take forever. The bridge felt infinitely long. All three were out of breath and only making a fast-walk pace by the time they reached the other side.

They climbed over the guardrail and sat for a few minutes in the bushes.

They were panting and out breath. Martin shushed them. He wanted to listen for voices or a humvee starting up. It was hard to tell, between his own heavy breathing and Kevin's wheezing. Nonetheless, the guardsmen did not appear to be moving.

Once they had caught their breath, they moved down the embankment. They all made a fair amount of noise navigating through the brush. They stepped out to the lot of a used car dealer. Martin stopped to listen again before taking to the road. All seemed very quiet. The dim gray light of dawn was growing.

"I really appreciate you guys letting me come with you," said Kevin. "These past two days have been hell, I tell ya."

In the growing light, Martin could see that Kevin was a well-fed man, in jeans and a sport coat. He was dirty and had been wet.

"You guys got any food?" Kevin asked. "I haven't eaten in two days."

"Sorry. We ate the last of our food this morning," said Martin.

"Dang. Got some water? I'm really thirsty too."

Martin was reluctant, but their water jugs were not hidden. "Here." He handed Kevin one of their half-gallon jugs. Kevin began guzzling as if he intended to down the entire jug. Martin grabbed it away.

"Hey. *Some* water, yes. All of it, no."

"Oh, sorry. I haven't had anything to drink either."

"So, where were you coming from, Kevin?" Martin asked, hoping to get Kevin thinking about something other than his privations and appetite.

"Beverly. My company's headquartered in the Cummings Park there. I'm the president of Optilux Worldwide," he said with a proud tone.

"Never heard of Optilux," Martin said. "What's that?"

"Oh, ho HO. We are *the* premier interagency infrastructure negotiation and re-placement specialists. *World class* specialists," he added.

"What does all that mean?" Susan asked.

Kevin went on to explain, at some length. Despite all the trendy buzzwords, Optilux appeared, to Martin, to be a broker for other people's excess inventory. They didn't make anything, or even sell anything. They arranged for someone else to buy someone else's excess goods. They were an after-market middleman. This was clearly a job that would not exist when the economy stalled for lack of power.

"I was in my corner office on Monday," Kevin began. "When the lights went out. Phones were dead too. I kept working my accounts until I couldn't get a cell line anymore. I sent Carol, my receptionist home, and Don, my sales guy."

There's only three people to Optilux Worldwide? Pretty small world.

"So I was trying to get home, but traffic was horrendous. I had to stop for gas for my Caddie, but the stations weren't working. I ran out of gas right there in line. Can ya believe it? Nothing I could do, so I walked to the commuter rail station. Figured I'd go back into town and come out on the Haverhill line to Lawrence. My wife could come get me from there."

"But the trains weren't running?" Martin said.

"No!" Kevin sounded outraged. "Can you believe it? Of course, I don't usually ride the trains. They're more for the blue-collar types, but just when I need the stinking trains, they don't work! Well, I knew Carol lived up in Middleton, so started walking up there. I pay her a pretty darn good wage for what she does. I was going to have her drive me home. She owed me that, for sure."

Martin and Susan exchanged looks. They pitied Carol.

"But I didn't even get that far. While I was walking along, minding my own business, these three punks in hooded sweatshirts come up beside me demanded my wallet. Well, I told 'em no way and pushed one of them away. Blindsided me, I tell ya. Cheap shots. While I was down they were kicking me too."

"I'm sorry, Kevin," said Susan.

"Yeah, thanks. They got my wallet. I had over two hundred bucks in there! Got my Rolex too. But the laugh's on them," Kevin snorted. "It wasn't a real Rolex." He had a good laugh, though Martin was not sure who the joke was on.

"Did they leave after they took your things?" Susan asked.

"I told those punks they better not mess with me again. Shoulda seen 'em run off. Low-lifes. All cowards. But that wasn't the worst of it. What really galled me is that the cops wouldn't do a blasted thing about it! Not doing their job! When I got to 95, there was all kinds of cops around. I tried telling them that I got mugged and described the punks. The cops didn't care! They weren't gonna make a report or do anything. Can ya believe it? I mean, what do I pay these jerks' salaries for anyhow?"

"That was yesterday," Martin observed. "What did you do for shelter last night when it rained?"

Kevin flailed his arms in exasperation. "Aw, that was insult to injury, I tell ya. I tried pounding on peoples' doors for them to let me in. No one would so much as answer their doors. I knew they were home. I could see candles inside. People are so rude sometimes."

Martin thought Kevin was lucky to be alive. In Massachusetts, guns were zealously prohibited. It was less likely that one of those homeowners would have owned a gun, but if they had, they might have shot a big loud stranger pounding on their door in the night.

"So, it started raining harder," Kevin continued. "I had to do something. I found some cardboard boxes behind this 7-11. They didn't help too much. I still got wet. Didn't sleep either. When the rain stopped, I headed out again. I thought I was coming up on Lawrence, but there was nothing but woods."

"No, you came up between them," Martin said.

"I coulda swore, but like I said, I usually use my GPS. I left that in my Caddie. Well anyway, I was coming up through them woods and saw a light. I figured it was help of some kind, so I kept going that way."

"What about you, Martin. Where are you and the missus headed?"

"We're going…a bit further north. Actually, Susan isn't my wife. She's just a friend who needs a place to stay."

Kevin glanced at Martin's wedding ring, then at Susan. He got a wide 'knowing' grin.

"Oh. I gotcha." He winked. "Pretty sweet deal, eh? Not so bad traveling with your own…"

"KEVIN!" Martin snapped.

Kevin, evidently saw the anger in Martin's face. The sophomoric grin dropped.

Martin wanted very badly to punch that smug locker-room-humor face. His fists were clenched and his face felt hot. Kevin was a much bigger man, but Martin did not care. Big men can still hurt and, it seemed, sometimes should.

Then Martin remembered the promised ride, so he tried to dial things back and keep it civil. It was not easy to dissipate a rage.

"The lady might take that the wrong way," Martin said carefully, through clenched teeth.

"Oh, uh. Sorry." Kevin glanced at Susan. "I didn't mean anything."

You did too, you big dolt, Martin thought. He imagined knocking Kevin over, sitting on his chest and pummeling his head.

"Apology accepted, Kevin," said Susan graciously. She also knew when to change the subject.

"Where do you live in Salem? Is it a nice house?" she asked brightly.

"Uh. Yeah. Real nice. Only the best, ya know? Lake front property." Kevin was more comfortable boasting.

Martin mouthed a 'thank you' to Susan behind Kevin's back. She smiled. He hoped he had not ruined their ride.

Kevin rambled about his exclusive neighborhood and how he got such a good deal on one of the 'primo' lots because he 'knew this guy.' Martin was unable to pretend to be interested. He busied himself planning where he might tell Kevin to drop them off, that would be near enough to reduce walking, yet not reveal where he actually lived.

After a few more sparse suburban blocks, Martin got out his map and showed it to Kevin.

"Which way to your house? We're right here. If we go up this way we'd pick up 97, we could go in towards Salem."

"Nah." Kevin turned his head to squint at the map. "That would bring us up on the wrong side of my lake. Long way around, and I'm sick and tired of walking. If we could get on this road here." He pointed. "It would bring us up to the south entrance road."

Martin studied the map. "There aren't many streets going up that way. Looks like we'll have to go a bit further, then follow this one up and over."

In the gray morning light, the houses along narrow and winding streets looked normal enough. Martin wondered why they saw no one outside. He thought he caught a glimpse of someone peering out a window, but quickly closing the curtains, or a head disappearing behind a corner. Perhaps large strangers had been banging on their doors in the night too.

Once they had turned left onto the road Kevin indicated, the houses were fewer and farther between.

Martin noticed they had not seen any cars on the roads yet. Had people finally realized that gas was hard to come by? Perhaps they also realized there was no 'work' to drive to, and that stores were equally fruitless destinations. He was about to point out the lack of traffic when he spotted a car crest the low rise, perhaps a half mile ahead.

"Hey look," he said. "That's the first car I've seen today."

As he spoke, two men stepped out of the line of trees ahead of them. They moved into the road, their backs to Martin's group. Martin did not like that fact that he had not seen them earlier. He vowed to be more vigilant.

The two men waved their arms to flag down the approaching driver. Standing in the middle of the road made them impossible not to notice.

"I don't have a good feeling about this," Susan said quietly.

"Me either." The three stopped and watched.

The driver stopped. The hooded man on the right spoke with the driver. Was he asking for a ride?

Suddenly, the man reached in the open window, apparently opening the door. He pulled the driver out. It was a thin man with gray hair. The other man pulled out the passenger: a woman with short gray hair.

Martin, Susan and Kevin stood stunned at the sudden carjacking in progress fifty yards ahead of them. The second man clubbed the woman. She fell into the brush beside the road. The first carjacker sat straddled across the old man, beating him in the head over and over with savage energy. The whole event was over in moments.

The second carjacker shouted something to his cohort and pointed at Martin, Susan and Kevin. The carjackers started walking towards them.

Martin's mind quickly assessed the situation. There were two attackers, versus him and Kevin. Even-ish, but not great. They might have unseen weapons. He had his little knife. They were clearly brutal. To stay and fight them could go either way, but could be bad. Then he thought of Susan. She said she was not a fighter. If it did go badly, Susan would be left alone with them. That was unacceptable.

"Quick," Martin said. "Back this way." They needed to put distance between them and the threat. He turned, grabbed the roller bag and ran. The other two followed. *Better to avoid a fight if the stakes are too high,* he told his inner John Wayne. The carjackers consulted each other for a moment then gave chase.

Martin turned right up a subdivision road. It was a dead-end loop, but offered more cover than a lone road with grassy meadows on both sides. The first few houses he passed offered little concealment. Wide yards, no trees. A quick glance behind him showed that both carjackers were running up the street after them.

"This way," Martin yelled back to Susan. He veered left, up a curving driveway.

"No!" shouted Kevin. "This way!" He kept running up the street.

Martin ran behind the first house, looking for anything to give a tactical advantage. The first house had a small raised deck with a single stair. It would be more defensible, but not if they had guns.

"Come on!" he called back to Susan. They ran across the backyard and through a line of shrubs.

"Did they just kill those people?" she asked, out of breath.

"Don't know, but it sure looked like it."

A piercing scream froze Martin in his tracks. Martin and Susan looked at each other, as if to confirm that they actually heard what they did.

"Kevin?" Martin whispered. It sounded like the shriek Martin sometimes heard on summer nights when an owl caught a rabbit.

Unfreezing, Martin saw that the second house had a utility shed built under its deck. The doors were open. He ran towards it. They could not out run the two carjackers, even if they abandoned their loads. The carjackers were young and rested. Martin and Susan were not.

It was dark inside the shed. A lawnmower sat in the center of the dirt floor. Rakes, hoses and sprinklers lined the walls.

"Quick," he whispered. "Up against the walls. Stay out of sight."

He pressed himself up against the short wall beside one door. Susan did the same on the other side. They would be hidden to a quick glance into the shed. He tried to slow down his breathing. They needed to be very quiet.

He could hear the carjackers shouting to one another. "They went back here!"

"No. I saw 'em run that way."

The fact that they could not agree gave Martin some hope that their route had not been seen.

"Well I'm looking back here. You check out that house up there. We can't let 'em get away."

Seconds seemed to take hours. Martin strained his hearing for some clue to their positions. He stopped breathing altogether when the doorway darkened. Martin glanced down. Wheel prints! The roller bag left fresh wheel prints in the dirt floor.

The carjacker jumped around the corner, his face within inches from Martin's.

"Gotcha."

Chapter 11: Escape into the void

Martin pulled at the carjacker's jacket, thinking he was off balance leaning into the shed. His flash mental plan was that the man would fall down inside the shed and they could run out.

It was not a very good plan. The man did not fall in. He was holding onto the door jamb with one hand.

As soon as Martin realized this, he did the opposite. His new half-thought plan was that the man, braced so he would not fall in, might not be situated to resist a push out. Martin lunged into the carjacker, throwing his shoulder into the man's chest. Martin was right that time.

The two of them tumbled out of the shed and onto the ground. Martin was thinking that if the man had a gun, it would be harder to use if his 'target' was grappling with him. Martin concentrated on trying to control the man's wrists. If he had a knife, Martin would have, at least, a little control.

Martin got a quick glance at one of the carjacker's hands as they rolled in the grass. One hand had a wad of Martin's jacket in it. No knife. The other hand, however, did hold a small knife with a wide curved blade.

The carjacker was trying to get on top of Martin, but Martin kept twisting. He had no plan other than to never let go of the knife hand's wrist, and avoid letting his attacker get into any kind of position of leverage. He wished he had a better plan.

The carjacker pushed himself out of Martin's grip and slashed across Martin's belly with his knife. He looked down for a second, as if expecting to see blood or guts. Martin did too, but there was nothing.

A loud clang rang out. The man fell forward onto Martin, who quickly rolled out from under him. Susan stood behind them, holding a small spade. When she saw the man fall, she dropped the shovel and covered her mouth, surprised at what she had done.

Martin scrambled to his feet and snatched up the spade. As the carjacker was shaking his head and pushing up onto his arms, Martin gave it his best swinging-for-the-fences swing. The flat of the spade caught the man behind his ear. The man fell flat on his face.

"Let's get out of here," Martin said. He grabbed up the man's knife and ran back to the shed for the roller bag. Susan still had on his backpack. They ran across the small backyard. Martin pulled the roller bag up in his arms and ran through the brush as best he could. Susan followed him into the woods.

Pushing left, right, ducking under, whichever way he had to move through the understory as quickly as he could, the roller bag was an awkward and bulky load to push through the brush. Martin wanted to put as much distance between themselves and the carjackers as he could before the man came to.

To the left, the trees were thinner, the woods brighter. A clearing might be faster going. He veered left.

The ground got soft. His sneaker sank into the dark mud. Swamp. The clearing was a pond. Martin ran back to the right, deeper into the pine and oak woods.

Amid all the thrash and crash of themselves running through the leaves, Martin could hear that the carjacker was up.

"Hey!" he shouted groggily. "They're back here! Hey!"

The other man's voice was indistinct.

"Back here. Over here," the first one shouted. "They ran in them woods. Cummon."

Martin could hear the carjackers crashing through the brush too. He thought that the men were likely to catch up with them. He resolved to veer off and lead them away. He would tell Susan to go straight. Hopefully, he could buy some time for her to escape.

He turned to tell Susan his plan, but never got a word out.

He fell instantly and hard. There was no time to put his hands out to break his fall. The impact knocked the breath out of him. He had mud in his mouth. Martin had fallen into the depression left over from where a tree's roots had been when the tree had blown over many years ago. The former root ball had decayed down to a leaf-covered mound beside the pit. The tree itself was little more than a raised line of moss in the leaf litter.

"This way," shouted one of the men.

Martin did not have the breath to leap up and run. A quick glance around showed that the understory was too sparse, or layered, to conceal them if they ran. The ground was fairly flat. The pit might be just what they needed to disappear.

Susan was trying to help Martin up, but he flailed off her help.

"No. Get down…in here. They won't see us," he whispered hoarsely.

Susan crouched down and pulled the roller bag that Martin had dropped.

"No. Lower. You'll have to lie down, like me, but not in the water. Make yourself as flat as you can. Keep your head down. Be very quiet. We need to disappear."

Martin pushed himself up the sloped bank of the pit to where he could just see with one eye over the leaf litter and under the spindly scrub of the understory. He rubbed the mud from his chin and neck up around his eyes, nose and forehead. He put a handful of leaves on his head, and laid dead still.

"Are you sure?" shouted one of the men. "I don't see 'em anywhere."

"They were right up there. I saw 'em running."

"Well they ain't there now."

"Shhhh," said the first man. "I think they're trying to hide. We'd hear something if they were still running."

Martin could make out the legs of the two men through the understory. They were roughly twenty yards away. The two stood motionless for a long time, listening. In the limited visiblity of the forest, this was an audio game. Martin intended for them to hear nothing.

When the men lost patience, one of them gestured to the other to spread out and search very slowly. They were slow, but not particularly stealthy. One of them headed to the right — towards the swampy pond — getting further away. The other one advanced slowly, stooping down frequently to peer beneath the understory and behind trees.

Martin laid completely motionless. His leaf-covered head would be just another small bump in the leaf litter.

The nearer man slowly zig zagged to the left of the pit, checking behind the bigger trees.

His cohort called out in pointless half-whisper. "Nothin' over here."

The man near the pit backtracked to where they had split up. He waved the other man to join him.

"We can't let'm get away," said one. "They saw us. And I wanna get even for that crack on the head they gave me. They'll pay for that, big time."

"Whatever, but we need to get movin'."

"They couldn't have gotten away that fast. You go get the car, and ditch those bodies. I'm stayin' right here. They gotta move sometime. And when they do…"

Susan whispered very softly without moving her head. "What do we do?"

Martin shushed her softly. "We wait. Lay totally still. We can't make a sound."

Eventually, the second carjacker returned. "Couldn't find one of them. Car's in the street. Cummon, let's get outta here."

"Shhhh. I'm still listening. They *can't* have gotten away. They gotta be out there."

"Man, let it go. We've got more important stuff to do than look for those two."

In the distance, far to the right, a branch cracked and something fell into the brush. Martin sometimes heard spontaneous noises like that in his own woods. It could have been a dead branch finally letting go, or a clumsy squirrel knocking something loose. Martin was often curious what such spontaneous forest noises were, but this time he did not care. He was delighted.

"Ha! Told ya!" shouted the waiting man. "I knew they couldn't stay quiet forever. That way. Fast!"

The two carjackers ran through the woods towards the sound. Martin was very thankful that the woods sometimes made its own noise.

"Hey, I found a footprint! They must be on the other side of this pond," shouted one.

"I'll go around this way. You go that way. We got 'em now." They crashed further away, sounding like a pair of charging moose.

"Now," said Martin quickly. "While they're going that way, and making so much noise, let's go the opposite direction as quietly as we can."

He finally dared turn his head to see her. She had wide frightened eyes, but nodded. She crawled out of the pit and began to take a few furtive steps away.

"Pssst," Martin hissed. "Your bag."

"Leave it. We can go faster without it," she whispered back impatiently.

"Yeah, but if they come back looking around here and find it, they'll know we weren't over there and maybe start looking in the right direction."

"Oh jeez," she gasped.

Martin took the wheels end, she took the handle. They hurried as quickly as they could, crouched as low as they could. Martin stopped periodically to listen. The carjackers voices still carried, as did their plowing through the brush on the other side of the pond. They did not sound like they were getting closer.

As Martin and Susan traveled deeper into the woods, Martin was mindful to not push through twigs and dead branches that would leave an obvious trail. He remembered seeing deer or turkey scrapes in the woods and looked back to see what sort of tracks he and Susan might be making in the leaf and needle litter. Martin did not want to be leaving an obvious trail for the carjackers to follow.

"Be careful as you walk," he whispered back. "Try to only step ON the leaves and not kick them as you walk."

"I have been. It makes less noise."

"Good, good. We have to avoid leaving broken twigs and branches too. If either of those guys have done any hunting, they might be able see traces of us, and follow."

Susan looked behind her then began stepping with more deliberate care. Martin had to take some convoluted courses to steer them around dense brush or tangled branches.

Martin stopped to listen. More faint crashing of branches could be heard in the distance. The carjackers were still on the other side of the pond.

"They sound even farther away now. Maybe they think we went back to the road, or they're going back to the car they stole."

"I can't believe it," Susan exclaimed in a harsh whisper. "Those guys killed that old couple? Maybe Kevin too?"

"Maybe they did, maybe they didn't," whispered Martin. "Regardless, they sure don't want us around to tell about it."

"I know. I've never been so scared."

"Let's keep going a little further, then listen some more. They don't seem to be coming this way at all."

"That's good. I feel a little better just being this far away from them."

"Me too," said Martin as he ducked under low pine branches. "I am so glad you kept your cool back there when we were in the pit."

"I knew I had to keep it together. Having a melt-down then, or now, would be…well…really bad."

Martin smiled. There was that pioneer spirit again.

"But don't let the calm exterior fool you," she continued. "A few times back there, I wanted to throw up."

Martin stopped. "Oo. That would have been beyond bad."

"I know, right? Talk about a trail to follow. And you were so worried about them seeing bent twigs." She smiled. That did Martin's heart good. Humor proved she was coping okay. Distance from a threat brought a huge sense of relief to both of them.

When they could hear no other noises behind them, Martin thought it might be safe to stop, rest and reorganize. Being quiet for awhile would be good too. They had come to a tumbled-down stone wall, marching arrow-straight through the forest. It was one of those lost traces of the old days when the land was farmed. Corn fields and cow pastures abandoned a hundred years ago had grown back into forests. The lichen-covered stones were the only traces that remained of an agricultural past.

"I'm wiped. Let's rest behind this wall," Martin said. "Those two hoodlums are way off in that other direction, if they're still there at all."

"You think we left too little trail to follow?"

"I think so. Also working our favor is that I don't think those two have the luxury of waiting and searching. I bet that when they realize how long it will take them to search, they'll opt to bail and run."

"I sure hope you're right."

"We'll have to keep an ear out."

Susan gasped as Martin turned to face her.

"Your stomach! That guy cut you! I saw him cut you. Oh my God, you must be hurt." She studied the gash in his jacket apprehensively — wanting to know, but not wanting to see.

"You're right, he did!" In the rush to escape, Martin had forgotten that too. He looked down at the gaping horizontal slash in his jacket. Not only was there no blood anywhere, he did not feel any pain. Martin probed around the gash. He pulled out wads of newspaper then let out a laugh — quickly stifled.

"What?" Susan was confused and a little annoyed. Slash victims are not supposed to laugh.

"My newspaper. Last night, I waded up pages and stuffed them in my jacket for extra insulation. Worked great, but I forgot I had them in there. Hmm. Looks like he nicked my flannel shirt a little, but not bad. It's mostly just my jacket. Zipper is shot now. Time to get out what's left of my duct tape."

"Oh, thank God you're not hurt. I thought he had really cut you. I was so upset that I..." she gasped and covered her mouth. "...I knocked that guy out."

"You did real good, Susan. Perfect timing." He took the carjacker's knife out of his pocket to see what his battlefield pick-up prize might be. It was a generic folding blade: nothing fancy, but better than his multi-tool blade.

"I've never knocked anyone out before," she said, as if pleading to a judge. "I've never even hit anybody before."

"That was a perfect time to start. You're quite the little fighter. Good thing I didn't leave you at La Quinta, huh? You'd have laid them *all* out."

"Oh, stop it." She frowned and leaned against a tree. Her face looked pensive as she tried to digest her newly discovered violent streak.

Martin leaned against one of the larger stones such that he could peer back over the rubble. He started cleaning the mud off his jacket, so the duct tape would stick.

"I thought they would find us for sure," Susan said. I was so scared. "I know we were hidden in that hole, but why did you think they wouldn't find us?"

"I was thinking of the second shot rule."

"Huh?"

"It's one of those old war wisdom things. A single shot in the woods alerts the enemy, but it's over too quickly. They can't tell where it came from. But, once the enemy is alert and listening, it's the second shot that gives away your direction. I figured that if we stopped making sounds, they would have no idea where we were."

"Oooh." Susan said. "You were in the military?" She sounded ready to be impressed.

Martin hung his head a little. He had no brag-able credentials: no tours in Afghanistan, no duty in Iraq, no Ranger battalion. *Who gathers around the bar to hear a software geek tell his 'battle' stories? 'There I was, searching every subroutine for this rogue conditional loop that was jeopardizing the success of our...' No. Software is about as un-Rambo as it gets.*

"Well, um. No."

"Then why would you know that second shot thing?"

Martin gave her an embarrassed smile. "It applies to hunting out of season too."

She frowned. "But that's against the law, isn't it?"

"Technically...yeah."

"Then why would you do that?" Her voice was hushed and sounded incredulous, as if she were interviewing a convicted felon.

"It was the strawberries," Martin said, in what he thought was a passable Humphrey Bogart impersonation.

"Strawberries?"

Martin took her blank look to mean she was not a fan of The Caine Mutiny. He started to chuckle at his own wit, but his ribs hurt. He flinched and gasped.

"Oh my. You *are* hurt" she said. "Is it when you fell in that hole?"

He nodded. "I'm a little sore is all. Nothing serious. I got this far, didn't I?"

"True, but look at you. Jacket ripped and cut. You've got mud all over your face and jacket. Here, let me get some water and help clean you up."

She wet one of the paper McDonald's napkins he was using on his jacket and handed it to him. He wiped at the crusty mud from around his eyes and off his forehead.

She gasped. "Wait. That's not just mud. It's blood! You've got a big cut on your forehead."

Martin looked up, as if he could see the cut. "Really? I don't feel anything." She wiped mud out of the cut with a wet napkin. "Ow, ow, ow. Okay, NOW I feel it. You can stop now."

"No," she said firmly. "This needs to be cleaned up. Sit still." She unzipped the front pocket of his backpack and pulled out his little first aid kit. "My turn to play doctor."

Martin was not going to get a lollypop for being a good patient. He squirmed and several times had his hands up by his face, trying to help. She swatted them away.

At one point she stopped, hands on her hips. "Did I wiggle this much when you put the bandage on my blister? Hmmm?" A chastened Martin sat very still.

"What did you mean, 'it was the strawberries'?" she asked while she applied the antibacterial ointment.

"Sorry, that was an old movie reference. Humphrey Bogart plays the captain of a navy ship during the war. He's going mentally unstable and his crew had to deal with it — sort of a soft mutiny. Captain Queeg got all paranoid and obsessed. The trigger was thinking someone was stealing his frozen strawberries. There's more to the movie than that, of course. Great movie. My point was that sometimes I think I sound like Queeg, all obsessed about 'my strawberries'." His first Bogart came off better than his second.

His eyes narrowed as he remembered run-ins with his rodent pests. "Every now and then, the squirrels discover my strawberry bed.

When they do, the little monsters can wipe out my whole year's produce in a week. I go all Queeg on them."

"Squirrels have to eat too." She took a bandage out of its wrapper.

"They can eat in the woods. I don't grow a garden to have fat squirrels."

"So you hunt them illegally? I didn't know squirrel hunting was illegal, or legal, for that matter."

"Well, there is an official season, but I try to keep the local herd small. Too many of 'em and they're all over my garden. I take 'em when I need to, regardless of any seasons. It's on my own property, so not really anyone else's business. Still, I try to remember the second shot rule to avoid any upset neighbors calling cops, or whatever."

"There. You're done," she announced. "Stop that. Don't touch. Just leave it alone."

Martin turned to look and listen for the carjackers. The woods were silent.

"I think they're gone."

"How can you be sure?" she whispered.

"They weren't the quietest at moving through the woods."

"True."

"So, I think we can get going again," he said. He stood to put on his backpack. "The more distance we put between us and them, the better. I'll take wheels again. We can go slower this time."

"Okay, but which way?"

Good question, Martin thought. They ran into the woods, going no particular direction, often changing directions. The sky was evenly gray overcast. No sun for bearings. The trees had moss all the way around them, so the old Boy Scout adage was useless.

Martin's map was a street map. It did not show creeks, ponds or rock walls. He located the dead-end street they had run up and traced a line into the large, featureless void. He knew they were near the New Hampshire border, but not much else.

"I think we're somewhere around here." He pointed to an empty area on his map. "We sure don't want to go back the way we came. If we go up this way, we'll eventually meet this road here. It leads up to this other road. I know this road up here. Not the most direct route, but it will work."

"Okay, but which way is 'that way'?" She looked around at the evenly distributed trees.

Martin dug out his little button compass — a freebie from a trade show. He turned the map so that map north aligned with the red needle, then off a bit for the deviation. "Looks like north-northeast will be the shortest path. Which would be that way." He pointed.

Avoiding thickets and denser stands of trees meant their course was anything but a straight line. Martin tried to 'dead-reckon' how much to compensate their heading for each deviation, but he knew it was just guesswork. He took some comfort in knowing that they would have to come to a road eventually. He was hoping for the shortest walk possible.

"You shoot the squirrels?" Susan asked.

He was surprised she was still thinking about the squirrels. "Yes."

They trudged without words, ducking under low branches. Martin imagined she was conjuring unpleasant mental images of bristling black guns, innocent-looking squirrels and pink mist. Maybe not the pink mist part. He did not use an assault rifle on them, nor were they innocent in Martin's mind. Sometimes, they were more akin to a biblical plague. *Nobody in the Bible ever said, 'Locusts have to eat too.' Ever.*

"What do you do with them?" she asked.

Martin was about to answer, *I certainly don't hold little funerals for them.* He knew that was far too sarcastic. Squirrels tended to bring out his dark side. He did not want her to think he was a vicious killer type. He was already on the margins of civilized society by being a gun owner. He decided that he should try a kinder and gentler style.

"Well, let's just say they don't go to waste."

"Oh."

After they negotiated a thicket of saplings, she asked, "What does 'don't go to waste' mean?"

Martin sighed. He did not want to go there. "We eat them."

After the words left his mouth, he realized it was a poor time for brevity. His words sounded barbaric, like he bit into their dead furry bodies and ripped off a strip of red flesh with his teeth.

"What?" Her shocked tone signaled that he *did* sound barbaric.

"I mean, I clean them..." (Clean, being a nicer word than butcher.) "Then we cook them. Not a lot of meat on a squirrel, but they taste okay."

He glanced back. Susan had a swallowed-a-bug expression.

"It's not that bad," he said. "People have done that for thousands of years. Hunt their prey, cook it over a fire..." Martin stopped himself. He was painting a barbaric picture again.

"I know, I know. But I don't even like looking at the packages of meats in the cooler at the supermarket."

"Oh. You're a vegetarian?" That spelled some future trouble. What food they had stored away had not been blessed by some Vegan priest-guru-expert. It was just plain food.

"No. I like meat well enough. I'm just used to it being already diced up and in my meal."

He was relieved to hear she did not have complicated diet restrictions, whether medical or 'ethical', but her phrase 'already diced up' stuck in his mind. He wondered what that meant.

"So you prefer to buy things like ground turkey, or hamburger?"

"Not so much that. I just don't cook much."

This was a does-not-compute comment to Martin. People eat every day. How could they not cook? Margaret was always cooking something. Pumpkin bread, pies, soups, casseroles, even her canned tomatoes, or salsa were cooked by her before going into the canning jars. Martin liked to cook too. His father always told him, 'If a guy's gonna eat, then a guy's gotta cook.' It did prove a useful skill in his bachelor days.

"You mean you eat out a lot?"

"Not a lot. Only like three times a week. It gets expensive."

Three times a week? Martin felt like a hermit. He tried to think of the last time he and Margaret had gone out to eat. He could not come up with one. He wondered if the drive-thru at Dunkin' Donuts counted? He thought not.

"Mostly," Susan continued. "I just buy frozen meals. You know, Stoeffer's, or Lean Cuisine. I usually get the store brand, though. Less expensive."

"Oh. Are those any good?" He had not eaten a frozen meal since college. Margaret would not abide them in her house.

"They're okay. A little salty sometimes, or bland, especially the low-fat ones. Still, couldn't be easier. Just pop it in the microwave and there ya go. That's how almost everybody does it in town."

"Hmmm." Martin still had a hard time imagining that lifestyle. "You mentioned, the other day, about waiting through that last power outage. What did you eat while you couldn't use your microwave?"

"Graham crackers," she said flatly.

"For two days?" Martin paused to point at a mossy log. "Oh, be careful with that log there. That's really rotten."

"Thanks." She stepped over the log. "Technically, it was only a day and a half, but yes. They did get a little boring. I haven't been able to eat graham crackers ever since. I was so glad when the power came back on, but I had to throw out all my meals and buy new ones."

"You just threw them away?"

"Yeah. They were probably bad. They thawed out."

Martin felt barbaric again. He would sniff some meat past-its-date, from the back of the fridge, know it was iffy, but cook it anyway. Was he just one rung up from eating road kill? How charming was *that*? And why did it matter if he was charming or not?

"Sometimes the store would carry exotic meats like buffalo or mutton, but I never tried those. I'm good with plain ol' beef or chicken. Sometimes fish. I don't think I could ever eat anything like squirrel."

"I wonder what all those people back in the city are doing now," Martin mused. "If most of them shopped and ate like you, they would be running out of things like graham crackers n' stuff pretty soon."

"Yeah. Kinda scary, but let's talk about something else, okay? This is making me realize how hungry I am. I'm regretting that we did not buy that jar of olives from Andrew's. I don't really like olives, but even they sound pretty good about now."

The trees thinned somewhat. The ground ahead of them was muddy and had more tussock sedge than leafy bushes. Martin stopped and set down the roller bag.

"Looks like we've come to a strip of swamp. The ground gets higher again on the other side, see? But I don't feel like mucking straight through there."

"So what do we do? Go around?"

"Yes, but no sense both of us walking back and forth looking for a way around. How about you stay here with the bags and rest. Maybe on that log over there. Looks dry. I'll go up this way and see if there's a way around."

Martin pushed his way through the spindly brush for what he guessed was thirty yards. He had lost sight of Susan. The marsh was getting wider, not narrower. Another fifty yards ahead, there was open water: a pond. This was not the easy way around.

Susan was watching, nervously, and eagerly, when Martin emerged from the brush.

"Can't go that way," he said. "The swamp starts turning into a pond. I'll try the other way next, after a bit of a rest. Didn't get that much sleep last night." He sat on the log with the roller bag between himself and Susan.

"Um…Martin?"

There was something in her 'um' that sounded like trouble. "Yeah?"

"I didn't get a chance to finish what I wanted to say this morning."

"This is about when I scared you, isn't it? Look, I'm really sorry that I…"

"Hold on." She interrupted. "You didn't do anything. That's why I'm trying to apologize to *you*."

"What? Why?"

Susan looked away, sheepishly. "For thinking that you…"

"Well, I wouldn't!" Martin did not want her to finish her sentence. He could feel a blush of embarrassment coming on.

"I know. That's why I feel terrible.…It was just something about the fall, I guess. I got scared."

"These are scary times," Martin conceded. "We've seen that."

"True, but it wasn't right. I know you're not like that."

"Not your fault. You couldn't really know. Five minutes a week through a teller window? A couple of days of chaos on the road? Still plenty of room for reasonable doubt." Martin was trying to excuse her fears as reasonable, but wondered why he was trying to leave the door open that he might be a terrible person. He needed to fire his lawyer.

She glanced at him. "People skills, remember? There's a whole lot of guys out there that…well, a girl can just tell that they *would*…you know, given half a chance, no matter how nice they talk. Something in their eyes."

She looked down and fidgeted with the buttons on her coat. "But you…"

Martin could see an inner struggle playing out on her face as she searched for words. Something inside of him suddenly realized that he did not want her to find those words. Things said in the flush of emotion usually went horribly wrong. Many times in his past he had said things too spontaneously, too candidly, and regretted it. All those times, he had wished that someone would have doused him with ice water, or set a trashcan on fire — anything to distract him and derail his tongue.

He had no ice water or trashcans, but he could change the subject for her. "We'll just both have to be more careful, right?"

Her small smile told him she appreciated the derailment. "Yeah. That's it. More careful."

"With that in mind…" Martin handed her the folding knife. "You should carry this."

Susan tried to decline, but Martin insisted. "I've got the blade in my multi-tool. You should have something too. We might run into more trouble."

She reluctantly took the knife: a physical symbol of the brutality that had so quickly risen around them. "It's hard to believe that people are acting this way. Out there, I mean. They didn't act like this during the last big outage. Why is this time different?"

Martin had to think. *What was the difference?* Were people losing hope so quickly because they connected the dots like Leo had? Did they sense that help would not be coming quickly, that 'normal' would not return soon? Was it a sudden lack of law enforcement? After Katrina hit, people looted and committed crimes pretty quickly. It could be that law enforcement gets overwhelmed at times like these and people are on their own. Being on your own is scary.

"Maybe it's that bad people, who are always there, feel like they can get away with things now," he offered.

She frowned. "With all the policeman piddling around with roadblocks, of course they can."

Martin matched her frown. "There wasn't much stopping those two carjackers. Who knows what they've already done and what they would have done if they caught us. Thank God we got away."

This thought sent Martin down a dark rat hole. If he had not stuffed newspapers in his jacket, the thug might have killed him, then and there. Then Martin realized that would have left Susan alone with them. He felt a flash of fear, quickly followed both rage and terror swelling inside him. His rage surprised him. The Good Samaritan in the Bible felt compassion and concern for the wounded stranger, but not rage at the robbers. Was Martin even entitled to the emotion of rage?

It was Susan's turn to derail deep thoughts. "I got away okay, but *you're* not looking so good." She pointed at his muddy, duct-taped jacket

He appreciated her interruption of his dark mood. It was kinder than ice water. He looked down at his jacket. "Yeah, I seem to be kind of accident prone lately."

"You said you were going to go look for a way across this swamp, right?" she added brightly.

"Yes I did."

"I'll wait here." She patted the log. "Don't be gone too long...and try not to fall down so much, okay?"

He gave her a give-me-a-break eye roll, then pulled out his invisible note pad and pretended to write. "Don't - fall - down. Got it. Like my new notepad?"

"I like it. It's pink." She winked.

The swamp tapered down to a muddy stream, roughly a dozen yards southeast. It took a bit of careful balancing on wobbly tussocks to get across. They traveled back up the other edge of the swamp until they spotted the log they sat on.

"Okay. Now we're back on course. North-northeast. Ready?"

"Sure. I'm really getting hungry, though."

Pushing through the woods had the same perpetual quality that walking the railroad tracks had. There always seemed to be more trees ahead.

"Hey, look up there." Martin pointed through the tree trunks.

"That looks like a shed or a garage or something."

"Cool. That means we're almost to the road."

They walked with more enthusiasm. Their ordeal in the woods was almost over.

"Hmm. This is more of a little barn," said Martin. "I wonder what they keep in this little pen."

Susan cupped her hands around her eyes as she peered in a dusty window. "Rabbits. There's a bunch of cages of rabbits in there."

"Interesting. I wonder if they…" Martin trailed off. He realized the owners were raising them for meat. He had already bungled that topic with squirrels, so felt it was best to avoid round two. "That must be the house up through there. The road is probably just on the other side."

Martin welcomed Susan to New Hampshire officially with a theatrical bow. Somewhere back in the woods, they had crossed the line. Susan chatted about traveling, but never making it up to New Hampshire, as the two of them walked up the path from the rabbit barn to the house's back yard.

"Stop right there!" shouted a man's voice from the house.

Martin and Susan looked up, startled. Stepping off the back porch was stout little man with salt and pepper hair. He had a shotgun to his shoulder, one eye squinted, the open eye behind the bead. The gun was aimed at Martin's head.

Chapter 12: Captured as looters

"You two just stop right there, or I'll blast ya. So help me, I will."

Martin and Susan put their hands up. The roller bag clattered onto the path.

"Um, hey, Mister, we don't mean any…" began Martin.

"Shaddup you," hollered the angry man.

As he took a few careful steps toward Martin and Susan, he was muttering to himself. "I knew them low life scums would be coming. She said I was nuts, but I knew. Dang mass-holes. I knew they'd come sneaking up here eventually. Well, I was ready for 'em."

To Martin, he yelled. "What did you do to my rabbits?"

"Nothing, sir. We just came through the woods and…"

"So, you DID come from Mass. I knew it. I knew you low-lifes would come sneakin' up here as soon as yer precious system collapsed. It was only a matter of time. Get out here in the yard, both of ya. And don't try anything or I'll blow a hole in ya." He waved the shotgun barrel to point to a spot in the back yard.

Martin tried to walk slowly but keep himself between Susan and the angry man. As he walked closer to the man, Martin got a far better view of the muzzle than he liked.

12 gauge Mossberg, he thought. *Rifled barrel. Slugs. Oh great.*

"Now both of ya. Lie down on the ground with your hands out where I can see 'em. Go on. Lay down. Now!"

Martin knelt down, then Susan. It was not easy to lie down without using one's hands.

"Keep yer hands out! None of yer stinkin' tricks. I'll just shoot ya where ya lay." The man's voice had a nervous tremble to it.

Martin lay facing Susan. She had a worried look, and rightly so.

"Sorry," he whispered. "Don't do anything to…"

"Shaddup!"

They laid on the cold ground for what seemed forever. The man with the shotgun continued muttering to himself as he paced back and forth.

"Now what am I gonna do with these two? Can't just shoot 'em in cold blood, even if they are thieving looters. Be easier if they made a move on me. Then it'd be self-defense."

Martin saw Susan's eyes get a little wider.

"Can't just let 'em go, neither. They'd go back and tell their gang about that old softie on the back road thats got rabbits. No, no. They'd be back here in big numbers. These two would tell 'em how I had guns and defended my place. They'd put two n' two together and figure I had lots of good stuff worth defending. That's how they think. Dang looters."

"We're not looters," Martin said.

"Quiet!" the man hollered.

The man resumed muttering to himself. "What do you do with criminals when there ain't no law? Slave labor, maybe? Nah. Not that much to do around here. I don't fancy feeding a pack of slaves with little to do. They'd run off, first chance they get anyhow. Too much trouble." The man continued to pace and mutter. He was the dog that finally caught the car he was chasing, and had no idea what to do with it.

Not daring to move his head, Martin moved only his eyes to check out a crunching sound coming from beyond the house. He caught a glimpse of a faded red station wagon pulling up the gravel driveway. It disappeared from view behind the house. After a car door creaked and slammed, a woman's voice called out.

"Linny? You out there?"

"In the back, Pat." Linny hollered. He did not relax his aim as he continued muttering. "She didn't think they'd come, but this'll show her."

"I tried shopping at the Shaw's in Plaistow," said the woman. "But people there were going nuts." A dowdy woman with short gray hair rounded the corner. She gasped. "Linnwood Varney. What on earth are you doing?"

"I captured me some looters, Pat. Caught 'em red handed, I did. They were sneaking up on our house through the woods, but I saw 'em. I was watchin'. I've been monitoring our perimeter ever since things went down, and this right here is why. I told ya they would be coming. Didn't I? Only a matter of time."

"Looters," Pat said slowly with wonder.

After what seemed like an eternity of awkward silence, Pat stooped down for a better look at Martin.

"We're not looters, ma'am," Martin said. "We were just trying to…"

"Shuddup you!" Linny kicked dirt at Martin's head. He got his eyes shut just in time.

"How do you know they're looters, Linny?" Pat asked. "They look like plain folks to me."

"Bah. Looks don't mean nuthin. You think looters always wear striped shirts and masks and carry canvas bags? Looters is looters. This is just like I told ya. As soon as things got bad down there, there'd be a horde of these mass-holes crossing the border to loot and pillage for supplies cuz they were too stupid to…"

Pat cut him off with a wave. "I know, Linny. You've told me. But how do you know these two are your horde of looters?"

"They got some loot right there. Check out that guy's backpack first. Then that bag they dropped over there." Linny waved the shotgun barrel at the roller bag. "Probably find all kinds of stuff they stole from other people's houses."

Pat squatted down and began looking through Martin's backpack. "Socks, a torn shirt. Oh. He's got a laptop in here."

"See? Didn't I tell ya? Stealin' computers. Dirty thievin'…"

"That's my laptop," Martin said.

"I told you to shuddup!"

"Hold on," Martin interrupted. "I can prove it's mine, Just open the cover. A little white box will come up in the middle." Pat opened the laptop. "Now type in k-r-o-n-o-s-1-9-5-7. A looter wouldn't know the password for a computer he just stole, would he?"

Pat held the laptop on one arm and pecked out the password.

"Hey. It worked. Ooo. Pretty pictures," said Pat. "I just love mountains."

"See?" Martin turned his head towards Linny. He squinted, expecting more dirt to be kicked at him.

"Okay, so that's his computer," grumped Linny. "Don't prove they ain't looters. Maybe he uses that computer to hack into people's security systems. Could be that, ya know. What's in that big bag? Check it out. Probably been stealin' people's pre-64 silver or their ammo, or maybe their food."

Pat squatted down, unstrapped the bundles and unzipped Susan's duffle bag. "There's no silver or ammo in here. Sweaters, pants and ladies underwear." She held up a bra. "Linnwood, do you really think they were stealing ladies underwear?"

Linny lowered the shotgun. "How am I supposed to know what people steal, woman? I ain't no mind reader of the criminal brain. Maybe they're perverts."

"Oh Linnwood hush," snipped Pat. "You're just getting silly now." She stooped down beside Susan. "So who are ya, honey?"

Susan turned, keeping a wary eye on Linny and his shotgun. "My name is Susan. This is Martin. We're not looters, honest. We didn't mean any harm. We were just trying to get to Cheshire."

"Ask 'em what they was doing in my woods, and back by my rabbits. Go on. Ask 'em," shouted Linny.

"Okay, okay," replied an irritated Pat. She turned to Susan. "You're both a long way from Cheshire. What were you doing in our woods?"

"We were trying to walk to Cheshire from Boston, you know, because of the power outage, and we got chased into the woods by two really bad men, who we think might have killed some people."

"Oh my," exclaimed Pat.

"They chased us into the woods, but we hid and they lost us. We got away," Susan said.

"We came out the woods to your place," added Martin.

"Load of hooey," said Linny. "Can't trust no mass-holes."

Martin rolled slowly onto his side, hands held out in plain view. "Look, sir. I'm *not* a mass-h...I'm not from Mass, okay? I live in Cheshire. Lived in New Hampshire for many years. Here check out my wallet." He slowly pulled it out of his pants pocket with just his thumb and index finger. Linny had his eye behind the bead, ready for any sneaky moves.

Martin held out the wallet. "We work in Boston. We were stuck there when the power went out. We've been walking home since Monday."

Pat opened Martin's wallet and studied his driver's license. "Oh Linnwood, you old ninny. You didn't capture any looters. These are just poor folks trying to get home."

"Well how was I supposed to know, huh? They came a traipsin' out of the woods from Mass, all sneaky like. Violated our perimeter."

"All sneaky like," Pat mocked. "You're so fired up for looters and zombies that you'll be shooting at shadows."

"We can't take no chances, woman. This is serious. There's gonna be trouble. Big trouble. You'll see. Them city people are gonna be swarmin' up here lookin' to steal food or whatever they can get cuz they were too stupid or lazy to prepare."

"Yes, yes. I appreciate how you're protecting our little home, dear," Pat said diplomatically. "But these two aren't your swarming horde of city people. This here's just a man and his wife trying to get home." Susan blushed slightly but attempted an agreeable smile. Martin gave Susan a little look to say 'go with it.'

"That's right. Just trying to get home," Martin repeated. He minced his words so as to not lie, technically. He was a New Hampshire resident, but Susan being a Massachusetts resident was an inconvenient truth best avoided for the moment, if possible.

"Could we get up off the ground now?" Martin asked.

"Of course you can," said Pat. Linny backed up a step, but kept the stock at his shoulder.

"Linnwood!" Pat scolded. Her husband reluctantly lowered his shotgun.

"No hard feelings," Martin said with a smile. "Simple misunderstanding. We'll just gather up our stuff and be on our way." Martin slung his backpack around so he could push the loose clothing back inside. Pat handed him the laptop. Susan reassembled her bundles while keeping a careful eye on Linny.

"It'll be lunchtime soon," said Pat cheerily. "Did you two have lunch plans?"

"Um..no ma'am?" Martin answered. He was taken aback by the sudden shift from a being a prisoner to a dinner guest.

"Actually, we haven't had much to eat for the past couple days," he said.

"Ah, then you must be famished. You should stay for some lunch." Pat seemed almost giddy at the opportunity to be the gracious hostess. "I started a big pot of soup this morning. I'm sure it's done by now. How about I pour you both a nice cup of soup to help make up for Linny's...um, enthusiasm?"

Pat stepped towards the back door, motioning for Martin and Susan to follow her.

Linny stepped between Martin, Susan and his house. "They ain't comin' in the house, woman. Ain't no one comin' in the house. That would totally blow our OPSEC. No one's gonna recon my defenses and scout out my preps."

Pat cut him off with a wave. "Fine. Fine. I'll bring the soup out to the picnic table. That be okay?"

Linny grumbled, turned and stomped back to the house.

"I'm sorry my husband was a little rough on you. He's really not a mean man. This outage has him spooked pretty badly, though. He's been certain that hordes of desperate city folk will come streaming up from Mass since Y2K. After the elections and the crash in 2008, he was certain the country would go to pieces in a few months and the hordes would be coming through our woods. Now with this outage being so widespread, he's all on edge again."

"I can understand," said Martin. "Things have been going a little crazy down there since everyone's lost power."

"Yes, well, they can go crazy later, after you've had some soup, eh? There's the picnic table over there. You go have a seat. I won't be but a few minutes. It's already hot." She turned and scurried into the house. The screen door smacked shut behind her.

Martin and Susan sat on the same side of the picnic table, so they could face the house. They kept a wary eye on the door. Linny was not as inconspicuous as he imagined, peering at them from the kitchen window.

Susan spoke in a half whisper. "Mr. Varney is a Doom People, isn't he."

"It would seem so," said Martin.

"Doom People are soooo weird."

"Maybe he's just a bit too enthusiastic, like Pat said. One of those people who are so ready for trouble, it doesn't take much of a 'boo' to make them jump."

Susan nodded. "I'm getting pretty familiar with jumpy. Seems like whenever I say to myself 'I've never been so scared in my whole life,' something even worse happens. I've decided that I have to stop saying that."

"I've gotta say," Martin said quietly. "Ol' Mr. Varney did have me worried. I noticed he had his finger on the trigger the whole time. I was afraid he'd flinch out of nerves and blast me by accident. All I could think to do was lay totally still and hope he'd calm down."

"I couldn't think of anything. My mind went blank."

The screen door creaked open as Pat backed out. She carried a mug in each hand. "Here we go." Her voice had the musical tone of a grandmother dispensing cookies.

"Thank you," Susan said. "I hope we aren't an inconvenience…you know, eating your food and all."

"Nonsense," assured Pat. "We have plenty. I'm sorry the biscuits aren't ready. I wasn't expecting guests."

"This will be just fine," Martin said. He sipped the hot soup from the spoon. The salty broth eased his chills. It felt great to chew boiled carrots, potatoes and diced meat. A hot meal is magical medicine. Susan was devouring her soup too.

"I am soooo hungry," said Susan. "This has to be the best chicken soup I've ever had."

"Oh, it's not chicken," said Pat. "It's squirrel."

Susan stopped in mid chew. She shot a glance at Martin.

Oh, please don't spew, Martin thought. *Please don't spew.*

She held his eye for a couple seconds, then resumed chewing and swallowed. "You don't say," she said in sing-song voice.

"It's true."

"There's a different spice or something in there." Susan continued to play the good guest.

Martin realized his mouth was hanging open.

"Oh, you're probably tasting the dill." Pat beamed as she sat next to Susan. "I put in a little dill and lemon juice. Takes away any gamey taste. Not that they get gamey. Linny's real good at cleaning 'em. He's always saying 'why should we eat our rabbits when we got meat growin' on trees.' " Pat laughed at her impersonation of her husband.

Pat peered into Susan's empty cup. "You must have been starving, you poor thing. Would you like another cup?"

Susan looked like Oliver Twist as she handed Pat her cup. "If that's alright."

"Of course it's alright. I'll be right back." Pat took Martin's cup too, and shuffled back into the house.

"Squirrel soup?" Susan said. "I thought it was just dark chicken meat."

"From the look on your face, I thought you were going to spray it all over."

"Well, I have to admit I started to gag. But then I thought that would be really rude, considering how nice Pat was to give us something. You talked about eating squirrel. Then I asked myself if it really tasted weird or not. I had to admit that was actually a good soup. Add to that, the fact that I am really hungry."

"But what was that whole spice thing all about?"

Susan waved off his comment. " I don't know spices. Salt, pepper, garlic sometimes. Just being a gracious guest."

Martin glanced around the Varney's back yard, trying to be careful not to look like he was looking around. Linny, with binoculars, was poorly concealed in a bedroom window. Martin did not want to appear to be "recon-ing" their spread.

A long garden flanked the house and driveway. Most of the plants had died back or been cleared. Many rows of corn stalk stubble hinted at a recent harvest. They had their meat rabbits out back and plenty of trees for firewood.

"The Varney's have a pretty nice setup here," said Martin.

"Oh? Looks a little dumpy to me."

"Don't look around," Martin said out of the side of his mouth. "Mr. Varney is watching us." He continued, looking only at his spoon. "Sure, the house and buildings could use a little TLC, but they have a nice big garden over there and he has a winter's worth of wood laid up." Martin gestured with his eyes to a several cord of wood, split and stacked beside the back deck.

"He's got some sort of small scale solar thing going on with a couple panels on the roof. We know he's well armed."

"Pfft. Ya think?"

Martin chuckled. It was easier to laugh afterward. "So my guess is that the Varney's are pretty well situated to handle the outage."

"Do you think he's right? That there will be hordes of hungry people coming up through the woods like we did?"

"Hmm. Hordes, maybe, but through the woods? Not so much. That was a lot of work."

"Tell me about it."

"I figure most people — the hordes — tend to be creatures of habit and take familiar paths of least resistance. I figure they'll follow the roads. The Varney's are set so far back here, that we can't even see the road. Odds are, most of any horde will pass them by looking for the obvious."

"That would be good. Pat's nice. I like her."

"What about Mr. Varney?" Martin teased.

Susan scowled at him. "He needs to be less weird."

Pat used her rump to push open the screen door. "Sorry I took so long. I had the dough rising while I was shopping. Put a few in to bake. I just took them out of the dutch oven, so they're kinda hot." She set a mug and a biscuit in front of them.

While he finished his soup, Martin gave Pat a quick summary of their trials since leaving downtown. He was not trying to sensationalize, but Pat kept inserting a periodic 'oh my'.

"You two have been through so much," Pat said. "I wish I could just drive you two back home up to Cheshire. But Linny would be furious with me. He's all strict about 'no unnecessary trips' and trying to conserve our gas. I know he's right and all, but still..."

Pat stood up quickly, her eyes brightened. She turned so her back to the house. "Ooo. I've got an idea. You two get your things together and set off walking down the driveway. Turn left on the road."

She gathered up the empty cups and spoons, then said, rather louder than necessary, "Well, goodbye you two. Safe travels." She waved exaggeratedly and let the screen door slam behind her.

"I wonder what that was all about," Martin mused. Susan shrugged. They carried her bundle down the long dirt driveway.

They had walked only a few yards down the pavement when Martin heard the crunch of tires on gravel. A car was coming down the Varney's driveway. Pat's red station wagon lumbered out onto the pavement.

Pat pulled up beside them and rolled down her window. "Hop in you two. We gotta be quick." Martin motioned for Susan to sit up front. He muscled the roller bag into the back seat.

"I had to run to the store," Pat said over her shoulder. "We still need a few supplies and couldn't get them at Shaw's. I figured I could give you two a ride up as far as Harstead."

"Thanks Mrs. Varney," Martin said. "This helps a lot already."

"Oh, you can call me Pat. And you're welcome. I wish I could drive you two all the way home, but Linny would have a fit. I'm only supposed to go to the store and straight back. No wasting gas."

"It's good to conserve what you've got," said Martin. "Might not get any more for a long time."

"I suppose you're right," said Pat. "But we're not hurting for gas. Linny's been storing cans of it in our basement for years. Must have twenty of those five gall…" Pat clamped her mouth shut tight, her eyes grew wide.

"Oh dear. I'm not supposed to have said anything about that. Linny says it will ruin our app-sack, or something. Please don't tell anyone, okay? He would be so cross with me."

"We won't," assured Susan.

"But you will have to be more careful, Mrs…Pat." Martin said. "Gas is hard to come by already. Most people won't conserve and will run out pretty quickly. A few people might turn nasty trying to get more. We've seen some of that nastiness coming out already. Best not to let anyone know what you have."

Susan chimed in. "Your husband is a little weird, no offense, but he's right to be careful. The two guys who were chasing us were definitely not good people."

"I know, dear. I know. I just wish he had a bit more manners."

"Aw Shoot," Pat said as they approached the intersection. "Hannaford's is just as mobbed as Shaw's was. Look at that. People are parked all along the highway too."

"Somebody's pulling out over there." Susan pointed up the road. "You could park there."

"No, honey. It's not just the parking. I don't think I want to go in there. It looks a lot like Shaw's. That was a madhouse. People pushing, shoving, running up and down the aisles. Right in front of me, two women were pulling each others' hair over a box of Minute Rice, of all things. I just left. I wanted nothing to do with such craziness. I'm gonna try a different store. Hopefully, it's not such a zoo." Pat turned onto the highway.

"I would have thought that you and your husband were pretty well stocked up already," Martin said. "What are you shopping for? That is, if saying won't compromise your OPSEC?"

"I don't really understand his app-sack thing," Pat said. "So I have no idea."

"Truth is," Pat continued. "I'm hoping I can get a little more cooking oil."

Martin waited for more items on her list, but none came. "That's it? Just oil?"

Susan looked puzzled. "I thought you were going to say fresh veggies or something. Why oil? "

Pat gave a little embarrassed smile as she turned onto a side road. "Heh, well, I blame my mother for that. You see, she was a girl back in Germany during the war. The family lived in the country, near a little town named Wiesenbronn. Things got terrible lean for people, especially late in the war, to where they were eating mostly turnips -- which is what they grew for the cows to eat -- or bread made with sawdust. Mom's family had it a bit better than the city folk, since local farms grew grains. What they couldn't get, though, was cooking oil. You need oil for just about every kind of cooking, but it was nearly impossible to get, even on the black market."

"Well, after the war, mom married an American soldier — my dad — and moved to the states in the early 50s. She used to tell my sister and me how she could not believe her eyes that American shops had gallons of cooking oil on the shelves and no one was rushing to grab any of it."

Pat laughed. "But Mom did. She always had several gallons in her kitchen, at least. She would never throw away bacon grease, and rendered down beef fat. Her advice to me, growing up, was to always have lots of cooking oil when I got married. 'You can grow grains, Patty,' she used to say, 'but you can't grow oil'."

"Your mom sounds like an interesting woman," said Susan.

"Oh yes. I loved my Mumu a lot."

The trees and old homes that lined the road, gave way to a triangular park with a few stately old maples still decked out in flaming orange. On one side of the Common stood town hall — a big white building in a mixture of the ornate styles of the latter 1800s. Beyond the trees rose a tall pointed steeple. A few squarish colonial style buildings, painted in earthy tones, also faced the Common. Such large houses were once the homes of the prosperous locals, doing double duty as inns and taverns. The Common had probably looked the same for over a hundred and fifty autumns.

The third side of the Common broke the antique mood. A brightly painted gas station asserted the crass dominance of the twentieth century. Flanking the station were small shops attempting to look as colonial as limited budgets allowed. Modern clutter of newspaper boxes, parking signs and advertising posters filled all available gaps.

Pat pointed beyond the gas station. "That's better. Center Market has cars in the lot, but it doesn't look like a mob scene. Maybe only the locals know about this store."

Pat pulled her big red station wagon into the parking lot of the modest grocery store set back from the road. There were many cars already parked, but she found a space quickly.

"Do you think they'll check IDs?" Susan asked. Pat looked confused.

Martin leaned in between the seats. "We tried to shop at a store down in Stoneham, but the manager said people had to have a local ID."

"Hmm. I have no idea. That would leave me out too. Let's go see."

There was no manager with a bullhorn outside of the store. There was no line. People were coming and going with small bundles under their arms, but there was no pushing or shoving.

When Martin got through the glass doors, he felt like he had finally beaten a tough level in a video game and leveled up to something totally new. He half-expected a heavenly chorus and beam of golden light from above.

There was no beam of light: no chorus. The interior of the store was dim. Daylight from the street-front windows did not carry far. A hand-lettered sign announced that purchases were limited to $20 per person, cash only. A hawk-faced man sat on a stool at the checkout station.

"We're actually inside," Martin said. "I didn't think we'd get this far. I just realized that I don't know what I want to buy."

"It's looking kind of picked over here too. You might not have much choice," Susan whispered.

"I'm going to go look for my treasure," Pat said cheerily.

"Thanks for the ride, Pat," Martin said. "We really appreciate it."

"Glad I could help. I do hope you two get on up to Cheshire alright."

"I'm sure we will," said Susan. "We hope you and your husband will be okay too."

"You're such a dear," Pat said, laying a hand on Susan's arm. "Well, I'm off to do what Mumu told me!" With that, Pat shuffled off into the dark aisles.

Coleman camp lanterns in the far corners of the store provided just enough twilight to navigate the aisles, though not enough to read labels. Dark silhouettes of other shoppers drifted through the aisles. Martin used his flashlight, as the other shoppers did, to survey the shelves. There was not much to survey. He gave Susan his other flashlight so they could split up and search faster.

The bottled water shelves were completely bare, as were the shelves for juices and sodas. Promotional placards taped to the shelf edge announced what was no longer there. The bakery shelves were cleared too, leaving only empty cardboard display boxes. The boxed cereals were gone, except for a few ruptured boxes. Very few flakes or Cheerios remained on the shelves from the ripped boxes. Someone must have scraped up the spillage to take home.

The canned soups aisle had several cans, though all were missing labels. Placards announced a sale on Dinty Moore canned meals, but there were none.

"I was hoping we could pick up something easy to eat for this last leg of our walk," Martin said as he met Susan. "Easy-to-eat seems to be the hardest hit."

"I've been looking for easy foods too," said Susan. "There's no breads, no cereals, no soups — unless we want to play mystery-meal with those label-less cans. The produce cases were empty. No veggies or fruit. There's no cookies or crackers of any kind. I even looked for graham crackers. Nothing."

The next aisle looked promising. At least the shelves were not empty. It was the stationary and housewares aisle: Air freshener, dish soap. pens, calendars, greeting cards. An older man pulled the last bag of barbecue charcoal off of a bottom shelf.

"There's some pet food left," said Susan.

"Hmm. I'm not quite that desperate yet. Are you?" Martin asked. She squinted and shook her head.

There were still jars of mustard, bottles of ketchup and barbecue sauce.

"Hey look." Susan reached up. "A jar of olives!" She set it back down with a chuckle. "New Hampshire's locusts don't like olives either."

Martin chuckled too.

While Martin was moving empty display boxes on the shelves, a small can rolled out. He snatched it up before it fell. "Ugh. Vienna sausages."

"What's that?"

"You've never heard of them? They're like little hotdogs, but weird," he said.

"Sounds like you don't like them."

"Oh, they're not terrible, I just got really tired of them as a kid. I made the mistake, one time, of telling my mom that I liked them. All that summer, she was buying me cans of vienna sausages as my summer snack food. I was never so eager for school lunches to start. Still, it's the only thing we've found so far that we could eat on the road."

"Sounds like your mom wanted to make you happy."

"I know. Mom's are funny that way, though. After I connected the dots on the endless supply of vienna sausages, I told her I really liked Cap'n Crunch. It didn't work that time. I still only got that once in a blue moon."

Susan laughed. "That's funny. My mom was the same way."

"No way. You got vienna sausages too! I thought you hadn't heard of them."

"No, no, no. I've never heard of those before. For my mom, it was owls. I once told her I thought this picture of an owl in a book was really cute. She must have figured 'oh, she loves owls!' For years afterward, I was getting owl sweaters for Christmas, owl nick knacks from yard sales and owl birthday cards. I was getting kind of tired of owls, but didn't have the heart to tell her. I knew she meant well."

Martin and Susan made their way to the checkout counter. Martin set the can of vienna sausages on the black belt.

"I didn't see a price on this, sorry," Martin said. "It just came rolling out from behind a box."

"That's okay," said the hawk-faced manager. He studied the can. "This would be aisle four, left side, third shelf...hmmm..." The man muttered to himself, eyes closed as he imagined his inventory. "These are $1.29. That'll be a dollar twenty nine."

Martin was surprised he did not say five dollars. "Oh, and this too." Martin pulled the jar of olives from his pocket.

"You kept those?" Susan said.

"Aisle three, right side, top shelf...hmm...$2.29."

"Why did you get those?" she asked.

"You said yesterday how you wished we bought that jar back at Andrew's, remember?"

"Um, yeah?"

"You said it again today. So, I decided to buy you the next jar of olives I came across." Martin presented her with the jar like a trophy. "Here ya go. No more olive regrets. Now you have your very own jar."

"That'll be three fifty eight," said the manager.

Martin fished out his cash, handing over four badly wrinkled ones. "Doesn't look like you'll be open for business too much longer, eh?" Martin said to him.

"Nope. Pretty well cleaned out." The manager jotted down the transaction in a notebook. "You missed the biggest day: yesterday. It was a store-owner's dream, it was. Place was packed. Of course, I usually get a shipment every morning, but Monday was the last one I got. By the end of the day yesterday, we were outta most everything."

He scooped out a few coins from an open register tray. "Here's yer change. I'm surprised you found that can there. Meats were the first thing to…no, actually water was the first thing, then batteries, and other drinks. But meats were right up there. Went fast."

"Sounds like we were lucky to get this little guy." Martin rolled the can in his fingers. "Guess we should savor it. Thanks."

Martin and Susan waved to the manager as they stepped back out into the bright of day. They walked out onto the long, winding road up to Cheshire.

Susan regarded her jar of olives. "That was thoughtful of you, Martin."

Martin could feel a blush coming on. He coughed and fussed with his hat.

"But let's not let this become like owls, okay? I'm still not fond of olives."

Martin chuckled. "Okay. Deal."

Chapter 13: Deadly problem

The past two days had provided more than enough exciting events to put anyone on edge — a house fire, a gunfight, a dead body, a knife attack. Martin had noticed that even during the quiet times when adrenaline was not running strong, he still could not relax. He chalked it up to heightened situational awareness as they traveled through unfamiliar territory. He had expected that when he got to more familiar roads, he would feel some degree of relief, some sense of comfort. He was in familiar country at last, but felt *more* uneasy, not less.

Haverhill Road was part of his old daily route to his car pool. That job connection set him to thinking about his job downtown. The long walk had given him ample time to run out the "what-ifs" of the grid-down situation. The prospects were not encouraging.

From what little news he had gleaned, many major components of the power grid around the nation, perhaps even the world, had all failed around the same time. Unlike the popular EMP scenario that Brian often talked about, this crisis had left all the delicate electronics intact. Cars with computerized engines still ran. Smart phones still functioned. Even his laptop still powered up. The problem was not the delicate electronics, but the power that supported them: the grid.

Without the grid, consumer communications systems had fallen away, piece by piece. Some of the cell towers stayed alive — their generators chugging along on a week's supply of propane — but the network they were connected to had too many components relying on the grid. Martin's phone still powered up, but there was no network for it to connect to.

Highly computerized cars still ran, but without the electrical grid to power the gas stations, storage depots and refineries, how long would there be fuel to run them?

No power and no internet meant his job could not be performed. As of two days ago, he probably did not have a job any longer. In the career-sense, it could be the end of the world as he knew it. But not the end of the world. Aside from hunkering down to deal with the power outage, what was he going to do with himself long-term?

"You've been awfully quiet," Susan said.

"Huh? Have I?"

She rolled her eyes. "At least back in the city, there were horns and sirens and people yelling at each other. I'd welcome some crickets about now. How far is your house from here?"

"Hmm. Eight miles, maybe."

"At our pace, that's roughly, what, maybe four hours?"

"Sounds about right."

"Four long, *quiet*, hours," she added with melodrama.

Martin chuckled. "Okay, okay." He was about to summarize his dark musings but stopped. He had been theorizing how the economy that everyone relied upon would collapse for lack of power and fuel. He had imagined how millions of the average citizens would be cast adrift without supplies and without an income to acquire more. An improvised economy might develop, but most people would be like himself with skills no one needed. Many would become desperate. Trouble was certain. He had run out the ramifications for himself, but what about Susan?

If his pessimistic side was right, a bank branch in downtown Boston would not be open for business-as-usual for a long time —

maybe never. He felt some relief that he was able to help Susan not to get stuck in a mess like La Quinta, but what was she to do long-term? Did he expect that she would simply stay living in Lindsey's room forever? He realized he had not thought very deeply on that score.

Susan cleared her throat. "You know, I was expecting a bit more conversation than 'okay, okay'."

Martin smiled apologetically. He did not want to parade his pessimism. People prefer hope. His optimistic side could imagine that the multiple equipment failures in the grid could be resolved — much like that substation in San Jose was eventually repaired. Maybe it would take three months instead of one, but come Spring, things could begin to return to normal. Hope made for better conversation.

"Oh, I was running through various what-to-do plans in my mind," he said. "Things like, what I should do right away when I get home, what I need to do later. I was getting stuck on the 'later' stuff. It's a lot harder to figure. I mean, maybe they can get things fixed in a…while." He tried to smile. "Might get fixed slowly. So until then, things might be…well…different than usual."

"Yeah, I've been thinking about that sort of thing too," she said.

"Oh?" Martin was curious how *she* was picturing her future. It would make for better conservation to take a cue from her vision than run off down his own dark trails.

Martin pointed to a section of guardrail. "What do you say we take a rest up here? I'm feeling pretty tired already." Susan nodded. He passed her the water bottle and tore in half the big biscuit Pat gave them in the car.

"I've been doing a lot of thinking too," she said after taking a long drink. "I've never been in a power outage that lasted more than a couple days, so it's hard for me to imagine things *not* returning to normal fairly soon. I mean, they always did before, right? I just have to wait it out with candles and graham crackers and the lights all come back on. I *really* want to think that this might last a week, maybe two. The branch will reopen, I'll go find some other apartment, and pick up where I left off. Take my test. Become an Associate. Life would go on."

"It would be nice if things got up and running in a few weeks," he said with his mouth full. He was trying to curb his pessimism and let his optimist speak.

"Yeah," she said as she tore off a tuft of her half of the biscuit. "But what if things *don't* get fixed anytime soon and the lights don't all pop back on? Mr. Skinner used to lecture about revenue streams. You know, for personal loans and stuff. She imitated Mr. Skinner's voice. 'The bank expects our loan customers to dependably make repayments. Applicants must have an income stream that is regular and dependable'."

Martin chuckled. "You do a pretty good Mr. Skinner."

Susan smiled. "Thanks. I've had practice. Whenever he talked about reliable incomes, I always thought of myself as having one. I won't say I felt smug, or anything, but I thought I had a pretty reliable job. I was okay."

"Thought?" Martin noticed her use of the past tense.

"Yeah. I think it was while we were in those neighborhoods in Stoneham, seeing all those people standing around because they couldn't go to work. I got to realizing that if this outage is going to be as bad as it sounds, all of the retail customers that I would have dealt with will be out of work, and probably fighting over boxes of Minute Rice. The odds are that my State Street branch isn't going to reopen for a long time, if ever. I could easily see the home office scaling back the number of branches. I might not have a job anymore."

Martin pushed his last bit of biscuit into his mouth and nodded sympathetically.

"That was one of the reasons I decided to take you up on your offer," she said without looking at him. "It still sounds crazy for me just to walk off to the North Pole." She flashed a brief smile at him. "But if I've got to start over again, the North Pole sounds better than a city full of fights. I had my little future plans built around moving up to Associate. Now, I have no idea what starting over will look like."

Martin sighed and nodded. "Me either. But, we'd better get going. Need to get home first before we can do much of anything." Susan popped the last of the biscuit in her mouth and handed him his backpack. It was her turn to pull the roller bag.

As they approached a cul de sac of newish homes, the puttering hum of several portable generators grew louder.

"Sounds like almost everyone up here has a generator," she said.

"Many do. Sales usually boom after an ice storm. With houses like those down there, they're kind of crucial. Did you notice that none of those houses has a real chimney?"

Susan squinted down the cul de sac. "Now that you mention it..."

"Usually oil heat. Sometimes propane, but they need electricity to run their furnaces, so they need a generator."

"How long can one of those generators run?" She pointed to the houses.

"Lots of variables, but if they were careful, I'd guess most folks have enough gas on hand for a week. That's usually plenty for the yearly ice storm."

"They're so loud," she said. "I don't think I'd like all that noise beside my house."

"Yeah, you'd think they could make them quieter. Don't know why they don't. I mean, whole-house generators are pretty quiet. Why can't these be too? I was helping a widow lady in the church with her big whole-house generator set up. I was surprised how quiet it ran.

"Seems like we haven't gone all that far," Susan said, "but I think I'm going to be ready for another rest soon."

"Sounds good. This hill is wearing me out too. It's not all that steep until nearer the top, but this slope is like a couple miles long. Not much for seating along this stretch. Mostly just trees." Martin pointed to a small yard in front of a modest blue house. "What isn't just trees is somebody's yard. I feel a little odd just sitting in someone's yard or driveway."

"How about up there?" Susan gestured with a tip of her head. "There's a low rubbly line of rocks up ahead there. We could sit on a couple big rocks."

"Good enough for me," Martin said.

The tumbled down rock wall bordered the yard of an old gray ranch style home.

"This house must have one of those whole house generators you were talking about. I wouldn't mind that sound so much," Susan said.

Martin could hear the well-muffled putt ,putt, putt, but something struck him odd. Big wattage stationary generators cost several thousands of dollars. They are typically optional equipment on McMansions. The little gray house was old and shabby. The shutters needed paint years ago.

"It does kinda sound like one," Martin said. "But this doesn't look like the kind of house to have one of those."

As they walked past to the house, Martin kept looking at it. The asphalt driveway had many cracks and weeds growing up. One window was broken and patched with packing tape.

"Something's not right here," Martin said. "Look at this house. Whoever lives here has been scrimping on upkeep: even the inexpensive maintenance stuff like paint. Why would they spend several thousand dollars on a fancy generator, yet leave broken windows? I want to take a quick peek, just to satisfy my curiosity."

"Peek at what? Where are you going?"

Martin walked up the side yard, "Just a look around back to see their…" He stopped.

"There's no generator back here." He leaned his ear near the small attached garage. "It's coming from inside the garage!"

His eyes quickly scanned the back of the house. All the windows were closed except the back window of the garage, which was open a few inches at the top. He ran back around to the overhead door and peered in through the small windows.

"There it is," he said. Susan came up to peer in the other window. "A little portable. See that? The extension cord runs to the back door, which isn't fully closed."

Martin ran up to the front door and knocked urgently. He paced back and forth on the small wooden porch.

"What is it?" Susan asked. His worry was contagious.

"Carbon monoxide. I'm worried that someone might be in there."

He pounded on the door. "Hello! Hello! Is anyone in there? Hello?" No answer came.

Martin stood on tip toes to peer through the high fanlight in the door. "Maybe no one is home. Maybe they left the generator to charge some batteries while they were gone."

"No," said Susan, her hands cupped at the living room window. "There is someone sitting in a chair in the living room."

Martin jumped down and rapped on the window. "Hey. Hey in there. Open the door. Come open the door!" he shouted.

The old man in the stuffed chair turned his head slowly and stared blankly at Martin and Susan.

"Hello!" shouted Martin. He waved. "Hey. Please come unlock the front door! You're in danger."

The man stared with no expression, then burped up a small thread of vomit.

"Oh my God," said Martin. "He's stuporous. He won't come to the door."

"Then we have to get him out of there!" Susan exclaimed.

Martin ran to the rear of the house. The back door was locked. He tried to lift up the lower sash of the garage window, but it would not budge. The upper sash would not slide down either.

"They must have these pinned. I can't get in this way," he said to himself.

Martin ran back to the front and jumped onto the porch. Remembering movies he had seen, he began kicking at the door latch. It looked easier in the movies. The door held. Susan picked up one of the rocks that lined the sidewalk and pointed to the small sash beside the picture window.

Martin jumped down amid the bushes. "Pull the roller bag over here. I need some height." He stepped up, looked away, and struck the upper window. He carefully cleared a pair of shards, unlocked the window and pushed up the sash.

He hopped off the roller bag. "Okay, now take a deep breath and go unlock the door."

"Me?"

"Yes you. It's a really little window. I won't fit. You will. Here, I'll give you a boost up. Remember, deep breath first then try to hold it. Avoid breathing the monoxide. Be careful of any glass on the floor."

Martin helped her step up. Susan had to angle herself and wriggle through the narrow window frame. She eased down to the floor and scrambled over to the front door. Martin could hear the locks turning.

He took a deep breath as Susan flung the door open. The air was stale and smelled of vomit and acrid with exhaust fumes. They both rushed over to the man in the stuffed chair. They each took an arm and tried to lift him, but the old man was dead weight and hard to lift. He stared at them with a vaguely confused look. Martin pulled, Susan pushed to roll the man over the arm of the stuffed chair. They struggled to drag the man toward the open door.

"Stop right there!" shouted a nervous bearded man in the doorway.

Martin was staring at the muzzle of semi-automatic pistol, held in a tense full-extension grip. The man's finger was on the trigger. He was breathing fast and shallow.

Oh geez. Not again, Martin thought.

"What the hell do you think you're doing?" the man shouted. "What have you done to him? So help me I'll…"

"It's carbon monoxide!" said Martin, as loudly, but as calmly as he could before the bearded man could rant further.

"What?" The man looked up over his sights.

"Carbon monoxide. There's a generator running in the garage. This man's unresponsive. We're trying to get him out of the house fast!"

The bearded man looked at the old man, yellow drool dripping from his chin.

"Holy cr… Dad!" The man hastily stuffed the gun into his waistband and took the arm Susan was holding up. Martin and the bearded man struggled to get the old man down the front steps and laying in the front yard. Dead weight with rubber legs was an awkward load.

"Dad! Dad! Can you hear me? Dad?" The old man turned his head toward the bearded man, but stared past him.

"Is there anyone else in the house?" Martin asked.

The bearded man gasped and looked back at the house. "Mom!"

"I'll help you look," Martin said. "Susan, try to keep him on his side, so if he barfs again, he won't choke on it." Susan looked shocked, but nodded.

Martin and the bearded man ran back into the house. There was no one in the kitchen, or the side bedroom. They found the old woman, sitting on the bathroom floor, barefoot, with a brush tangled in her hair.

"Oh good God. MOM!" The man squatted in front of the woman and patted her face. "Mom?"

"Uh. Jimmy?" she said with half opened eyes. "Be a dear…uh…help me to bed?"

"We need to get her outside too, and fast," said Martin. They carefully lifted the old woman. She was much lighter and felt fragile. It was easier to get her out into the yard.

"You need to lie down here, Mom," Jim said. She tried to get up off the brown grass. "No, no. Lie down, Mom. That's right. You just rest."

"So cold. Must be a window open," she said.

"I'll get the window, Mom." Jim was scared, but tried to sound comforting.

"We'll watch them," Martin said. "Run back in and get a bunch of blankets. They need to stay out in the fresh air." Jim ran into the house.

Martin turned to Susan. "I'll be right back. I want to shut off that generator. Try to keep them lying down."

Martin took in as big a breath as he could, then ran through the open front door. Moving through the living room, he saw a coffee mug on the floor and a big coffee stain on the carpet. More coffee was splashed on the lamp table. Across the arm of the stuffed chair were splotches of yellow vomit.

He followed the orange extension cord from the kitchen to the back door and out into the garage. He flicked off the switch on the little generator. It puttered to a stop. Martin burst out the rear door of the garage to gulp in a lungful of fresh air. His eyes watered from the exhaust fumes.

In the front yard, Susan and Jim were wrapping blankets around the old couple.

A young woman came running down a path between the trees that separated the two house lots. "Ohmygod Jimmy! What's going on? Are they hurt?"

"I don't know Mira. They're alive, but I don't know."

"What happened? Who are these people?" Mira asked her husband.

"We were walking by your parent's place," Martin said. "I heard the generator running in the garage, so I knocked on the door. No one answered."

"Aw Dad," Jim squeezed the shoulder of the old man. "He's been so worried that someone was going to steal his generator. I tried to tell him we could work something out. I'm surprised he tried something stupid like this."

"He had the rear window open," said Martin. "He must have thought that would be venting enough. But the extension cord kept the rear door open a crack. The exhaust was going in the house too."

"We could see him sitting in his chair," added Susan, "but he looked all groggy."

"We had to get him out fast," said Martin. "Sorry about the window."

Jim waved off Martin's apology. "I'm glad you guys came along when you did. And, I'm sorry about coming at you guys with my gun, but I thought you were breaking into my parents' house."

"That's okay," Martin said. "I'm sure that's what it looked like. It's a good thing you were watching and came right over. We might not have gotten your mother out in time. You probably saved her."

Jim looked up from wiping yellow drool off his father's face. Martin helped Jim adjust the blankets around the old man. The old man's eyes popped open and latched onto Martin. He turned on his side, pointed an unsteady finger at Martin and ranted something incoherent. His son knelt beside him, coaxing him to lay back down.

Mira stroked the old woman's hair. "What do we do, Jimmy? We can't call for an ambulance. We can't take 'em to the hospital. You don't have the truck put back together yet. All we've got is your motorcycle."

"I'm not sure how much the hospital could help now anyhow. They'll have their hands pretty full with the outage," Martin said. "If the ambulance came, they'd give them oxygen. Do you or your parents have oxygen tanks in the house? CPAP machines, do you do any welding, anything like that?"

"No," said Mira. "Does this mean they're gonna die?"

"Not necessarily, but they are in rough shape." Martin tried to summon his doctor voice again. "Their bodies need to work out the monoxide. Without pure oxygen, it could take a long time."

"How long is a long time?" Jim asked.

Martin shrugged. "Hours? Could be a day or two."

"They can't lay in the yard for two days," objected Mira.

"No, but they can't go back in their house until it's really well aired out."

"We'll take them to our house," said Jim.

"Good," said Martin, "but they need to stay as inactive as they can, so their bodies don't use up what little oxygen capacity they still have. They can get oxygen from the fresh air, but it takes a lot longer than from a tank of oxygen."

The old man sat up and began to rant again. "Hoo iz zziz…Ar anna…"

This time, Mira knelt beside her husband, providing additional screening.

"He gets agitated when he looks at you," Mira said to Martin.

"I see that. They need to be kept still. Minimize their bodies' oxygen needs. They could still pass out."

"Araggh..na..oudda…muh…" The old man had propped himself up again, peeking at Martin over Mira's shoulder. He stared, wild-eyed at Martin. Jim and Mira had to work at laying him back down.

Jim spoke over his shoulder. "Look, we're really *really* grateful you guys came along and saved my parents, but he gets all worked up whenever he sees you. If we're supposed to keep them quiet…"

"I know," said Martin. "It seems like I'm doing more harm than good by staying here."

"They're just still really confused," said Mira. "We'll explain it all to them later, when they're better. Thank you both so much."

Martin motioned to Susan to back away and stay low. "Maybe you can carry them into your house later: when they seem a little more coherent," Martin said quietly, "they still need to be kept inactive for a day or two before the monoxide is really out of their systems." He recalled what a paramedic told him about possible lingering damage from carbon monoxide poisoning, but thought it would only add stress. They were doing what they could.

Mira smiled a worried smile and gave a little wave. Jim was busy talking to his father, who was finally laying back on the blankets, muttering.

Martin walked briskly up the road. "Maybe we can get some of their neighbors to help them," he said over his shoulder.

Martin remembered how Kevin had trouble getting people to answer their doors, so he tried to keep his tone light and friendly, and invoke the names of Jim and Mira as much as he could. Nonetheless, no one answered the door of the blue cape, or the gray colonial. At the little black and white cape, the lady cautiously answered the door. She and her husband knew Jim's parents somewhat. Martin explained the problem briefly. Neither the man, nor his wife had any oxygen tanks, nor did they know of anyone who did. Martin suggested they could help by bringing more blankets and helping Jim and Mira move the parents indoors. Maybe drive into Nutfield to get help of some kind.

The two rushed back inside, a flurry of activity. They loaded several blankets into their car and sped off. Martin could see through the door window that they had left their teenage son in charge of the house, with a 12 gauge shotgun. The boy looked nervous at his sudden new duties.

"I need to sit down awhile," Martin said. The quicker pace of rushing from house to house had left him more winded than he expected. "But let's go out to the road. Maybe sit on that planter they have out there. I don't want to make this young guy any more nervous than he already is. I sure don't need anyone else pointing guns at me." Susan nodded.

Martin eased himself down onto the rock wall of the planter. His thighs ached. "I don't know what else to do to for those folks."

"At least Mira and Jim will have some help," Susan offered. "Do you think they'll be okay?"

"I don't know. I'm no doctor." Martin rubbed his face. "They had a pretty heavy dose of monoxide. Even in a hospital with oxygen, it could take a long time. No telling how long it will take to clear their systems with plain ol' air. Hopefully, there's no lasting damage."

They resumed their trudge up the long and gradual slope of the hill.

"This outage is the craziest thing I've ever been in," Susan said. "I've been through a few outages, but people didn't go around robbing anyone, or stealing cars. No one I knew ever died in one. This is just…well, crazy."

"I'm a little surprised too, to be honest," Martin said. "Somehow, I think I always figured people would tough things out, you know, with stiff upper lips, as the British say. Boston Strong and all that. I really didn't picture fist fights at hotels, or criminals getting so bold. Now, if someone told me L.A. or Detroit had broken out in riots and looting, on the first day, I wouldn't have been surprised, but Boston? Stoneham?"

"My dad was all worried because I was moving into the city," Susan said. "I remember reassuring him that there were only a few rough neighborhoods and I'd stay well clear of them."

Martin nodded in agreement. "Yeah, by and large, sleepy old Boston's a pretty quiet place. I really didn't picture people getting that bad, and certainly not that fast. That nagging voice inside me must have, though. That's why I was so pig-headed about not waiting around in the city. I sure didn't want to be stuck down there if riots did break out like we heard on Isabel's radio."

"That kind of trouble always seemed to happen someplace else," she said to herself. "Do you think things will get bad up here?"

"I don't think we'll see any riots around here." He could not picture a riot in Cheshire. The little rural towns still had some of the old self-reliant Yankee farmer ethos, despite the decades of dilution by soft 'city people' who had made the farm villages bedroom communities of Boston or Manchester. The worst Martin could picture things getting in Cheshire was some loud whining by the unemployed city people having to endure evenings without cable TV. Riots in Cheshire? Martin shook his head.

"There might be riots in Manchester and Portsmouth," he said. They have their share of 'entitled' residents". I suppose no place is ever totally safe from trouble, but Cheshire is out of peoples' way. I remember reading newspaper articles where people bemoaned the lack of tourism business because Cheshire wasn't on any main highways. Times like this, I think that 'curse' will be a blessing."

"I sure hope you're right. Being out-of-the-way sounds great," she said. "I've had more than my fill of being in the middle of the action."

"Me too." He patted the duct tape across the front of his jacket.

"What? The road goes uphill *again*?" Susan said. "I thought we were over the top of the hill back there."

"Yeah, this little dip is deceptive," Martin said. "Let's take a little rest before we start up." He pointed to a scruffy patch of yard beside a detached garage. Susan laid on her back and blew out a long breath.

"I've never felt so tired in my life," she said. "My legs ache, my feet hurt. Even my arms ache. Why would my arms ache? All we're doing is walking. I know we haven't been eating or sleeping properly, but still."

"I feel extra beat too," said Martin. She had a point. Granted, he was not in the best of condition, but he felt more exhausted than a several mile walk should have made him. Then a cold shiver ran down his back. Carbon monoxide.

"Listen, maybe we got a dose of carbon monoxide back there."

Susan sat up. "Really? I tried to hold my breath, but I know it didn't always work. I didn't think a couple of breaths would matter."

"Me either, but now I'm thinking maybe it did."

So, what do we do? We can't just lay here beside this garage."

"No. I don't think we're that bad. We're out in the fresh air. I think if we just take it easy, take more breaks the rest of the way, we'll be okay. Probably really tired, but okay."

Chapter 14: Walnut Hill and homecoming

"I don't feel any perkier for having rested," Martin said as he slowly stood up. "But, we'd better get going. Only a few more miles to go."

"I suppose. But now we have to go up another hill?"

"Yes, and I'm afraid the 'best' is yet to come. Up ahead is the steep part to the top of Walnut Hill. My old two-wheel-drive truck couldn't get up this stretch in the snow."

"I don't find that very encouraging."

"Sorry." He tried to have a perky tone. "There's no snow now, so we'll make up it just fine. How's that?"

Susan glared at him and shook her head.

His attempt at humor failed, yet again. "No. That didn't work on me either." He passed her the water bottle. "We'd better save a little for when we get to the top."

As they neared the crest of the hill, Martin's legs ached; his shins in particular. Susan was taking slower, smaller steps. He noticed that he was taking smaller steps too.

"I can see why…my old truck…didn't like this hill," he said between deep breaths. "But we're doing better…than my truck did. I never got it…any higher than…that driveway back there."

"How much farther to your house now?" she asked.

"Three miles? Maybe four."

"That doesn't sound as close as I had hoped it would," she said wearily.

"Know how you feel. This here's the top — for real this time. We need to take another break and catch our breath. There's a good spot. Bet you're thirsty too," he said.

They sat on a low stone wall that bordered the yard of an old house with several ad hoc additions. While they finished off their water, they heard a woman singing softly. Around the corner of the garage came the singer with a plastic bucket. She was strewing food scraps onto the yard. Greedy chickens were racing to get the best bits first, then running away, lest another chicken steal their prize.

"Oh, hello," the woman said. "I didn't notice you there before."

"Sorry. We're just taking a bit of a break from walking up the hill." Martin wanted to reassure the woman that they were not trespassers. "Don't worry. We'll be moving on real soon."

Looking past the woman, Martin noticed a tall radio antenna in the back yard.

"Excuse me, but I just noticed that you have an antenna back there. Do you have a radio set, a transmitter?"

"My husband does. Why?"

Martin explained about the old couple down the road and the carbon monoxide poisoning. She motioned for Martin and Susan to follow her behind the house. They came in the back door of an old kitchen.

"Walter! Walter! Wake up!" the woman called into the next room.

"Huh? Is it time?" came a groggy reply.

"No, but get up anyhow. You need to radio for help."

A man with tousled gray hair and rumpled clothes staggered into the door frame. "What is it? What's the problem?"

The woman summarized quickly then let Martin take over telling about the old couple in the little gray house. "Do you think there's anyone in their area that might have oxygen? If not medical tanks, then maybe some for welding? Anything?"

"Hmm. Might be a couple people. 'Scuse me." Walter pushed between Martin and Susan and out the back door.

Through the walls came the muffled sound of a generator sputtering to life. Walter strode back into the house with a gait of a young man. He plopped down in a swiveling chair in front of several pieces of radio equipment that lined a bench and shelf at the far end of the kitchen. After watching some gauge needles flicker for a moment, he fiddled with several of the knobs and muttered to himself about frequencies and bands.

"There's a guy down Haverhill Road that monitors 20. 'Nother guy near Ordway I've heard watching 6. I'll see if any of them are on."

He cleared his throat and put the mic to his mouth. "CQ CQ, K1NTZ on Walnut Hill. Got a medical emergency. CQ. Anyone in North Harstead? Medical emergency." They heard nothing but static.

Walter tuned a different frequency. "CQ CQ. K1NTZ Walnut Hill. Anyone in North Harstead on this frequency? CQ. Medical emergency. Anyone monitoring in North Harstead?" He listened to the static. As he reached for the tuner, a voice broke in.

"This is Thompkins, North Harstead. What is the nature of your emergency?"

Walter recounted what he heard from Martin.

"Oh Cripes," said Thompkins. "Young Jim's folks? I know them. I don't have any kind of oxygen, but the guy across the road from me still does gas welding. I'll see if he's got any O2. Over." The channel returned to soft static. Everyone in the kitchen stared at the radio. Martin caught a small movement out of the corner of his eye. A dark-haired woman sat at a little round table in the corner of the kitchen. He had missed her and the table when they came in.

"Walnut Hill, this is Thompkins. Sent my grandson over across the road. Neighbor does have a tank of oxy. They're loading up in his truck now. Gonna drive up to Jim's place. I'm going with them. Will report back later. Same channel. Thompkins Out."

"Well, sounds like help is on the way." Walter flicked off the power switch to his equipment and leaned back in this chair. "They'll have to rig up something for breathing masks once they get there, but anybody still doing oxy-welding tends to be a make-things-work kinda guy."

"Yeah. Might not be hospital-official, but it's something, anyhow," added Martin. "Thanks for calling for help."

"No problem," said Walter. "See, Sally? All this stuff? Might've saved them people's lives."

"Yes dear," Sally said patronizingly.

"Darn right, yes dear," Walter said. He pushed himself up out of his chair. "I see it's not long before 3:00. Gonna switch the gen to charge some batteries for a few minutes rather than restart it. Be right back." With that, Walter toddled out the back door, steadying himself on chair backs and countertops.

With the rush of the moment passed, Martin glanced around the kitchen. It had been state-of-the-art new in the 1950s; a proud twentieth century modernization of the nineteenth century farmhouse. The kitchen was small and tidy, but had clearly seen heavy use.

"Thanks for helping. I guess we should be going. But, could we ask you for some water first?" Martin asked.

"Of course. Give me your bottle. How far do you have to go?" Sally said.

"Not far," Martin said. "I live on Old Stockman Road."

"That's still a bit of a hike from here." Sally pointed to the round kitchen table. "This here is Holly. Family friend. She lives up your way. I'm Sally, by the way." She ladled water from a large galvanized bucket into Martin's bottle.

"I'm Martin Simmons. This is Susan."

"Simmons?" Holly tipped her head. "On Old Stockman Road?"

"Um, yeah?" Martin wondered if he knew this Holly, but could not think of where.

"I'm Holly Baldwin. We met a couple years ago. I live in that old gray colonial on the other side of the hill from you. You and my husband, Micky, were talking about that beaver dam problem in the swamp behind your place?"

"Oh yes." Martin's memory finally located her file. "I think the beavers are still back there."

"I don't think I ever met your wife," Holly said, glancing at Susan.

"Hi," said Susan. "I'm Susan Price. I used to live in Boston, but my apartment burned down so Martin offered to let me live with him."

Her last few words struck Martin as sounding all wrong. He could feel his face getting warm. *Is that how this is going to sound to everyone? I've invited an attractive young woman come live with me? Oh man. Margaret is gonna kill me!*

He rushed in some disclaimers. "Yes, um, I figured she could stay with my *wife*, Margaret, uh, and me until the power comes back on." He turned to get his water bottle and conceal any obvious blushing.

"I see. Well, if you would like a ride part-way home, I have a friend meeting me outside in a few minutes."

"That would be great," Martin said. He felt relieved at the change of topic. "We're both pretty wiped out by the walk from Boston and maybe some monoxide from helping those people."

"Boston?" asked Sally.

"Yes," said Susan. "We met while Martin was walking home from work downtown. It's been quite the long trip, but we're almost done."

Sally peered over Susan's shoulder, out the storm door. "Uh oh. Here comes Walter. Better step aside. He's going on the air again," explained Sally. "He's been doing this since the power went out. Top of the hour for three minutes. Fancies himself a news man."

"Ham radio?" Martin asked. Sally nodded with the weariness of a golf widow. "Would it be okay if we stayed and listened in, just for a couple minutes?"

"Pfft. Mind? He loves showing off. He takes the 'ham' part far too seriously."

"Just for a minute or so?" Martin asked Holly. She acquiesced with a shrug.

"I'd like to hear what's been going on out there," Martin said.

Walter rushed through the storm door. "Excuse me. Comin' through."

"This young couple walked all the way from Boston," Sally told Walter as he brushed past her.

"Really? Boston?" Curiosity replaced annoyance on Walter's face. "What did you see? I heard some stories about riots and fights and roadblocks or checkpoints or something. Did you see any of that?"

"We did." Martin nodded. "We didn't see any riots, but we heard of a few. We saw some fights. We encountered our first roadblock at 128. They were only letting through residents of Reading, Andover and such. We found a way around it, but they were trying to block that off too. There was something weird going on in Reading; police in riot gear pulling people over. We didn't stay to find out what that was all about. We saw another roadblock at 495. They let people through if they lived in Lawrence. We had to take a long way around that one too."

"Police?" asked Walter.

"Most were by state troopers, some local police, but we did see some National Guard on 495. They said their job was to keep 495 clear."

"Why in blazes were they blocking the roads?" Walter asked.

Martin could only shrug and shake his head.

Walter glanced at the wall clock. "Shoot! It's nearly 3:00. Gotta get on the air. Excuse me." Walter slid into his desk chair and flicked his equipment back on. He fussed with a few knobs, listening with one ear to the static. He cleared his throat and brought the mic to his lips.

"CQ, CQ, K1NTZ on air at the top of the hour. CQ, CQ." Walter leaned back and listened to the light static. He fiddled with the knobs a bit more.

The speaker crackled. "KA1YRK. Evn'n old man."

"Evenin' yerself, Ray. You're comin' in five by nine tonight. You fix that antenna?"

"Kinda sorta. Actually, it wasn't the antenna proper, but some bad connectors."

Walter took in a breath and put the mic to his mouth, but the speaker crackled again. "N1WGF."

"K1NTZ. Evenin' Joyce. Looks like you're buying the donuts again. Got Ray on air already. Over."

"KA1YRK to donut lady. Evenin' Joyce. Punkin' spice, please."

"Aw shoot," said Joyce. "I gotta set my clocks ahead or something. I owe you guys too many donuts already."

"Well, we may not get eyes on for awhile, YL" said Walter, "So don't you fret. Score might even out before this is all done. Anything new Joyce?"

"Okay, I'll go first," replied Joyce. "Second-hand: Area 3 Contact in Maryland reports DC still under lockdown. Tense protests, but no riots. Government issued statements, but nothing new in them. More comments against the Russians than the Chinese today. Only two on terrorists. Heard there's supposed to be some big meeting with the FEMA director, Homeland Security and somebody else. Didn't say who. No word on when. Unclear if Prez is still in DC or bunkered. Over."

"This is Ray. Any updates on those riots, Joyce?"

"A little. Lockdown of New York extended to Staten Island and all of Nassau County. Fires worse in Chicago. Sounds like protest in Philly went bad. Twenty or so dead. The Governor sent in the

Guard. Things are worse in Baltimore. Police pulled back, abandoned whole riot area. Lots of fires. Over."

"What about your local, Joyce?" asked Ray. "I've been hearing about roadblocks? Can you confirm?"

"Roger that, Ray. First hand: this morning, Mass state troopers closed the border on 93, just south of Exit 1. Seen it myself. They're letting some people through, but most not. No idea why.

"Joyce, this is Walter. I've got a couple at my QTH that confirm. They report roadblocks at some major intersections in Mass. Troopers and National Guard. Some are allowing residents only into blocked areas. Over."

"Residents only, huh. That matches a report I heard from Salem. Lots of people stuck at border on 93. Contact in Tyngsboro says same for Route 3, too. Lots of people were trying to head south. Hundreds sleeping in cars, waiting to get through. Some set up tents in the median. No word on when the border will open. Over."

"K1NTZ. Thanks Joyce. Any news from up your way Ray? Over?"

"Not much. Marine traffic pretty much stopped now. Two new ships arrived, anchored offshore. Nothing moving in port. Not offloading or loading either. Folks pretty much waiting it out here."

"Thanks Ray. We've only got a minute or so left for this session. Let's do our BBS. You first Ray, anything new?"

"Yeah. Two new ones to pass along: Area 1, ARL 23 W, K4VGM: To M. Scully, Hartford CT from Little Teapot. We have Gram at summer house. All good. Come when you can. To Ali Jaffarian, Halifax VA from Marcus. TT did not make it. Will bury here. Can't come. That's it, Walter. Over."

"Copy Ray. Got any new BBS posts, Joyce?" asked Walter while he finished writing down the message on a note pad.

"Roger, Walter. Got one for each of you, both in Area. For Ray to pass on up. Area 5, ARL 312 W, N1TFN, To A. Lishness, Portland, ME from Duck Buddy. Heather had baby boy. Steven. All okay. Cannot travel now. And a new one for you, Walter. ARL 15 W, K4QEC,To B. Hillard, Hooksett from Missy and kids. All okay, but car broke. Cannot come as planned. Will go to uncle Eli's. All from me, Walter. Over."

"Well...I don't have any..." began Walter.

"Um." Susan touched his shoulder. "Could I send a message?"

"Sure," said Walter softly. "Hold on a sec Joyce."

"Roger. Holding."

Walter turned in his chair. "Okay, Who do you want to send it to?"

"To my dad, Mr. David Price, 1212 Cramer Street in Lakeview, Ohio. Tell him his daughter Susan is okay and staying in Cheshire, New Hampshire."

"Well," Walter said. "For security reasons, we try not to use whole names and don't include locations others could recognize since these'll get posted on public bulletin boards. Safer to keep things kinda cryptic. Is there something personal that only *your* D. Price in Lakeview would recognize as coming only from you?"

Susan's brow knit as she stared out the window for a long moment. "Okay, how's this? To. D. Price, Lakeview, Ohio. Pixie found a place."

Martin turned and smiled."Pixie?"

Susan squirmed. "It's a long story. Never mind. Will that work okay, Walter?"

Walter nodded and turned back to his microphone. "K1NTZ with one more BBS for you Joyce. For Area 8, ARL 4 W, K1NTZ: To D. Price, Lakeview, Ohio. Pixie found a place. Over."

"Got it, Walter," said Joyce. "Will pass along to the next contact with Area. I see our time's up. Seventy threes, gentlemen. N1WGF clear."

Ray keyed back in. "I won't be on at 6:00, Walter. I'm gonna see if I can work some skips tonight. Let ya know tomorrow if I get any useful news. KA1YRK."

"G'nite Ray. K1NTZ Clear." Walter leaned forward and powered down his equipment. He slumped back in his chair for a long sigh then pushed himself up from his chair. "It'll probably take a couple days before your message gets posted around Lakeview, young lady, but it'll get there." Walter toddled unsteadily outside. The drone of the generator rumbled down to silence. He shuffled back into the kitchen looking more stooped and tired than before.

"Well, folks, this old man is feelin' beat. I'm gonna go finish my lie-down. Nice meeting you two. Thanks for the news update. Holly, thanks for the meds. Headache's gone! Sally, you make sure I'm up by quarter to 6:00 this time, okay? Don't want to miss the contacts. Might work me some skips tonight too."

"You go rest on the couch, dear," said Sally.

Walter disappeared into the flickering firelight of the living room.

"I've half a mind to 'forget' and let him sleep," Sally whispered. "He's been taking this news-man thing too seriously."

Holly leaned back to look at the wall clock. "Uh oh. Five after. I told Jen I would be out by the road at 3:00. You two better gather up your things. Thanks for the tea, Sally. I'll come back by in a couple days to see if you need anything else."

"You're such a dear." Sally patted Holly's shoulder. "You two take care now, and get home safe." Martin and Susan waved as they stepped out the door.

In the grassy shoulder of the road stood a dark brown horse, fidgeting nervously. It was rigged up to a two-wheel cart made of thin metal tubing, all painted black. It was a minimalist buggy with a pair of wire-spoked wheels and thin tires like a moped might have. A plain woman in a brown barn coat and beret pulled down over short curly gray hair sat on the thin bench seat, holding the reigns.

"Hi Jen," Holly called out. "Thanks for waiting. Walter was on his radio again. Think Jasmine could handle a couple more passengers?"

Jen looked skeptical. "I don't know. She's not all that used to the trap yet. I guess we can try."

Jen pointed behind the thin bench. "There's a package shelf back here. I think you two could sit on it if you hold onto the bench back. You'll have to dangle your legs. Best I can do. Trap's only made for two."

"That's okay," Martin said. "This will be great." He and Susan took a seat. The package shelf felt precarious at best. Holding on was not an option. Martin curled one arm around the top tube of the bench. He held the roller bag handle with his other hand so it could trail along behind them.

"No new messages from Walter to post in town?" Jen asked. Holly shook her head.

Jen flicked the reigns, "K, girl." The horse jerked forward and seemed to want to veer right and left. Jen spoke softly and worked the reigns.

"I have only had Jasmine on the trap a couple times before all this. She's doing pretty good for only her third time, but she's still not comfortable with it. The road is mostly down hill from Sally's place, so we'll be okay that far. I'm not sure how she'll handle the extra load when we start up Wilson hill. Just have to play it by ear, I guess." Jen chuckled. "We're both learning this rig."

"When I first saw you on this thing," Holly said. "I thought it was adorable. You looked like something from an old postcard. Now, it looks pretty darn handy."

"Yeah, since Robert's not back from Concord with the truck, I thought it was a perfect opportunity to take her out for real: get some distance practice. The Cauloff's are doing pretty good, considering. They really appreciated my visit."

The two of them continued to share news of the people they had visited. They were all people Martin did not know, so his attention wandered. He watched the roller bag trundling and hopping behind them. He hoped the improvised bigger wheels could handle the speed.

He glanced at Susan who was watching the trees go by. Their trek was nearly done. Soon, he would have to introduce Susan to Margaret, and explain how he offered up *their* home without consulting her first. But then, how could he have? He wanted to imagine a happy meeting and generous hospitality, but that felt like a fool's optimism.

Years ago, Margaret was none too happy with him when he brought home that little homeless kitten. She did not want a cat, *and* he had decided to adopt it without consulting her. That was what rankled her more than adding a cat to the family. It took a long time for the ice to melt.

Susan would be Cat 2.0 and a much bigger deal. One does not simply graft a pretty young woman into the family. *Hi Honey.*

Look what I found! Martin shuddered. The "fine" factor would reach toxic levels. He was doomed. Martin wondered what Siberia was like.

On the other hand, Margaret did eventually warm up to the kitten. Those big cute eyes finally melted the ice. Pudge even became Margaret's faithful lap buddy. Perhaps Susan's natural charm would win Margaret over too. Martin's gloom was fading. Maybe the two women would become friends — not best friends, perhaps, but at least cordial. Margaret might take Susan under her wing and teach her cooking and canning.

Martin tried to figure out words of introduction that would not sound like he had brought home another cute orphan: which was pretty much what he had done. He recalled that Margaret's feelings about the cat turned a corner when the kitten got a cute name, and not just 'that cat.' It was harder to resent a newcomer named Pudge.

Susan is too silky of a name, he thought. *Almost sultry. Guests should not have sultry names.*

What if Susan had a cute nickname, like Susie or Missy? Maybe Button? How can anyone be angry with someone nicknamed Button? What was that Pixie thing all about, he wondered.

"So," he asked without taking his eyes off the trundling roller bag. "Was it a school play?"

"What?" Susan was lost in her own thoughts.

"Pixie. Character in a class play or something?"

Susan rolled her eyes. "Didn't I say 'never mind'?"

"Yeah," Martin said slowly. Now he had a frog in his pocket. The trees still had most of their colorful leaves, so he could only get brief glimpses of the swamp or meadows beyond the woods. *Pixie is too childish. Maybe shorten it to Pix.* He imagined Margaret calling out from the kitchen, 'Pix, could you help me kneed this dough?' *That could work. Pix isn't sultry.*

"A Halloween costume, maybe?"

Susan leveled a glare at him. "You aren't going to leave it alone, are you."

Martin could not completely suppress a smile. "I *could* keep guessing."

Susan sighed. "I suppose you would too."

Martin smiled.

She shook her head in resignation. "Alright. But you can't tell anyone. It goes back to when I was six. I was playing with my pixie dolls out in the woods behind our house. I was their pixie mother, see and…agh, this sounds so stupid when I say it out loud."

"That's okay. Kids play games," Martin comforted. "What did you do in the woods?"

"Well, I was making a little house out of sticks for my pixie dolls. I wanted to make special beds for them using this soft moss I found. I needed more moss, since I had three pixie dolls. So I took my pixies in my arm and we all went looking for more bedding moss."

"And you wandered out of familiar territory?"

Susan nodded. "From where I was building my pixie home, I could clearly see my house. Once I was over the hill, though, I lost track of where I was. Too focused on finding moss, I guess. Well, this big storm came up fast. I didn't notice until it got really dark and windy. It started to rain. When the lightening started, I ran as fast as I could down the hill. I thought I was running toward home, but my house wasn't there. I knew I was lost."

"You must have been pretty scared, huh?"

"Actually, no. I was being the brave mother — too busy telling my pixies not to be scared."

Martin could see that her pioneer spirit had been there since childhood. *How could Margaret not be charmed by Susan?*

"I came across this little house, like a dog house, only a bit bigger. It had a little door, so I went in. It was dark inside, but a little light came through some cracks between the boards. It had a big motor thing in the middle. I jumped when it started up the first time, but it wasn't bad once I got used to it."

"The rain got really heavy. I kept telling my pixies that they would be okay. I found a nice dry place for them where they'd be safe. The motor thing got warm so it was actually pretty comfortable in there. It got dark outside and I got sleepy, so I curled up with my pixies on a squashed cardboard box and fell asleep."

"You do have a knack for falling asleep during a crisis," Martin quipped.

"Oh stop it." She tried to slap him on the shoulder but her free arm could not reach him.

"Go on with your story. You fell asleep in…in what I gather was a pump house? Did you sleep there all night?"

"I did. My parents were out in the storm looking for me, calling my name. But with the noise of the motor, I didn't hear anything. In the morning, the door opened and my dad looked inside. He got on his knees and cried. I felt really bad. I tried to tell him not to cry, that we were all okay. I told him I was a *good* pixie mother and found my pixies a safe place."

"So that's what your message meant. You found a place to be safe from the storm."

Susan nodded. "I'm sure he's worried about me. That's what he does best, I think. He'd know that message was from me. I only hope it reassures him. He never let me forget that night, you know. It took years before mom and dad let me out of their sight — always hovering over me. I felt so bad that I made my dad cry. I tried to make it up to him by never doing anything that would scare him. Always be safe, you know…for him."

Martin looked at her, expecting more.

"That's all," she said. "And you still can't tell anyone about it. My dad used that Pixie name on me whenever he was worried about me, which was most of the time. I don't want you or anyone else latching onto it, thinking it's a cute nickname or anything, cuz it isn't. Promise you won't tell anyone? You have to promise."

Martin smiled. "Promise." *But it might leak out somehow. It's cute, like Pudge.*

"*And,*" she added with emphasis. "You have to tell me some embarrassing story from your childhood too, so I have some leverage to keep you honest."

Martin smiled, but cringed inside. He had done so many stupid things as a child. Where to begin? Saving rabbit 'eggs' in his sock drawer, incubating them with his desk lamp. The stink never came out of his socks. Or that time in first grade, when he and his cousin Pam took off all their clothes under the rhododendron so they could play Tarzan and Jane? They never lived that down. Or his bike with cardboard wings and the shed roof? It really did seem like a good idea at the time. Blackmailing him into silence would not be difficult.

The trap jerked and faltered. Jasmine whinnied and reared. Jen had her hands full trying to calm the horse.

"I'm afraid we're too heavy for her," Jen said. "Sorry to say, but you two will have to walk up the hill on your own." She pulled up Jasmine to an unsteady halt.

Martin and Susan stood up off the shelf. His arm hurt from the sustained grip. Holly stepped down too and faced Martin and Susan. "I was thinking of taking my little backroad shortcut anyhow. It's just a little ways up ahead there. See that split rail fence? I usually take it to avoid walking up either Stockman or Wilson hills. You can come with me, or go up and meet Jen at the top of the hill?"

Martin glanced at Jen, who was trying to calm down her skittering horse. "Shortcut sounds good to me. Jasmine doesn't look happy. How about you?" he asked Susan. "Feel up to a bit more walking?"

"I suppose."

Holly raised her voice to be heard over the hoof clatter. "Tell you what, Jen. We're going to take the back road from here. You go on without us."

"You sure? We could wait for you up top. I'm sure she'll settle down and behave the rest of the way."

"That's okay. Thanks so much for the ride."

"Alrighty then," Jen said. "See you Friday at the meeting?"

"Yes. Friday." Holly waved as Jen got Jasmine started at an erratic trot.

Holly turned to Martin and Susan. "That was fun, eh?" They both nodded. "Jen's place is other side of Stockman Hill. If we rode to her house, we'd have to walk up and over. I'm not feeling like doing that today."

"Me either." Martin could sympathize. He had walked that road a few times, coming back from the little general store. It could be a wearying hill even when feeling fresh. Walnut Hill and the monoxide had consumed any freshness he might have had left.

The shortcut was little more than an ATV trail through the woods. "Your short cut isn't much of a road," said Martin. He and Susan were acting stretcher-bearers for the roller bag again.

"No, not anymore, but back in the day, this was *the* road. Horses hauling freight wagons from the east would take this way so they could skirt around Stockman hill on their way to town. Once cars and trucks came along, the road just went up and over the hill. Nowadays, only a few dirt bikes and hikers use this old road. But, like I said, it saves me walking up and down two of those hills, so I like it."

"How have you and Micky been handling the power outage?" Martin asked.

"Oh, taking it in stride, I guess," Holly said. "We could always use a few more supplies. That reminds me. I have a friend who is a checker at the Market Basket over in Londeville. When the power went out, the manager closed the store right away. So, it didn't get cleaned out like Walmart, Hanaford and Shaw's did. Well, he's going to re-open tomorrow morning. I'm going early to get in line. I'm sure Market Basket will get picked clean too, probably by the end of the day."

"What time will the store open?" Martin asked. His truck was parked near that store. He did not know what supplies his house might need, but he was sure there was something.

"She told me 9:00."

"Thanks. I just might be there."

"You won't have heard about the special town meeting then either," Holly said. "There's a sign up in the center of town. The selectmen are holding a special meeting at town hall on Friday: an informational thing, I guess."

Martin had an automatic aversion to town politics. The petty egos and sandbox power plays of the previous town he had lived in seemed to better fit the Biblical expression, 'brood of vipers,' than 'democracy in action.'

Holly must have seen the disdain on his face. "Oh come on now. Our little town's got a bit of a crisis on its hands. Cheshire residents need to step up and help each other."

Martin knew she was right, but could not imagine what good could possibly come from his participation. He rather liked his civic-wallflower status. Fewer vipers.

"Besides," Holly continued. "With phones and TV out, it'll be the best place to find out what's going on around here."

"I suppose," Martin said reluctantly. Again, she was right, but visions of new vipers dampened any enthusiasm he might have felt.

"Ah, see?" Holly pointed ahead of them. "Stockman Road. That wasn't so bad, eh?"

Once on pavement again, Martin could pull the roller bag alone and give Susan a break. She was starting to limp again.

"There's my house," Holly said. "Do you want to come in for some water or a snack?"

"No, but thanks," Martin said. In truth, his stomach rumbled at the suggestion of a snack. "I appreciate the offer, but I'd rather get home as quickly as I can."

"I understand. If you just go past my barn and over the meadow, it'll save you a quarter mile of walking."

"Thanks!" Martin and Susan waved as Holly pressed on down the road to her house. The two of them turned onto the dirt driveway that led to the barn. The tall meadow grass was tan and gold. Colorful maples and oaks lined the meadow. The leaves of the autumn-berry trees were still a lush green. Martin found a few bushes that were still loaded with berries. He was not fond of crunching on the seeds, but he was too hungry to care. He raked off a big handful of berries.

Susan gasped. "Aren't those poisonous?"

"No." Martin stuffed in his handful. "They're a little bland, but okay." He knew it was tacky to talk with his mouth full.

Susan skeptically bit into one then looked in the distance, as if expecting to feel something.

Martin's driveway was directly across Old Stockman Road from the Baldwin's meadow. He offered Susan half of his second handful of berries.

"They're okay, really," Martin said. "Margaret makes jam and stuff out of them."

He stretched out his arms towards his house. "Man, I can't tell you how great it feels to be back home." He climbed the stone steps of the front walk.

"I just want to sit in my comfy chair, by my cozy fire and sleep for a week," he said.

Susan lingered at the bottom of the steps, securing the duffle bag that had worked loose.

Margaret threw open the storm door. "Martin! It WAS you! You made it." She ran up to him, but stopped short, aborting a hug. "Eww. You're all dirty and bristly. And *what* did you do to your jacket?"

"That's kind of a long story."

Margaret rolled her eyes. "I suppose I can fix your jacket. I'll have to give it a darn good cleaning first. Were you rolling in the mud, or what?"

Margaret took a deep breath and launched into a rapid-fire update. "Anyhow, I got your message and sent you one back, but then there was no signal. I was going to tell that I had things working pretty good since the power went out, but yesterday the generator just died while I was running it for a half hour to keep the fridge cold, but it just conked out and I couldn't get it started again, but I remembered what you said about the spark plug getting fouled if the choke was partially on, so I got the spark plug wrench from your workbench — you are really going to have to clean up that workbench. It took almost forever to find anything. I don't know how you can work in a space like that."

"So was it the spark plug?" Martin asked, hoping to derail the critique and get her back on her original topic.

"Yes. I took the spark plug out, cleaned it and sure enough, it started right up and I was so glad because I really needed to run the blender just a little while more to finish processing the berries which reminds me that I still need to get out there and pick the rest of them before we get a real frost and…"

"Wait." Margaret interrupted herself. "I heard you talking. Why were you talking as you came up to the house?"

Susan took a step sideways to make herself more visible at the bottom of the stone steps.

"Oh. Hello." Margaret was taken aback for a moment. She looked at Martin, her eyes expected an explanation.

"Um. Margaret, this is Susan Price. Susan, Margaret. Susan works for Bank of Boston downtown. I met her while I was walking home, you know, when the power went out? Her house was destroyed in a fire and she had nowhere else to stay…so I thought, well, Lindsey's room is empty and…" He did not sound as self-assured and casual as he had hoped.

Susan stepped up the stairs with her hand out for a handshake. "I thought it was so kind of your husband to offer some help. I really had nowhere else to stay, and the hotels I tried were either full or damaged."

Martin appreciated Susan's tact at calling him 'her husband' instead of using his first name. That would have sounded far too familiar. Nonetheless, there was a long silence while Margaret took in this clearly unexpected development.

"No problem," Margaret said flatly as she shook Susan's hand. "I am glad my *husband* was able to help a *stranger* in need." She gave Martin a firm look that said his explanation was insufficient, before looking back to Susan with a hostess smile.

Her emphasis on 'husband' was a gentle territorial challenge. The emphasis on 'stranger' signaled the category she expected Susan to fit into.

"I do appreciate your kindness," Susan added, with emphasis on 'your.'

That was a good touch, Martin thought. Margaret cast in the role of generous hostess was far better than *him* having a woman stay with *him*. The two women walked ahead of Martin up the walk. He pulled the roller bag.

Martin was relieved that they were getting along fairly well for a first meeting. Margaret was being politely territorial. Susan was being especially tactful. Things were cordial. Perhaps he had worried too much for nothing.

"Hopefully, the power will come back on soon, and I won't have to stay long," Susan said. "I don't want to be a burden."

Margaret held the front door for Susan. "Oh, I'm sure everything will be *fine*,"

Fine. Martin's fragile hope for peace crumbled. That dreaded word came up during their first minute together.

Two hens in a nest. He was doomed.

The End of Book One

Book Two: Siege Fall

Book Three: Hunger Season

Made in the USA
Middletown, DE
13 February 2017